Healey's Cave

By Aaron Paul Lazar

Best wishes from Aaron P Lazar
8-9-11

Twilight Times Books
Kingsport Tennessee

Healey's Cave
A Green Marble Mystery featuring Sam Moore.

This is a work of fiction. All concepts, characters and events portrayed in this book are used fictitiously and any resemblance to real people or events is purely coincidental.

Copyright © 2010 by Aaron Paul Lazar.

All rights reserved. No part of this book may be reproduced, stored in a retrieval system or transmitted in any form by any means electronic, mechanical, photocopying, recording or otherwise, except brief extracts for the purpose of review, without the permission of the publisher and copyright owner.

Twilight Times Books
P O Box 3340
Kingsport TN 37664
http://twilighttimesbooks.com/

First Edition, August 2010

Library of Congress Cataloging-in-Publication Data

Lazar, Aaron Paul.
  Healey's cave : a green marble mystery, featuring Sam Moore / Aaron Paul Lazar. -- 1st ed.
      p. cm.
  ISBN-13: 978-1-60619-162-0 (trade pbk. : alk. paper)
  ISBN-10: 1-60619-162-4 (trade pbk. : alk. paper)
  I. Title.
  PS3612.A97H43 2010
  813'.6--dc22
                                            2010032667

Printed in the United States of America.

Dedication

To my grandchildren,
Julian, Gordon, and Isabella.
Savor the delights of childhood
and keep the memories close.

> Your loving Papa

Preface

I blame this book on my wife.

I was minding my own business, wrapping up the fifth novel in the LeGarde Mystery series, when she turned to me and said, "You need to write a book from the killer's point of view."

I laughed out loud. I'd always written in first person, from a man whose character was diametrically opposed to villains. He was a good man, a man I admired and wanted to share with the world. Sure, he had his faults, but how could I switch from that kind of mindset to the inner thoughts of a killer?

Dale reads Stephen King and James Patterson. She loves psychological thrillers and even a little horror. Not like me with my relatively wholesome mysteries that skirt around the gruesome details of murder.

I put aside the thought until shortly thereafter, while rototilling my garden, I unearthed a green marble, a cat's eye. I held it in my hand and wondered about the little boy or girl who lost it. I imagined how neat it would be to be able to hold the marble tight in my hand and have it whisk me back in time to the boy's life. I'd be able to see what he saw, walk beside him, and maybe witness some horrible crime. And what if the villain was still alive today? What if he was my next-door neighbor?

That was all it took to dislodge me from the LeGarde Mysteries for a few months. With my wife's urging, I gave into the desire to create a new world. I didn't expect it to turn into another series. But it did.

This is book one in the green marble series, otherwise known as Moore Mysteries. And yes, I blame my wife for the whole thing.

Aaron Paul Lazar

Acknowledgments

Special thanks to Peggy Adamson, Sonya Bateman, Jeanne Fielding, Dale Lazar, Nancy Luckhurst, Kim Smith, Pat Thomas, and Lesia Valentine, the gracious friends who provided extraordinary editing. Thank you all!

The following supportive friends and family read *Healey's Cave* before it was finalized. Some supplied enthusiastic feedback that fueled the fire and provided encouragement. Others painstakingly noted typos or logical errors and took time to document their findings. Both approaches were necessary and much appreciated.

Sherrie Coleman, Sue Clark, Don Harman, Eva Douglas, Anne K. Edwards, Jason Jarvis, Mum, Bobbi Scranton, Linda Slade, Scott Slattery, Mina Sniderhan, and Jane Soan.

Chapter One

SAM MOORE WAS FREE. Free from the tether of the alarm clock, pushy pharmaceutical reps, runny noses, and waiting rooms packed with patients. On the first day of retirement, at the age of sixty-two, he was ready for a change.

He stood behind the barn and looked toward the garden. It lured him with a peculiar intensity he'd never been able to explain to Rachel. The pull was visceral, infused with a strong lust for the land. Cirrus clouds skated across the sky, racing eastward and the cool May breeze ruffled his hair, caressing him.

He *should* be happy. But a familiar sense of melancholy washed through him. It was always there, ever present. It retreated occasionally, when he was busy caring for patients. But as soon as he stopped—to take a breath, to look out the window, or to eat his lunch—that undercurrent of sadness, born of loss, returned.

It had been this way for fifty years. Fifty years of longing for the truth, of missing his little brother.

Where are you, buddy?

A flurry of starlings swooped past him. Their trickling waterfall calls resonated, frightening the goldfinches feasting at the thistle feeder. He watched the birds settle on the branches of the black walnut tree. Their blue-black plumage glistened in the sunlight.

The breeze rose, stirring the leaves in the cottonwoods.

Is it a sign?

Sam shot a glance toward the house, embarrassed to have such thoughts. He was glad Rachel couldn't hear the foolish ideas that ran through his mind.

Was Billy dead or alive? Snuffed out on his eleventh birthday, or whisked away by a kidnapper? Was he living somewhere? In Alaska? Canada? Forced to change his name as a child, brainwashed to forget his life as a Moore? Did he have grandchildren, like Sam? Or…

Sam's heart blackened. He hated this part.

If Billy *were* kidnapped, he would've tried to come home once he gained access to a car. He had been old enough when he disappeared to remember what town he grew up in. So...if he hadn't returned, he must be gone. Gone for good.

Sam sighed and ran a hand through his thick gray hair. Two starlings lit on the birdfeeder and pecked at the seeds. The wooden feeder had suet holders on each end, and his hands were still greasy from the peanut-flavored cakes he'd refilled earlier. A woodpecker hung upside down on one end, tapping at the treat.

He realized it would be harder now to ignore the persistent questions about Billy's fate. He'd have time on his hands. Lots of time. Besides tending to Rachel and babysitting his grandsons, he'd have hours to imagine the best and the worst.

He slid a hand into his pocket and jingled his keys.

I'll just have to keep busy.

Squaring his shoulders, he walked into the barn and yanked on the starter cord of the rototiller. It coughed, belched black smoke, and stalled. He nudged the choke back and tried again. The engine roared to life. Sliding the choke all the way down, he shifted the tiller into reverse and backed out of the barn.

Sam guided the tiller over the wet grass toward the garden. Its knobby tires dug into the ground, drawing him past the bearded iris bed. His mind drifted to patients and the young doctor who'd taken over his practice.

I wonder how Garcia's doing?

He'd dreamed about retirement for the past forty years. And here he was, on his first day of freedom, about to embark on a full day of gardening until he dropped into the lovely sleep born of physical exhaustion—and his first thought was about Garcia.

Doctor Andrea Garcia had worked by his side since she graduated from the University of Rochester Medical School. She was good. Very good. And she'd take excellent care of his patients.

But would she remember to retest Jenny Boyd for strep?

An annoying voice hissed inside his head.

Forget about it. It's not your job. Not anymore.

It was hard to sever himself from a practice that flourished for forty years. Forty years of growing this "limb" that became such a part of him, and everyone expected him to simply chop it off. Just like that! It wasn't going to be easy.

He stopped and looked at the cloudless sky. The strong sun shone through pure azure, although it was just eight in the morning. Leaves rustled in the whispery willows and sugar maples that dotted the grounds. He smiled, drank in the scent of honeysuckle, and propelled the tiller forward.

The jungle grew to his left. He'd hacked away at the bamboo-like shoots for weeks after tending to patients all day in his family practice in Conaroga, New York. The official name of the weed was Japanese knotweed, a rapid-spreading invader that killed everything in its wake. Last year's stalks were dry and crisp. They towered twelve feet high, crackling in the breeze. He imagined them taunting him, calling to him.

You can't stop us. We're taking over.

Sam had worked hard to clear half the knotweed spreading behind the barn near the woods, but a lot remained standing. His bonfires had been impressive. Fueled with dried knotweed, dead apple tree limbs, and bundles of crispy weeds, they roared into infernos, inciting stares from passersby. The coals were usually warm the next morning, when Sam added more branches to the pile each day.

He reached the vegetable garden near the above ground pool and set the tiller in motion between the wide rows of sugar snap peas and asparagus. Rachel and he had feasted on purple-tipped asparagus for the past few weeks.

His stomach growled. He'd skipped breakfast and bolted outdoors before the sun had crested over the hill. The idea of a brunch of asparagus on buttered toast nearly drove him inside, but he resisted and kept working.

Sam muscled the machine around the row of peas and started on the other side. The soil churned like butter. Baby beets grew thick within the row. He smiled again, pleased with the result. He'd defied upstate New York conventions and had boldly planted the beets at the same time as the peas. He'd marked it in his garden journal: March 27th, a rare, eighty-degree day, perfect for the first till.

Lila trotted toward him from the woods, hopping over felled logs and skirting piles of knotweed stalks. Her sleek, white body moved with feline fluidity. She meowed twice, raising her tail in greeting.

Sam switched off the tiller and leaned down to pat her. She pushed her head against his hand and turned in small circles beside him.

"What's the matter, Lila? You hungry? You missed your supper last night. What have you been up to?"

She purred and placed her delicate paws on his knees as he crouched beside her. He stroked the smooth fur on her neck and scrubbed his fingers behind her ears.

"That's a good girl. Good kitty."

When Lila was satisfied, she abruptly trotted toward the house, probably to claim her missed meals. Sam restarted the tiller, finished working the soil between the corn and potatoes, and headed to the knotweed patch.

He was ready to dig today. Although the job of clearing wasn't yet complete, he ached to set tine to soil and stir it up. It would allow him to smooth out the area, rake it, and eventually mow the knotweed to death.

He maneuvered the tiller over the lawn to the knotweed jungle and slowly worked the soil. The weed colony was founded when he and Rachel owned horses, years ago. When her multiple sclerosis worsened and she needed the wheelchair, the animals were sold, and the knotweed multiplied, infesting the edge of the woods. By the time Sam retired, it had grown expansively, creating "the jungle." Sam was obsessed with ridding the landscape of the infectious weeds. Listed first on his retirement list, he planned to turn the area into a lush lawn, opening it to a line of heirloom apple trees that edged the woods.

Something sparkled from the earth. Sam poked at the soil and uncovered a clear glass bottle. He brushed off the dirt. "Bayer Aspirin" ran down the side of the tiny vessel in raised letters. He pocketed it. Rachel would want to clean it and add it to her collection. Such treasures frequently popped out of the earth around the house and barn. Long ago, it was common practice to bury trash, before the emergence of the town dump. Since the house was built in 1815, Sam anticipated an abundance of finds.

He continued tilling until he connected with the woody root of a knotweed plant. The tiller bounced up and down, trying to unearth the root. Eventually, after coming at it from several directions, it popped out of the ground. The offender was ten inches long, knobby, and misshapen. It resembled a piece of wood. Pink shoots of baby knotweed sprouted from the chunk. He threw it into the wheelbarrow. After letting it dry in the sun for a few days, he'd burn it.

Another object flashed from the dirt. Sam backed up the tiller and dug until his fingers closed around a small marble. He picked it up, rubbed it on his jeans, and held it to the light.

The sphere was small and partially opaque. A cat's eye. He turned it in his fingers. Light sparkled through glass the color of lichen; muted, pale green overlaid swirls of deeper green within. He smiled, put it in his pocket, and continued until hunger drove him in for lunch with Rachel.

Chapter Two

"Want some more, Sam?"

Sam wiped the napkin across his lips and pushed back from the kitchen table.

"Thanks, but I'm stuffed. How 'bout you? There's a little asparagus left. I could make you another piece of toast."

He walked past her wheelchair with his dirty dishes.

Rachel smiled and patted his hand when he passed. "No, I'm fine." She paused. watching him. "Stop that, now."

He reached the sink and looked over his shoulder.

"Huh?"

She motioned toward the sink.

"I'll do the dishes. I'm not helpless, you know. "

He kept working and smiled.

"I know, but now that I'm retired, I want to pitch in more."

A look of surprise crossed her face, followed by a frown. Sam returned to the table to collect the glasses and pan of asparagus.

"What? What's wrong?"

She brushed aside her graying bangs.

"Much as I love you, Sammy, I have to admit I've been dreading this day."

His eyes widened and he dropped into the chair.

"What? *Dreading* it? Dreading my retirement?"

She covered a smile. "Don't sound so hurt, honey. It's just that I don't want you to mess up my system. You know, I've got everything organized and if you start helping out, I'll have nothing to keep me busy all day."

Her voice fell at the end of the sentence. Sam reached for her hand.

"Really? I thought you could use the help."

She shook her head. Tears welled in her rich brown eyes.

"Since my legs got bad, I've needed things to keep me busy. To keep my mind off this rotten illness. The way you fixed the house is perfect. I can reach almost everything, now. I keep to my schedule every day. It makes me feel useful, Sam. I need that."

He digested her words as memories of their past flashed unbidden across his mind. The diagnosis came when their children were born, over thirty years ago. Sam took Rachel to the best neurologists in the country, but as the symptoms worsened he knew before they did. Multiple sclerosis. It progressed slowly over the decades, relapsing and remitting as it ran its curious and elusive course. The exacerbations were periods of unusual exhaustion, facial and limb numbness, and weakness in the legs accompanied by frequent bouts of depression and anxiety. Six months ago, Rachel's legs gave out. She'd tried a cane for a while, but fell three times. Finally, and with much angst, she accepted the small scooter Sam purchased for her. She swapped between a lightweight wheel chair and the electric scooter, depending on the circumstance.

Sam looked into her eyes. They were still beautiful, after all these years. He leaned over and ran his rough fingertips along the soft down of her cheek.

"Okay, honey. Don't worry. I've got plenty to keep me busy outside, anyway."

She brushed at her eyes and squeezed his hand, flashing a familiar look of affection.

"Thank you." Her voice shook, husky with emotion. Changing the subject, she put her dishes in her lap and wheeled to the sink. "Are you working on those nasty weeds today?"

He nodded. "Uh huh. It's slow going. And I have to mow again."

The thought of the cool blue air called to him. He felt the pull of the garden as he fidgeted in his chair. His hands ached to be in the soil again. There was weeding, mowing, planting, mulching, and clearing to be done.

"Well, then, you'd better get out there. That lawn won't mow itself. And don't forget, the boys are coming later."

He had forgotten about his grandsons' visit, but didn't want to admit it. "I won't." He kissed her forehead and walked back into the sunlight, refastening the Velcro on his back brace. A simple arrangement, the stretchy straps worked like suspenders, and the wide, nylon brace rode low on his back. He repositioned it, took a deep breath, and started toward the knotweed colony.

As he headed out, a memory flashed through him—brief, but palpable. Billy and he, aged twelve and eleven, had walked barefoot on the hot pavement after a spring rain. Soft tar warmed their feet. Rain puddles sizzled and misted on the road. The boys laughed, then raced home to dinner. Steak, corn on the cob, baked potatoes, and salad. Billy's favorite.

Sam checked the date on his watch. *May twenty-fourth. Billy turns sixty-one today.*

The little boy who slept in the bottom bunk, who breathed hot, sweet breath on his face when they hid in the closet beneath the stairs, who offered his sticky hand during scary movies, and who mysteriously disappeared on his eleventh birthday—would be sixty-one today.

He closed his eyes and let the wind blow across his face. The breeze lifted his hair. Sam felt the cool soft touch brush his leathery skin. He pictured his brother communicating with him from Heaven. He'd often imagined it, and was comforted by the thought.

Happy birthday, buddy.

He opened his eyes, sighed, and ambled toward the stone fire pit behind the barn. He dropped onto the old iron bench and wondered for the millionth time what had happened to his brother.

Sam reached into his pocket and fingered the green marble. It reminded him of the marbles they played with as children.

Could it have been Billy's?

He closed his eyes again and rolled it in his hand. The smooth glass slid between his fingers, warming his hand, then grew almost too hot to touch. Surprised, Sam plucked it from his pocket and inspected it. Strong sunlight glinted on its surface, but it seemed to glow from within. He cupped his hands around it, puzzled by the intensity of the heat.

Instantly, a green flash blinded him, forcing his eyes closed. Shimmering, ghostly images danced before his mind's eye. The sound of children playing reverberated in the air. In seconds, he was transported to another realm, wrapped in a rolling cloud of green effervescent swirls.

Chapter Three

AN ORANGE SCHOOL BUS BOUNCED along the country lane and stopped at the corner, red lights flashing. Black smoke spewed from the tailpipe. After two boys disembarked, the doors whooshed shut.

Sam floated in the air, hovering over the two boys. They skipped along the road with lunchboxes banging at their sides. His lungs constricted when he recognized the younger boy.

Billy.

He tried to get a look at the other boy, then recoiled in shock.

It's me.

There was his old Lassie lunchbox. And his Dodgers cap. And his little brother. Right there. Close enough to touch.

The boys turned and waved at the kids on the bus. Several faces peered through the windows. The names came back to him in a flash.

Bruce McDonald. Harvey Allen. Doug Smythe. Renée Snell.

Doug, the youngest, stuck out his tongue. Renée fluttered her dainty fingers. Young Sam's heart quivered in response and Sam felt it resonate in his adult body, as if he were actually experiencing it.

Harvey and Bruce, Sam's best friends, waved goodbye. Harvey collared Bruce and rubbed his knuckles against Bruce's crew cut.

Noogies for the nerd.

The bus lumbered on its way. Sam remained suspended, observing his childhood self and Billy as they bounced down the road, but with each breath he linked closer to the young boy beneath him, feeling his small chest rise and fall, sensing the energy pulse through his slim arms and legs.

The wild sense of disbelief was curbed by his loss of control and tempered by the sensations rushing through him as he experienced the emotions of his twelve-year-old self. Reeling with puppy love for Renée, he felt the memories crystallize.

She'd offered him a fireball today on the way home. He'd blushed furiously, and accepted. He'd done well on his English test and couldn't wait to show his mother the A on his paper.

Thoughts flooded his brain and the connection to his past snapped into clarity. Today was Friday. He'd invited Harvey and Bruce to the backyard sleepover scheduled in his yard tonight, and could barely contain his excitement.

The memories gelled, and Sam whooshed into his young body.

Sam and Billy tripped down the lane, laughing and chucking rocks into the fields on the side of the road.

They slowed when they approached the Healeys' house. It seemed to glower from the yard. Unpainted clapboards sagged away from the rotten frame. Dirt smeared the cracked windows. Mr. Healey rocked on the porch. Back and forth. Back and forth. He stared at the boys through slit gray eyes. Sam's heartbeat quickened.

A car roared behind them. Manfred Healey squealed to a stop in his white Belair near Sam and Billy, honking the horn. The boys skittered past the driveway. Manfred peeled out and sped into the gravel drive, screaming at them.

"Vermin! Outta my way."

The sound of Manfred's shrill voice tapped icy fingers along Sam's spine.

The boys ran for their lives, tearing up the road in their Keds until they reached the safety of home. Sam put his arm around Billy's shoulders after they'd stampeded up the porch steps.

"We made it," he panted.

Billy's hazel eyes crinkled with unspoken words of relief, bathing in the bond of brotherhood and shared fears.

The vision turned to green mist. Sam lost touch with the past and instantly heard the thoughts of another.

Little bastards!

The ferocity of the words nearly jolted him out of the reverie. Or trance. Or whatever it was.

It came again. Smoldering. Pure hatred hammered against his brain as the thoughts screamed through his head.

Sons of bitches!

༄༅

Sam's back ached. His joints had stiffened. He opened his eyes and stretched his arms. The harsh tones of the voice resonated in his brain.

Whose voice was that? And why were his joints so sore?

The sun had traveled far across the sky since lunch. Surprised, he looked at his watch. Two o'clock.

Two o'clock?

He'd been sitting on the bench for an hour and a half, clutching the marble in his hand. It was warm from his skin, but not hot. Or glowing. He looked at it, shook his head, and dropped it back into his jeans pocket.

"I'm losing it."

A chickadee landed on the black walnut tree and chirruped, as if agreeing with him.

Chickadeedeedeedeedee.

Sam unfastened the back strap, shifted on the bench, and massaged his back. It throbbed from yanking the tiller around. He sighed long and loud.

It must have been a dream. I'm not used to so much physical labor.

He tried to convince himself, figuring he had dozed while he sat in the fresh air.

But the memory was authentic. The kids on the bus. The Healey boy. They'd all been real. Harvey Allen and Bruce MacDonald were his boyhood pals. Together with Billy, they'd hung out together and often included Doug Smythe, a year younger than Billy.

Sam laced his fingers behind his head and thought about his childhood friends. Doug inherited his folks' house and lived about a mile away. He'd always been a little annoying, constantly begging to hang out with the older kids. Even now, Doug was cocky and exasperating. He had become progressively overbearing as he aged.

Harvey, tall and athletic, was a straight shooter and honest to a fault. After joining the Marines at graduation, Harvey returned eight years later to Conaroga to open a family restaurant. It still thrived. He lived with his family halfway between Doug and Sam's house.

Chuckling to himself, Sam thought about Bruce, the nerd. Small, klutzy, and smart as a whip, Bruce had attended elementary and middle school with Sam, then left his pal in the dust and moved on to an elite private school in New Hampshire. Bruce graduated first in his class and had been welcomed to Harvard, where he served in the ROTC. After graduation, he worked his way up the political ladder until elected to the Senate thirty-six years later. Bruce had sprouted and reached the respectable height of five-foot-eleven by the time he graduated high school. Now he jockeyed for a presidential nomination in the Republican Party.

Sam glanced toward the house; a flash of guilt trickled through him. Renée was his first love. She'd mesmerized him in sixth grade. He remembered watching her in fifth period social studies. She sat right in front of him, with her white puffy-sleeved dress with the satin sash and red roses appliquéd on the front. He'd absorbed every detail of her appearance, every day. Every nuance of her motions, her words, her expressions. Even down to the part in her hair. He'd lost his voice each time he saw her, becoming a stuttering lunatic.

That is—until Billy disappeared.

Sam stood and massaged his back again, remembering the black time in his life. When Billy left, he simply died inside. He'd dried up, evaporated, almost blown away. They made him talk to a psychiatrist, who locked him in an institution. The guy smelled like disinfectant mouthwash and powdered hand soap. The forced incarceration hadn't helped, and the patients with whom he'd been surrounded made him feel even crazier. The doctors at the institute tried to convince Sam that Billy's disappearance wasn't his fault. But he'd known better.

He lost interest in girls for a long time. Throwing himself into his studies, he'd graduated with honors and advanced to Med School at the University of Rochester. Years later, Sam started his own practice and met Rachel. She waltzed into his office to apply for the secretarial position, and immediately landed the job. Sam remembered her from high school, but the woman who'd appeared in his office had been radically different. Poised, elegant, soft, and appealing, she breathed warm, sweet life into him. He'd re-awakened, and married her within the year.

In spite of Rachel's affection and friendship, however, Sam never completely regained his balance after losing Billy. Even now, fifty years later, it ate away at him.

He crossed his arms and stared into the woods, fighting the melancholy that threatened to break through.

The dream had seemed so real. Billy was alive. *Alive!*

He sighed again.

Billy? Little buddy? Where are you?

Chapter Four

SAM SURVEYED THE KNOTWEED PATCH and mopped his forehead with his sleeve. Two hours of drilling into wooden lumps beneath the soil brought tingles to his fingers and arms. When he let go of the tiller handgrips, his hands still vibrated. The wheelbarrow overflowed with the chunky roots he'd wrenched from the ground.

Enough is enough.

He leaned against the rough bark of a black walnut tree and eyed the front lawn. Shaggy and lush, it mocked him.

Sam walked the tiller back to the barn and grabbed the keys for the lawn tractor, embarrassed he'd let the grass become so unkempt. Cricket's former horse stall was now home to the tiller, tractor, and snow blower. Gardening tools, hoses, Christmas lights, and a croquet set hung on the walls. When Rachel's Morgan mare was donated to a working farm for the mentally disabled, Sam had removed the stall door to provide easier access to the equipment. He rested a hip on the tractor seat and sighed, picturing the mare.

Nimble and fleet, she'd carried Rachel safely through the woods and fields for years. Until his wife's illness progressed, of course. She had been a great equestrian in her youth; it was her passion, second only to raising Beth and Andy. When the multiple sclerosis weakened her muscles, riding became dangerous, and she'd been forced to stop.

Giving up Cricket had been a tough decision, but Rachel knew the mare would be better off with people who'd lavish attention on her. When the horse trailer rolled down the driveway with Cricket inside, she'd cried for hours.

The loss of her horse signified the end of an era. The end of Rachel's mobility, her energy, her freedom.

Sam's insides twisted. The memories washed through him. He closed his eyes and massaged them with gritty fingers. Rachel's pain had been so palpable; it had ripped his heart out.

The beginning of the end of "life with horses" had started with Bucky. Sam's gentle buckskin gelding was sold when the children were teenagers. With swim team meets, drama club rehearsals, orchestra, and piano lessons, Sam spent all his free time chauffeuring the kids to and from school. There was simply no time left in the week for Bucky.

He fingered the lead rope that still hung from the metal ring on the wall. Old Bucky had been a smooth ride. Steady as a rock. He still missed the gelding and longed for the good old days when he and Rachel would saddle up and ride for hours through the rolling hills of the Genesee Valley.

Sam checked the gas level, even though he remembered topping it off a few days ago. Satisfied, he swung one leg over the yellow padded seat. It was the closest thing to a saddle he'd ridden in years. He pushed the throttle to full, depressed the clutch and brake, and turned the key. The venerable tractor started on the first try. Shifting into reverse, Sam backed it up, performed a K-turn, and headed for the front lawn.

Starting with a long cut down the middle, he drove in increasingly larger rectangles, shooting the grass toward the outer edges of the yard.

He ducked and received a shower beneath the lilac branches that hung heavy with moisture from last night's downpour. The lavender blossoms had faded to rust in the past week. But the fragrant scent still lingered in the air when he brushed past.

Leaning down and pulling in his legs to avoid the thorns, Sam rumbled past the white shrub roses, inhaling the sweet smell. Pure and clean, it lifted his spirits.

He edged the lawn around the white garden. Flanked by the shrub roses and white lilacs, it backed up to a rustic split rail fence separating it from the gravel parking area. Five young floribunda roses lined the back of the plot, girdled by double Aglaia daisies, sneezewort, lupines, bleeding hearts, and Asiatic lilies. All were pristine white, including the dianthus that separated them from the lawn. Sam had just weeded and mulched the garden two weeks ago. He spied some surviving dandelions that poked through the mulch and his fingers itched to pull them from the soggy ground. Sam rode round and round the yard, comforted by the rhythm of the routine. He forgot about Manfred Healey, Harvey, Bruce and even Billy for a while. With growing enthusiasm, he began to plan the next day's gardening activities.

His temporary plot of re-blooming iris near the woods was ready to flower. When the petals showed their colors, he'd move them to strategic locations around the property. He'd thrown them into the ground last fall when they arrived on an unusually cold October day, heeling them in without marking their colors. Sam habitually ordered far too many perennials, and Rachel didn't hesitate to remind him of the fact when the boxes started arriving in September.

The herb garden was in terrible disarray and needed at least a half-day of devotion. The strawberry patch, although sopping wet, bore small green berries, but the weeds were spreading rapidly. There was so much to do—and plenty of time to do it, now that he was retired. He shrugged, chuckled to himself, and relaxed. Having loads of free time was such a strange feeling.

Sam mulled over the tasks, automatically circling the big spruce. He tried to avoid the prickly branches, yet cut as close to the base as he could. It was a delicate balance. Just as he finished the front yard, his son's white minivan pulled into the drive. He gunned the tractor toward the parking area.

Andy jumped out and slid open the side door.

"Hi, Dad. Someone's been asking for you."

"Papa! Ride! Ride tractor? Vroom, vroom!" Timmy's voice sang in needy anticipation. "Papa? Ride?"

Sam smiled and held out his hands for the boy. Andy unbuckled him and lifted him from his car seat, handing him to his father. Sam sat Timmy on one knee.

"Where's Evan?" Sam asked. He'd been looking forward to a visit from his eleven-year-old grandson.

"Sorry, Dad. He's at track practice."

Sam hid his disappointment. "Oh. Okay."

Timmy, who had just turned nineteen months, grinned at Sam and immediately leaned forward to shove the throttle lever up and reach for the key.

"Ride?" He lifted cornflower blue eyes in supplication.

Sam kissed Timmy's downy soft cheek and laughed.

"Okay. Let's go."

He started the tractor. The baby's legs dangled on either side of his knee, bopping back and forth in excitement.

"Ride."

Holding one arm firmly around his grandson's middle, Sam slid the tractor into first gear. He leaned his face against Timmy's dark copper curls, occasionally kissing his ears and cheeks as they rode around the grounds. They headed back toward the knotweed, around the blueberry patch, into the paddock garden where the horses used to graze, past the monstrous rectangle of black mulching plastic, home to sixty tomato plants and assorted vegetables. Circling the fruit trees, Sam slid the throttle up and aimed for the old perennial garden originally planted to hide the wellhead.

"Tractor. Fun," Tim said, reaching for the steering wheel.

"Good job, Timmy. You're driving!"

When they passed various objects, Sam would name them, and Timmy would repeat. A fast learner, he'd been picking up words and phrases all season. Sam was sure the boy had developed ahead of the curve, especially with his help.

Timmy kicked his legs. "Bird! Bird flyin'."

A cardinal flew past them and landed on the spruce branch.

"Right. And what's that?" Sam asked.

"Mulch. Big pile."

"Good! Now we're almost done, Timmy."

Tim looked at his grandfather in alarm.

"More?" His lower lip trembled. He flailed his legs. "More?"

Sam looked into his pleading eyes and relented.

"Okay. One more time. Then we'll be done, okay?"

"Okay," Tim said, surprising Sam with his new word.

They repeated the cycle, driving around the yard again, naming birds, flowers, trees, and other items of interest. When it was over, Sam parked near the back porch. He sat still for a few minutes with Timmy cuddled in his arms. They talked about what they'd seen. Finally, Timmy stirred impatiently.

"All done," Timmy said. "Tractor sleepin'."

Sam burst out laughing. Last week, Timmy had screamed and thrown a tantrum when the ride was over. Today, he used Sam's own line about the tractor sleeping. He smiled and carried the baby into the house, realizing that the best part of retirement had just begun.

Chapter Five

S<small>AM RAN A FINGER AROUND</small> the dessert plate, picking up the last of the crumbs. "That was so good," he said. "Delicious."

Andy had picked up Timmy just before dinner, after he and Sam had played with toys on the edge of the garden for an hour. Sam missed him already, but was also secretly relieved he'd be able to get back to his gardens in the morning. After demolishing three salmon cakes with dill sauce, a mountain of yellow rice, two helpings of spinach salad, and a huge piece of key-lime pie, he wasn't sure he would ever walk again.

"Glad you liked it, honey." A satisfied smile played across Rachel's lips. "Should we have our coffee in the living room and do a little reading?"

Sam pushed back from the table and stretched.

"Sure. Coffee sounds good." He loosened his belt a notch. "And I'm at a really good part in my book. I have to find out what happens."

Sam cherished their evening reading ritual. Summer or winter, he started a blaze in the fireplace for atmosphere. They would read for a few hours, then retire when the first one started to yawn. The television went on for an hour or two upstairs, but it usually didn't last. Most nights he fell asleep by nine.

"Okay. I'll start the fire, you make the coffee."

She tossed a smile over her shoulder. "It's a deal."

He ambled into the living room. Kneeling before the hearth, he bunched newspapers under crisscrossed kindling beneath two dry logs. Thoughts of Billy rattled unbidden into his mind, darkening his mood. Rachel wheeled in, picked up her book, and reached for her glasses on the coffee table.

"Which one are you reading?" Sam asked.

She held the book up.

"*The Scent of God*, by Beryl Singleton Bissell."

"Good one?" he asked. The fire flared into a satisfactory inferno. He set the screen back in place and straightened.

"Delicious. It's positively addictive. About a nun. And a priest. And how they fell in love."

Sam raised an eyebrow. "Really?"

"Yes. Listen to this. '*I woke that morning to the sound of waves crashing on the beach below, the pink and gold of the rising sun playing across my face. Despite my father's condition and my mother's frailty, I felt a wild surge of happiness. Eight floors below my window, a receding wave shimmered back toward an oncoming breaker, leaving a froth of bubbles to mark the edges of its ride. A solitary man jogged along the beach, the wet sand forming silvery halos around his footprints.*'" She beamed at Sam and loosed a long, romantic shudder. "Isn't that gorgeous?"

Sam nodded. "Wow. Maybe I'll read it next."

"You should. It's a true story."

In seconds, Rachel was lost in her book.

Sam didn't sit down, although he'd intended to read. He browsed through the movies in the cupboard over the mantle, hit with the sudden urge to rearrange them alphabetically. He glanced her way more than once, but she didn't respond.

When he was done with the videos, he sighed and moved onto the contents of the buffet drawers, sliding items around and aligning the items into neat sections.

"Sam?" Rachel asked. She reluctantly laid the book down.

He set the D batteries in a straight row behind the candles.

"Mmm?"

"What is it, honey? Is it Billy again?"

He cast a glance her way.

She always knows what I'm thinking.

Being married forty years did that to a couple. An intuitive spouse, Rachel was keenly aware of his moods, and could analyze his thoughts often before he recognized them as his own. But she was right. He'd been thinking about the dream all evening.

"Yeah." He collapsed in the leather armchair by the fire and put his feet on the brick hearth. "I can't seem to shake it tonight. I had a weird dream about Billy today."

"Today?" She peered over the top of her glasses and wrinkled her brow.

"I fell asleep on the bench by the burn pile."

She stared at him.

"Outside?"

"I know, I know. It's odd. But I was full from lunch, tired from working hard all morning, and…the sun was so warm."

"Still," she said with a trace of concern, "you've never done *that* before. Are you feeling sick?"

His face fell.

"Not really. Just sick at heart. Today's Billy's birthday."

Understanding flooded her eyes.

"Oh, honey, I forgot! It's May twenty-fourth, isn't it?"

He nodded; embarrassed that it still upset him. He'd been struggling with this unresolved issue for far too many years.

"He'd be sixty-one today, Rachel. Sixty-one. I can hardly believe it. Hell, let's face it, I can't believe I'm sixty-two."

She wheeled over to him and covered his hand with hers.

"Oh, Sam. I'm sure wherever he is, he's found peace."

He looked into her gentle eyes and sighed.

"I suppose. It's just that I remember him so vividly. And the dream was *so* detailed. I mean, it felt like I was really there. I was walking home from school, just like the old days. And all the kids were there. Harvey Allen, Bruce McDonald, Doug Smythe, and Renée Snell. Even Manfred Healey."

Her eyebrows drew together, creasing her forehead.

"Renée Snell?"

A trace of jealousy rang in her voice. Sam was glad to hear it, and knew it was intentional. For flattery. They moved back to the couch, where he sat beside her wheelchair.

Her mouth twisted to a pout. "Wasn't she your first love?"

He grinned and leaned over, brushing her lips with his. "Now, don't you worry, my dear. It was just a dream. I stopped liking Renée in the eighth grade. She ended up being a snob."

A smile crept to her lips.

"Well, okay. If you say so."

Settling back in her chair, she opened her book again, placing a finger between the pages to hold her place.

"Funny you should mention that Healey boy, though."

Sam's heart skipped a beat.

"What? Manfred?"

"Yes. I heard he's out of jail again. He's moving back into his parents' old house."

Sam's stomach spiraled.

"Oh my God. I thought he'd be in for life this time."

She shook her head.

"I'm afraid not. Maryellen saw him at the market. He was stocking up. Buying mops, cleaning stuff. Getting ready to move back in."

Sam sat still. The fire crackled beside him. It should have warmed him; instead, he shivered.

Manfred Healey would be around seventy years old now.

He shook his head in disgust. Now he'd have to drive by Healey every time he went anywhere in town. Passing that empty house was bad enough. But driving by the man who killed his little brother would be unbearable.

Sam was certain Healey was guilty. Healey hated the boys and treated them like dirt. Calling them vermin, he'd nearly run them over on several occasions. The police suspected the young hood of foul play weeks after searching for Billy. But they found no body. No evidence. No Billy. No trace of the little boy who drove his brand-new bicycle down the road and never returned.

Cold, greasy guilt rode over him again.

It was my fault. If I'd gone with him when he asked me to...

"What was he in jail for?" Rachel asked, dispersing the dark thoughts.

"Huh?"

"That Healey boy. I can't remember. What was he in for this time?"

"Oh. Well, he's hardly a 'boy' anymore. He's eight years older than me."

"I know, it's just a habit. My dad always called him, 'that Healey boy.'"

"It was for aggravated assault and armed robbery. He beat that poor gas station clerk unconscious and robbed the cash register."

Light dawned in her eyes.

"That's right. It's been a few years since he got convicted for that one, hasn't it?"

"I think so. I've lost track. The man's been in jail more than he's been free."

"Such a shame. To think he actually lives in our town. What a contrast," Rachel said.

"Contrast? To what?"

"Well, I was thinking to whom, actually. To folks like Bruce McDonald, naturally. For goodness sakes, Sam, I think he's actually going to be nominated for the Presidential race. Can you believe it? Oh! And I heard today that he's the one who's buying the old mansion on River Road."

Sam's eyebrows shot up.

"What? Bruce is coming back to town?" He got up to stoke the fire. "I don't believe it. After all these years?"

Senator McDonald lived in New York City for decades while carving his political niche. His seat had been well established. He'd taken an apartment in D.C. and commuted between both cities regularly. New York elected him in a landslide at the last election. It was unthinkable that he would return to such a tiny town in upstate New York.

"That old place is a wreck, isn't it?" Rachel asked.

"Oh, yeah. It's a white elephant. But if you've got the cash, as I'm sure he does, it could be almost palatial when it's all done."

"Palatial?" Her eyebrows arched. "Hmm. That will be fun to watch."

Sam reached into his pocket for the bottle and marble.

"By the way, I found this for you today in the knotweed patch."

He handed her the bottle. Her face lit up.

"Oh, how lovely. It's perfect, Sam. I'll clean it and add it to the collection. What else did you find?" she asked, eyeing the marble.

"This old cat's eye. Kind of unusual. It's opaque, except for this section here, see?"

He rotated it near the lamp. The soft green glass glimmered and flashed in the light.

"Beautiful," she said.

"I love the color. Reminds me of algae. You know, the kind that grows on the granite boulders at the lake?"

She took it from his hand and looked at it.

"You mean lichen, honey."

"Oh. Right."

She studied it in the light.

"Sea foam."

"What?"

"That's what the decorators would call it today. Sea foam."

Sam looked askance at her and sat back on the couch. She handed the marble back to him.

"Sea foam?"

"Yup."

"Okay. If you say so."

He flashed a smile, pocketed the marble, and grabbed his book from the side table, a mystery about a young Seminole detective in Florida, entitled *Tread Not on Me*, by R.C. Burdick.

I wonder if R.C. is a man or woman?

It would be fun to guess, to see if he could tell from the writing. Suddenly, he was anxious to get started. The small talk with

Rachel had helped him over his rough patch. He picked up the novel. In minutes, he was transported to another world, where the Florida waterways came alive with gators, mosquitoes, buttonwood trees, exotic birds, and slow moving streams that snaked beneath mossy overhangs. He didn't budge until Rachel started snoring two hours later.

Chapter Six

Morning sunlight danced across Sam's eyelids. He woke easily, eager to get into his gardens. The glowing blue numbers on the digital clock read six-fifteen.

Rachel slept soundly beside him, mumbling incoherently just before she rolled and dragged the covers over her head. She would sleep for another two or three hours. The multiple sclerosis dictated she get at least ten hours every night.

He used the bathroom, jumped into the shower, and emerged in seven minutes. He timed himself, pleased that he shaved a minute off yesterday's shower.

Funny how these things go so quickly when the land's calling your name.

Changing into yesterday's jeans and a fresh tee shirt, he brushed his teeth, took his blood pressure medicine, a multivitamin, and his calcium. After running a comb through his wet hair, he ignored the gray stubble on his chin and hurried outdoors.

Maybe I'll grow a beard. Less fussing around in the morning.

The air bathed his skin, fresh and cool. Drops of dew glistened on the leaves of the lady's mantle perennials near the back porch.

The leaves shimmered, heavy with condensation. The temperature had dipped to forty-five overnight, but had already risen to fifty. The grass soaked Sam's shoes, which quickly turned soggy. He wore thick socks beneath and didn't care.

I'm outside, I'm free, and I can work 'til I drop.

He wandered around the property, ducking wet low-hanging branches and noting each tiny variation from the day before.

The birds sang in glorious harmony. Soloists performed with flawless perfection, from the low hoot of the mourning dove to the caterwaul of the mockingbird. Loudest in the early morning, the divas swooped and dove as melodies intertwined in a chorus of pure joy. He stopped for a few moments to drink in the strains of the symphony.

He crossed the lawn, ambled through the smaller vegetable garden, then under the arbor into the large garden located in the rich black soil of the former horse paddock. Eight forty-foot rows of corn stood neatly on the bottom of the gently sloping garden. Strings tied to wooden stakes stretched along the rows, but sagged where the robins had pulled at the loose ends. They weren't needed anymore, as the corn had been planted, emerged from the ground, and now stood five inches high. Sam passed the rambling patch of Lincoln peas and began to gather stakes and strings from the corn rows.

When he was done, he walked past the corner where he started the herb garden last year. The new herbs he purchased a week ago waited in pots on a plastic tray. He decided to plant the herbs along the fence and transplant those overrun by the mint.

Sam nodded with satisfaction. He estimated the need for three wagonloads of mulch. Mentally calculating the square footage, he walked toward the American yellowwood tree. Overnight, its draping plumes of white flowers had opened. The fragrance floated on the air—intensely floral. Sam had always called it "the bees' tree," since the scent attracted thousands of bumblebees each season. Last winter he researched it online and discovered the tree was actually quite rare, typically found in Mississippi. The inner wood was deep yellow and American Indians originally used it for dye.

He patted the wide trunk of smooth gray bark and gazed at the crooked branches overhead. Hit by lightning thirty years ago, it had survived, in spite of its stark angle. As he pushed his way through the low hanging, wet branches, they drenched him. He laughed and wiped the moisture from his face.

He crossed toward the front of the property and passed the mock orange bushes that also miraculously blossomed overnight. Hundreds of tiny white blossoms remained tightly closed, but dozens were open, resembling small round butterflies with pearly wings. The mild sweet scent purportedly mimicked the aroma of orange trees. Sam had never smelled an orange tree, being an inveterate Northerner, but enjoyed the fragrance of the mock orange, nonetheless.

He made the turn around the side of the house, past the white garden, to the side porch. He feverishly planned the order of tasks for the morning, making a mental list that grew as he examined each new section of the grounds.

A few cars passed by.

Early birds on their way to work?

Sam felt oddly guilty, knowing he didn't have to go in today.

Or tomorrow. Or forever.

A sense of relief passed through him. The guilt he formerly felt when he took a day off to putter in the gardens faded. It transcended into a sensation of deep pleasure. Again, he laughed out loud and headed back to the paddock garden.

I'm free.

He entered by the lower gate this time, around the left side of the pool and beneath the cherry trees that had grown to such a height only the birds enjoyed the fruit. The strawberry patch, twenty-five by forty feet, was situated in a muddy section and featured six varieties of berries. It lay at the bottom of the slope where deep puddles formed during the recent persistent rains.

In spite of it, the plants thrived and were covered in white blossoms. He walked along the length of the patch, inspecting the plants. Abruptly, he stopped. A flash of red caught his eye. Then another. And another.

It was uncharacteristically early. Not even June yet. But there they were—fully ripened strawberries. Sam bent down with enthusiasm and plucked six berries from the wet plants. He dropped them in the pocket of his denim work shirt, then walked up the slope to the dilapidated glider near the fence.

He sat down and took out the first berry. Its tangy juice burst on his tongue. Chewing it slowly, Sam savored the flavor. He popped the next one in his mouth, and the next. As he swung on the old glider, thoughts of yesterday's strange dream returned. He dug around in his pocket for the marble, removed it, and rolled it between his thumb and forefinger.

It looked different in the early morning light. Muted, cooler. He laughed when he remembered the dream where the marble grew warm and he'd drifted into another world. Palming the sphere of glass, he popped another strawberry in his mouth.

The marble glowed.

Sam's jaw dropped.

It flashed and flickered and warmed his skin. He opened his hand and stared at it.

I'm awake. Wide awake.

Fog whirled around the glider. It vaporized from the grass and ascended in a thick cloud. Sam's feet, knees, and legs disappeared. He watched in a trance as the green swirling moisture enveloped him.

Chapter Seven

A DROP OF WATER FELL on Sam's face and woke him. He looked up through half-opened eyes. Moisture from the night air permeated the inside walls of the tent, forming droplets on the canvas. A Coleman lantern flickered in the dark, washing the sleeping boys with soft light.

Sam turned over in his sleeping bag to see Billy, who snored gently beside him. His little brother's honey-brown hair curled damp against his scalp and pale freckles covered his nose. One arm lay uncovered in the cold night air. A pang of affection hit Sam. He tucked Billy's arm back inside and pulled up the sleeping bag. The boy snuggled into it and let out a whispery sigh.

Bruce McDonald slept on Billy's other side, wedged against the tent wall. Sam watched their chests rise and fall by the dying light of the lantern. He tried to settle back to sleep, but felt wide-awake. His gaze drifted to Harvey Allen, who curled in a ball by the door, eyes completely covered by shaggy blond hair. A bag of cheese curls lay next to him, half-spilled on the floor. Sam smiled. Harvey had the appetite of a grizzly. He could eat a whole bag of cheese curls after polishing off five hamburgers and two shakes. Harvey's mother said he had a hollow leg and Sam believed it.

Something moaned outside the tent, and twigs cracked with the pressure of someone or something's weight. Sam sat up. Icy terror muted his voice. His worst fears bubbled inside him until he was sure a giant grizzly bear pawed at the tent zipper.

The wall of the tent moved, pushed in by a ghostly hand.

A laugh followed. Brittle. Harsh. Joined by several conspiratorial sniggers.

Someone's outside.

A shadow moved beyond the nylon zippered screen. It leaned down and drew closer. Sam's heart slammed rapid-fire beneath his ribs. The wind whipped the hair of the man silhouetted against the moonlight. Sam's mouth opened, but he emitted no sound.

As the man drew closer, the dim light of the lantern illuminated his features.

Manfred Healey.

Manfred screamed, hitting the sides of the tent with a baseball bat.

"Ayah! Vermin!"

Harvey woke and scooted back, falling over Bruce, who also woke with a start. Billy sat up and clung to Sam.

"Rahhhrrrr!" Manfred yelled. "Get the little pipsqueaks. Vermin. That's what they are. Vermin!"

Manfred wasn't alone. Drunken faces loomed at him through the nylon screen, shrieking and laughing. The boys in the tent shouted, and terror froze Billy's face into a macabre mask. Bruce put on his glasses, opened his mouth in shock.

"Guys!" He whispered fiercely, as if organizing a war maneuver. "Guys! Listen to me."

Billy whimpered and collapsed against Sam's chest.

"Shut up, Billy!" Bruce said as he jabbed the boy on his back.

Sam bristled and shoved Bruce. "Leave him alone!"

The hoodlums pounded on the tent, screaming obscenities.

"Come on out, you dorky girls. We just want to play!"

"I have my B-B gun!" Bruce picked it up and waved it around. "We can get them!"

Sam's fear deepened as a crazed look came over Bruce's face. Manfred and his juvenile delinquent buddies probably had real guns and knives.

"No!" Sam said. "No way. There are too many of them, and you'll make 'em mad. They're drunker than skunks, Bruce. Just wait 'til they get tired. They'll go away."

Manfred unzipped the flap and stuck his head inside the tent. His Coke bottle glasses sat skewed on his face and his breath reeked of alcohol.

"Come on, you little perverts."

He dragged Harvey outside by his collar. Hands reached inside and ripped Billy from Sam's arms.

Bruce was next, flailing against the teen who grabbed him. "I'll shoot your skinny butts! Let me go!"

Rough laughter exploded around them. Bruce squealed when one of the thugs jerked his BB gun out of his hands. Sam backed up, but Manfred snagged his leg and pulled him outside. The boys huddled together while the drunks taunted them, poking at them with bats and sticks. A tall scruffy boy dashed gasoline on the tent. Sam's heart fell to his feet.

Manfred struck a match.

"Sorry, ladies. You're on my land. Here's the price you pay for trespassing."

He tossed the match onto the tent. The conflagration whooshed up, crackling against an indigo sky. A chorus of wails went up, with Bruce's voice louder than the rest. Sam put his arm around his brother and glared, tight-lipped, at Healey.

"See ya in hell, girlies!" Manfred and his pals raced in a drunken gaggle toward the Healeys' house.

Heavy smoke drifted overhead, infused with the odor of burned canvas. Billy began to cough, choking on the fumes. The boys stepped back to avoid the acrid cloud. Sam stumbled, and fell into a cavernous void.

Chapter Eight

SAM WOKE ON THE GROUND, his face pressed against the metal leg of the glider. Feeling shaky, he sat up and tried to get his bearings. His head throbbed. He palpated a bump on his forehead while a crow cawed overhead in the Catawba tree, reminding him of the cries of Manfred Healey's sidekicks. Stringy black pods rattled in the branches in syncopation with the bird's squawks. Sam looked up, unsettled.

He rose, fought a surge of dizziness, and collapsed on the glider. Feeling dampness on his chest, he touched his shirtfront with trembling fingers. Drenched with dew, it clung to his skin like spandex. As he plucked at it, an odor curled up, assaulting him with its pungent stench.

Smoke. Burning canvas.

He shook his head in denial.

No. It's not possible.

He closed his eyes and the images returned.

The tent-burning event had actually happened, precisely fifty years ago. Sam and his friends ventured in the back woods with tents that night, and didn't realize they'd encroached on the Healey property. Old man Healey owned hundreds of acres and reportedly inherited a significant chunk of "old money," in spite of the contrary appearance of his dilapidated house and cars.

After the assault on the boys, Manfred and two of his drunken pals were picked up by the cops, kept overnight in jail, and subjected to a severe lecture from the police captain. In the months that followed, Manfred's revenge had been relentless. Furious that the boys had squealed, he seized every opportunity to terrorize them, particularly Sam and Billy.

Sam opened his eyes and glanced at his watch. Eight-thirty.

Over an hour and a half?

He shook his head to clear it. Still clutching the marble, he examined it. Cool, smooth, and innocuous, it lay quietly in his hand.

But it was more than cold glass now; it was his link to the past. His link to Billy.

Am I going insane? Imagining this?

He knew of cases where formerly sound patients had lost their minds, gone completely over the edge. It wasn't unheard of for someone to develop hallucinations out of the blue. Granted, they often had cases of latent schizophrenia or bipolar that had been successfully hidden or gone undiagnosed.

But Sam had been relatively sane his whole life.

Well, except for those few months after Billy disappeared.

But the dream, or whatever it was, felt *so real.* The sensations were tactile, the scents sharp, the sounds crystal clear.

He shook his head again.

I'm not crazy.

He unfastened his brace and massaged his lower back, wondering about the marble's owner. Had it belonged to Billy? It could be. They'd often played together in the back woods.

Carefully, Sam put the marble away. He leaned back against a scraggly mass of grape vines on the fence, and looked at the sky. Several cumulus clouds powder-puffed across the heavens. A pair of swallows swooped overhead, tumbling and chasing each other through the air. He ran rough fingers through his thick hair a few times and took a slow, deep breath.

Although the incidents alarmed and bewildered him, the contact with young Billy was also strangely comforting. A sense of longing overpowered him, luring him like Sirens from the rocks.

I want to go back.

No. Not now. He'd have to wait until no one could see him. He'd go outside in the middle of the night, or do it in his living room after Rachel went to sleep.

Guilt washed over him. He rarely kept things from Rachel. But he needed to see Billy again.

A robin hopped across the corn patch, looking for worms. Sam pushed the thoughts out of his head and began to review his list of jobs for the day.

He decided to start with the herb garden. Slowly, he stood, steadied himself, and walked to the barn to get tools, fertilizer, and peat moss. Stashing everything he needed in the tractor cart, he drove it to his badly overgrown herb patch. Next, he returned to the barn to get the rototiller. He walked it out to the garden, and started to churn the border along the fence. He tilled it over and over again. The black rich soil turned easily. When it seemed just right, he turned off the tiller and dropped to his knees to examine it. It sifted through his fingers, pungent and sweet. Satisfied, he added fertilizer and peat moss, and placed the curry, sage, marjoram, chives, rosemary, parsley, burnet, lemon thyme, and eucalyptus along the twenty-foot row that curved gently into the corner of the fence. The overgrown section would remain as it was—a mint garden extraordinaire. And if Rachel had a hankering for a cold fizzy Mohito when the July heat hit, he'd be able to crush fresh mint leaves all day all summer long, for her and every neighbor for miles, and he'd never run out.

He returned the tools to the barn and drove the tractor and cart out to the mulch pile. This year, he'd ordered twenty yards of the double-ground hardwood; aged four years. It was premier stuff, the best he could get. And he got a good deal due to volume. Nobody in their right mind ordered more than ten yards, unless they were a landscaping contractor. But nobody in their right mind had as many gardens as Sam, either. He chuckled and grabbed his pitchfork.

Because of last night's rain, the pile steamed, dark and wet. Sam worked hard to loosen the top layer with a pitchfork, and scooped shovelfuls of the rich mulch into the cart. He drove back to the herb garden and carefully layered it around the plants. After four loads, he stood back and admired his work.

By the time he'd shoveled all twenty yards of mulch, the effect on his arms and abdomen would be greater than that of a membership at an expensive gym. He wondered how much weight he'd lose now that he'd be working outside every day. He didn't need to lose much. Maybe twenty pounds at best. He glanced down at his stomach and patted it absentmindedly. Not too bad for an old geezer.

Sam moved onto the next job on his list. He circled the house and pulled all of the wilted tulip leaves from the flowerbeds. He mulched over some of them, then moved on to weed the strawberry patch.

The tall weeds pulled out of the mud with little resistance. After a half-hour of bending, pulling, and tossing, his back burned. He made three large piles of weeds and lifted all of them into the wheelbarrow. Carefully, he rolled the near-toppling load to the burn pile and tossed the greens onto the pit. They'd burn when he started a hot fire beneath them.

He'd just opened his box of matches when Rachel opened the back door.

"Sam! It's almost time."

Sam frowned.

Time for what?

He waved to his wife, pocketed the matches, and trotted to the house.

She waited at the door in her wheelchair.

"You forgot, didn't you?" A bemused smile played about her lips.

"What am I late for this time?"

"Honey, it's Memorial Day. Remember?"

His heart sank. Oh God. The day was shot. He'd have to attend the parade, listen to the boring speeches, cook a barbecue for a huge crowd, do the dishes, and stay out of the garden the whole day. But how could he have forgotten?

He rubbed his fingers over his stubbly chin and looked back at the property with longing, speculating furiously. He could leave the tiller out, then later, when everyone went home, maybe there would still be enough light to till the strip along the fence, where he would plant zinnias of all sizes and colors, calendulas, cosmos, California poppies, and bachelor buttons.

I'm completely obsessed. Two days into retirement and I've lost it. He laughed at himself and walked onto the porch.

Rachel rolled her chair back. Sam leaned down to brush his lips across her forehead.

"I'm sorry, love. I'll be ready in a jiffy."

"It's okay, you old badger. I can't believe you forgot!"

"What makes you think that?" He could barely conceal the smile that lurked behind his words.

She swatted his arm playfully. "Don't forget. I know you better than anyone on this planet. And I know you forgot, Samuel John Moore."

A laugh snorted from his nose. "Guilty. You caught me. I can't believe I forgot, tell you the truth."

He hung his back brace on the hook by the door and shrugged out of his denim shirt.

"So, what are the plans?"

Rachel wheeled up to him.

"We should get back from the parade around noon. I already did the dishes and marinated the swordfish and chicken. Maryellen's bringing the cucumber salad and a few pies. I'll start the salt potatoes when we get home. The guests are arriving around two. Oh, and I invited Bruce McDonald. Since he's back in town, I thought he might like to see some of his old friends. The Smythes and Allens are coming, too."

Sam smiled and leaned down to squeeze her hand. Her eyes looked tired, even though she seemed excited.

"You're so darned organized, my dear. But be sure you don't tire yourself out. You know, you should have asked for my help. I would've helped."

She looked sideways at him.

"I know. That's why I didn't tell you."

He laughed, kicked off his muddy shoes, and went upstairs to shower.

Chapter Nine

Sam sat in the lawn chair beside Rachel's scooter, enjoying the feel of the sun on his face. He stretched his long legs and waved to Dr. Andrea Garcia and her husband Ricardo, who'd set up camp along the parade route on the opposite side of Main Street. Thoughts of his medical practice raced through his mind.

I wonder how she's handling it? Will she need an assistant, like I did?

He still found it impossible to believe he was really retired, that he didn't have to care for patients any more. A sense of nostalgia washed over him, unimaginable days before, but patently real.

Andrea and Ricardo had many years of experience scouting the best vantage point from which to videotape their children, who marched in the high school band. Noting their prime location, Sam figured they had staked their claim over an hour ago.

The woman to Sam's left slid her chair further into the road, blocking his view. He sighed, scraped his chair ahead, and motioned to Rachel to roll forward a little. The parade hadn't started yet, but the inching had already begun.

"Do you see Maryellen and Timmy anywhere?" Sam scanned the crowd for his daughter-in-law and grandson.

Rachel stood halfway in her wheelchair to get a better look.

"There they are. Yoo-hoo!" She waved her arms in the air to get their attention, then plopped back onto the seat after the exertion.

Maryellen maneuvered the stroller across the intersection and wedged it with an apology between Rachel and a white haired gentleman in a beret who stood on the curb. Timmy's eyes flashed wide with excitement. He wore jeans, a red sweatshirt, and a blue baseball cap. After swiveling the stroller around to face the street in front of Sam, Maryellen dropped into the extra chair Sam had brought for her and started gabbing with Rachel. Timmy turned to Sam.

"Up?"

He obliged, unbuckling the boy and lifting him onto his lap.

A street peddler pushed a cart of balloons, pinwheels, and flags toward them. Timmy jumped down from Sam's lap, reaching for the goodies.

"Want it!"

Sam grabbed his hand before he could escape and motioned the hawker closer.

"What do you want, Timmy?"

He pointed to a small flag.

"Fwag."

"Okay, we'll take one."

He handed the flag to the boy, whose face bloomed with pleasure. Sam ruffled Timmy's copper hair.

"C'mere big fella. Papa wants to hold you."

The boy whipped his flag back and forth. "Fwag!"

Drums rumbled on the far end of Main Street. Sam's pulse quickened. In spite of his earlier feelings of dread, he had to admit he really did love parades, once he dragged himself out of the garden. He watched the townspeople settling along the street. Children ran and laughed, dogs trotted beside their owners, and old friends embraced. He smiled and shifted Timmy to his other knee.

What a perfect slice of Americana.

The town police blocked the road near the only stoplight, an indication the parade was about to start. Sam waved and nodded to most of the townsfolk, having come across them either as patients or through the school. Craning his neck, he stretched to catch a glimpse of the elementary and high school bands queuing at the end of the street.

A pack of Boy Scouts stormed the sidewalks, waving flags and offering red poppies in exchange for donations to the Veterans Memorial Fund. Names of the town's war heroes were inscribed on a monument at the head of Main Street near the grassy commons and the historic log cabin. There were plans afoot to update the memorial, make it grander, and include all of the town's veterans, including those from the current war in Iraq. Sam nodded to one of Evan's pals in the Boy Scout troop. He stopped to offer Sam a poppy.

"Would you like to…"

Sam had two dollars ready and pushed them into the boy's open hand before he could finish his question.

"Of course, Derek. I'll take two."

The boy's face lit up. He handed two poppies to Sam, folded the dollar bills, forced them into the slot in the can, and thanked Sam, racing to catch up with the other scouts.

Sam gave one poppy to Rachel. She stopped mid-sentence, smiled thanks, and picked up her conversation with Maryellen without skipping a beat.

He pushed the poppy's wire stem through a buttonhole in his white golf shirt. Timmy turned around on his lap to examine it.

"Flower. Pwetty." He plucked at the fabric petals.

The wail of a fire engine's siren launched the parade. Timmy twisted on Sam's lap and stood, staring with open mouth at the Village of Conaroga fire trucks and emergency vehicles. They honked and blasted their horns, inching down the road. The crowd erupted in applause when a contingent of officers and volunteers marched past.

Next, a long line of vintage vehicles appeared with their tops down. Elderly veterans waved from within, wearing their war uniforms with pride. Sam clapped extra loud, wanting these brave men to know they were appreciated.

Six horses trotted sideways down the street, tossing their heads. Their coats, buffed to a glossy sheen, sparkled in the light. Their necks curved gracefully, neatened with braided manes. Chestnuts, bays, a pinto and a dun pranced beneath their riders' skillful commands. The local hunt club wore traditional navy blue riding coats, black hats, and long black boots. Nostalgia stabbed Sam.

I want to ride again. I want to turn back the clock.

He looked at Rachel and melancholy washed over him. They'd had such good times together on horseback.

"Horsies. Yay!" shouted Timmy.

Sam shook off his despondency, clapped his hands, and hooted while stretching both arms around his wiggling grandson's middle.

Multicolored troupes of tee ballers marched by with parents who tried to keep them in formation. Purple, green, orange, and red teams meandered in wobbly patterns, waving their arms and tossing wrapped candies to bystanders. Children on the sidelines scurried to pick up the confections, stuffing them into their pockets.

The elementary band approached. The color guard came first, waving blue and white flags in graceful unison. Flags flipped over their heads, around their bodies, and sliced through the air. Louder now, the drums reverberated in staccato overture. With a sudden blast of brass, the band began to play. Sam stood up and lifted Timmy to his shoulders.

"Look for Evan, buddy. He's coming."

Rachel stood and leaned on Maryellen's arm. Sam smiled, pleased that she managed to get up without help.

Sam spotted Evan in his blue, red, and black band uniform. He stood on the near side of the street, holding his trumpet high in the air. He swung it back and forth, up and down, marching in time to the music. Evan's father, Andy, walked ahead of them, guiding the group as they split and marched around the fountain that anchored the intersection of Main and Center streets. Andy beamed and nodded to his family.

When Evan passed, Maryellen, Rachel, and Sam hooted and hollered.

"Yay, Evan! Go Conaroga!"

The high school band followed, playing a march that won first place in recent competition. Their tight, professional sound was far better than most community bands. Sam's heart swelled with pride.

This is Andy's legacy. Just listen to those kids.

When both the senior and junior high bands passed, a black sedan followed with flags flapping on its front fenders. Sam recognized Senator Bruce McDonald, mildly surprised at his youthful appearance. Rumors spread that the senator had everything "done." Eyebrows, chin, hair plugs, teeth, the works. Sam wasn't sure if it was sour grapes, or if his friend had just aged gracefully.

Bruce spotted Sam and Rachel and waved. The public appearance was brief, but probably good for his image. People exploded into applause when he passed. A popular man in Conaroga, Bruce brought substantial funds into the area for historic renovations.

When the procession stopped at the end of Main Street, they paused for a prayer and gun salute. Afterwards, the parade started over again in reverse direction. When the band returned to the starting point on the green, they dispersed. Evan ran toward his mother and grandparents.

"Evan," shouted Rachel. "You were wonderful, honey."

The boy smiled and ducked his head. He held his trumpet in one hand and his hat in the other. There was a small red line on his forehead where the hat had flattened his wheat-colored hair.

"You liked it?" he asked.

They nodded enthusiastically.

"Tremendous precision, Evan," Sam said. "The marching was right on."

Evan smiled.

"Thanks, Gramps. Yesterday, I kept getting out of step. But Dad said I nailed it today."

"He was right, honey," Rachel said. She motioned for Evan to lean down so she could kiss his cheek. He obliged, still chattering.

"Dad said he'd meet us at your house, Grandpa. Can we ride home with you?"

Andy shepherded students, collecting instruments and ushering children to their parents. He'd be busy tying up the loose ends for at least an hour.

Sam stood up and handed Timmy to Maryellen.

"You bet, buddy. Come over here. Let me give you a hug."

Evan fell into his open arms. Sam hugged him tight, then held Evan at arm's length and inspected him.

"You're getting so tall, my boy. Growing like a weed."

Evan's hazel eyes looked like Billy's. Mostly brown, their swirls of green mixed with flecks of gold. Sam stared at him and his heart turned to mush. The resemblance to Billy was uncanny. He loved the boy deeply, for his own special traits and personality. But whenever he looked at Evan in just the right light, he saw his brother. Billy had loved parades, too.

Someone tapped Sam on the shoulder. He whirled around, expecting Garcia.

"Hi, neighbor."

Sam stiffened. *Manfred Healey.* He wore wrinkled clothing, sported a gray, scruffy beard, and squinted at Sam through thick, cracked glasses wrapped in the middle with duct tape. His venomous black eyes had not changed from decades past when he'd tormented Sam and Billy for sport.

"Manfred. I see you're back," Sam said, keeping Evan close to him.

"Yep. Finally let me out. Say, who's this young fella? Looks like your brother," Manfred said, leering into Evan's face. Evan pulled back. Manfred's breath reeked of alcohol. Just like it had years ago, in the tent, on that awful night.

Sam steeled himself. "This is my grandson. Nice to see you again," he lied, "but we have to run."

Rachel led the way, parting the sea of people with her wheelchair. Maryellen hurried after her with Timmy, and Sam walked with his arm around Evan's shoulders.

Manfred laughed behind them, slurring his words.

"See ya 'round, neighbor."

Chapter Ten

THE CHARCOAL BRIQUETTES SPUTTERED with chicken and swordfish drippings when Sam poked them with a big fork. He'd been tending the grill for the past half-hour, chatting with guests who meandered around the backyard. Pushing away a stray strand of hair, he sighed, regretting he hadn't yet graduated to a gas grill.

He'd eyed them—passed by them in department stores, checked out the prices, and put a few on his list of favorites. He considered hinting around for Father's Day, but didn't want the kids to have to fork over too much for a present. Their daughter Beth made a good salary, but living expenses in New York City were ridiculously high. She struggled to make ends meet. Andy and Maryellen had decided to forgo Maryellen's salary when Timmy was born, so she could stay home and tend the boys. They clipped coupons, turned off the heat at night, and pinched pennies as hard as they could.

Just like we used to, thought Sam.

His mind wandered. He found it tough to enjoy conversation with his guests today. Harvey Allen and his wife, Mabel ambled over to him. They exchanged news about their children, talked a little about Harvey's restaurant and Sam's retirement, then ran out of fodder. The Allens wandered away to find someone more interesting to chat with. At least that's what Sam's brain told him.

Doug and Cindy Smythe made it a point to greet Sam when they came in at two o'clock on the button. Cindy, twenty years younger than Doug, was the topic of some pretty hot gossip when they first married. Doug remained single until he met Cindy while installing her computer ten years earlier. He still worked for the same national computer firm, and had apparently made his way up in the company over the past decade.

Cindy watched and giggled each time Doug snorted with derision when his opinion conflicted with Sam's. It happened frequently. He laughed at Sam's old-fashioned, non-techy ways, and couldn't believe Sam still used an "archaic" landline for the telephone. The topics of conversation strayed from Doug's opinions on the war, to how many amazing problems Doug solved at work that day, to what unbelievable deals Doug, the "deal maker," finagled at the hardware store last Saturday, to how his little sedan got nearly forty miles to the gallon because of the clever adjustment he made to the carburetor.

When Sam thought he couldn't fake interest for another second, Doug and Cindy wandered away to corner another unwitting victim. Sam moaned with relief and turned back to his grill, with uncharitable thoughts running through his head.

Yep. Still the most annoying guy in town.

He decided to tell Rachel his heart wouldn't break if she neglected to invite them next year.

He flipped one thick slab of swordfish after another and pushed them together as if fitting pieces of a puzzle, then poked at the chicken breasts that circled them. The marinade dripped on the coals and sizzled.

"Smells great, Sam."

Senator MacDonald was accompanied by a gorilla, apparently hired to defend him from the dangers of Conaroga's treacherous citizens. The bodyguard had a rhino forehead, a thick set of black eyebrows that met in the middle, and long arms with big hands and knuckles. The butt of a gun poked out beneath his jacket.

"Well, well, well." Sam said. "Look who's come home to roost." He nodded toward the bodyguard. "Who's your friend?"

"Oh, that's Rufus." Bruce flashed a disarming smile. "He watches after me. Keeps away the bad guys, you know?"

Sam raised an eyebrow.

"You really think there are bad guys in my backyard, Bruce?"

He smiled. "Of course not. But I couldn't leave Rufus to stew in the hotel now, could I? I guess he could go mingle. Go ahead, Rufus." He shooed him toward the table covered with bowls of chips, dip, and Maryellen's cucumber salad. Beside it was a tin tub filled with ice and beer. "Get yourself a drink and find a nice place to relax. We're among friends here."

Rufus grunted, looked suspiciously at me, and obediently plodded away.

"We're staying in a hotel until the mansion gets some running water in the kitchen. Guess those pipes have been busted for years, huh?"

Sam looked hard at his old friend. Flashes of baseball games, birthday parties, and the burning tent floated up from his memory.

"Do you want it straight?"

Bruce laughed awkwardly and nodded.

"Sure."

Sam wasn't sure he meant it, but continued in spite of his doubts. He had the right to know.

"I've been inside. It's gonna need major renovations, Bruce. You'll probably sink a hundred and fifty grand into repairs and redecorating."

Bruce's complexion grayed. He wobbled and grabbed Sam's arm for support.

Sam steadied him. "But, when it's done, it'll be a palace. The finest home for miles. Certainly worthy of the next President of the United States."

Bruce collected himself. He straightened and actually grabbed the lapels of his expensive suit coat.

"Well, Sam. That's all just speculation. But if I was bestowed with that honor, I'd do my best to serve our country."

He looks so pretentious. Sam laughed. He felt like he was being primed for a vote.

"I'm sure you would, Bruce. I'm sure you would."

Bruce's expression softened.

"Hey, Sam? I noticed how nice your grounds look. Would you like to stop by some time this week and give me some advice at the mansion? I could use some ideas, and might even try my hand at gardening in my spare time."

Sam looked at him with interest. It was a long time since he had a gardening buddy. His first and only gardening pal, Roger, moved to Florida two years ago.

"Sure," Sam said. "I'd love to. That old place has some rare plantings, as I remember. In the good old days it had one heck of a gardening staff. I think they employed three full time guys. Think you're up to that?"

Bruce wasn't deterred.

"No problem. Whatever it takes. I want to make it a home we can be proud of."

Sam smiled and flipped the swordfish.

Bruce spied Harvey and Doug on the other side of the lawn. His eyes lit up. The expression reminded Sam of a younger Bruce. They'd spent summers together when Bruce returned from his private school in New Hampshire every June. He spent most of his time at the Moores' house. Sam's mother loved the boy and often invited him to dinner. The warmth of the household had attracted him, time after time. His own home life was too proper, too formal. There were few hugs in Bruce's life. He took as many as he could get at Sam's.

Bruce headed for Harvey and Doug and began to pump their hands. Sam figured he was probably priming them for votes, too.

Bruce and his wife had no children, although Sam knew he'd kissed hundreds of babies in the last few months. He kept his picture-perfect wife, Kimberly, on a short leash. There was talk of an affair she had with an up and coming judge in New York City. Sam didn't know if there was anything to it, but heard Kimberly traveled everywhere with Bruce since the alleged affair was discovered.

Kimberly stood nearby, chatting with Maryellen, whose eyes had gone flat. She nodded while the Senator's wife droned on and on in her nasal voice. Sam recognized the expression on Maryellen's face. It was the same one he wore when Doug Smythe had bored him silly earlier.

Kimberly was too thin, with short platinum hair. Her fashion obsessions bordered on the absurd. She wore a tight silver dress with giant tortoiseshell buttons that marched down the front in two parallel rows. The skirt fell to her upper thigh, revealing far too much of her skinny legs for a backyard barbecue. Sam didn't know if it was actually supposed to be in fashion, or if she just lacked good taste. He shook his head and turned back to the swordfish. It was a waste of time even speculating about such nonsense.

The remaining fillets turned brown and crispy on one side. He flipped them over, taking care not to break them apart. Evan approached with a Frisbee in his hands.

"Grandpa?"

Sam brightened.

"Hey, how's my number one grandson doing?"

Evan scuffed his feet and looked embarrassed.

"You always say that."

Sam smiled broadly.

"You were born first, therefore, you earn the title of number one grandson."

Evan beamed at him. His eyes sparkled and the freckles across his nose stood out after being exposed to sunlight all morning.

"So, you wanna play?"

He wiggled the old purple Frisbee. It was their game. That, and their "indoor" game of gin rummy.

"Can you wait 'til I'm off duty?" Sam asked. "I need to finish cooking this stuff, then I'll be free for a while."

Evan nodded.

"Sure. Come find me when you're done?"

Sam nodded and smiled at the boy. Evan grinned, took off at a sprint, and disappeared behind the crowd.

Gus fingered the marble in his pocket while he finished up the cooking. A whisper crossed through his mind. It was foul and insidious; rustling like the wind on a dark, wet night.

Look at them. Milling around like a bunch of insipid otters. They make me sick.

Sam dropped the marble back into his pocket. He was stunned by the ferocity of the voice that whispered so viciously, but couldn't place it.

Where did it come from? The past?

Suddenly a thought struck him.

What if it's from the present?

He shivered, rejected the idea, and started serving his guests.

Chapter Eleven

WHEN THE CROWD had been supplied with swordfish, chicken, cucumber salad, beans, and biscuits, Sam wolfed his meal and noticed Evan, who sat quietly on the swing, rotating the Frisbee in his hands. He stared at the ground and scuffed his sneakers on the dirt patch that came from years of dragging his feet.

Sam sneaked up behind Evan, grabbed the ropes, and pulled the swing back.

Evan turned with wide eyes and a smile. "Grandpa!"

"Hang on tight!" Sam waited until Evan grabbed hold, and gave him a big push.

"Hey, I'm too old for this!"

Sam didn't stop. He pushed at the next opportunity, sending Evan even higher. The boy laughed out loud.

"Gramps! Stop!"

Sam suddenly grabbed the ropes, stopped it dead, and twisted Evan around until it could twist no further.

"Ready?" he asked.

The boy nodded.

"One, two, three, go!"

Evan spun like a cocoon on a silk string. The boy closed his eyes and gripped the ropes hard. As he neared the end, the revolutions slowed. Finally, it stopped. He looked at his grandfather and smiled. A flash of joy raced through Sam's heart.

"Ready for some Frisbee?"

Evan nodded, jumped off the swing, and ran through the garden toward the side yard where Sam had mowed a large section of the field just for this purpose. He glanced at his guests, feeling just a little guilty for abandoning them, and joined Evan in the field behind the hedgerow, where no one could see him goofing off.

A strange feeling of excitement coursed through him, suggestive of childhood. It was a sweet sense of anticipation, reminiscent of when a group of boys would gather at this very field to start a game. Sam and his father played catch out here, too. The summery, delicious sensation was exhilarating.

"Heads up, Gramps!"

The Frisbee whizzed toward him, coming at him from the right and heading straight for his hand. He caught it and smiled.

I taught him well.

"Here it comes," he said, spinning it in a gentle arc back to his grandson.

Evan leapt a few feet and nipped the disk from the air. "Got it!"

He landed lightly on his feet and whirled around to send one flying almost over Sam's head. Sam jumped, caught it, and whipped it back to the boy. His knees hurt when he landed, but he ignored the pain.

"Geez, you're still pretty good!" Evan said.

Sam grunted and missed the next catch. He ran toward the raspberry patch to pick it up.

"What do you mean? Considering my age?" He trotted back, slightly out of breath.

Evan grinned.

"Yeah. Aren't you like, over eighty now?"

Sam laughed out loud.

"What?"

He spun another good one toward the boy. Evan leapt in the air and stretched high to catch it.

"Yeah. You're like, ancient!"

Sam ran toward him and collared him.

"You know I'm sixty-two, you little knucklehead."

Evan broke away and danced around his grandfather with the Frisbee.

"Betcha can't catch me!"

He started sprinting back and forth, just out of Sam's reach. Sam lunged for him, missed, lunged, and missed again. He leaned over, with his hands on his knees, trying to catch his breath.

"Maybe I am ancient, after all," he laughed.

"Oh, Gramps. You're not so old."

Evan walked over to his grandfather and touched his arm. Sam straightened and reached for the boy, pulling him into a bear hug. Evan hugged him back, laying his head against Sam's chest.

"I love you, Grandpa."

Sam's heart skipped a beat. His voice was hoarse when he answered.

"I love you, too, my boy. Think I'll keep you around a while."

Releasing Evan, he ruffled his hair.

"You're a good kid, Evan. I'm real proud of you."

Evan smiled, then started doing handstands. Timmy emerged around the hedgerow and tottered toward them with Maryellen close behind. When she saw where Timmy was going, she slowed down and let the baby run toward his grandfather.

"You got him, Papa?"

Sam nodded and crouched with his arms outstretched. When Timmy reached him, he came so fast and hard that the force of the assault knocked Sam onto his back. He flopped down on the grass, picked Timmy up, and held him high.

"Plane!" shouted Timmy.

Sam raised his knees and propped them under Timmy's stomach. He held the boy's arms straight out from his sides and started making airplane noises.

"More!"

Sam continued for a while, until his arms ached. Finally, he let Timmy down. The boy rolled off and lay on his back beside Sam, looking at the sky. Sam pointed to the clouds.

"Clouds, Timmy. See?"

Timmy squinted in the bright sunlight and pointed.

"Clowns."

Sam laughed, leaned over, and kissed his little buddy on the cheek. The boy's eyes were bright and his skin glowed with health. One pudgy hand reached over and found Sam's. Evan sat down on the other side of Sam, and leaned back to look at the clouds. From where they lay, they could hear the party, but couldn't be seen over the wide hedgerow of raspberries. The scent of the freshly mowed grass smelled intoxicating.

"That one looks like a witch," Evan started.

"Which one?" Sam asked. His lips twitched.

"What? Oh, I get it," Evan smiled. "You're so corny, Grandpa."

"That's what you love about me, my boy. Now what about that one over there? Do you see what I see?"

Before Evan could answer, Timmy did.

"Clowns."

Evan and Sam laughed together.

"Hey! That one over there really *does* look like a clown. Gramps, Timmy was right!"

Timmy stretched out on his back, stared at the sky, and repeated with certainty this time.

"Clowns."

Chapter Twelve

SAM ROSE AT FIVE-THIRTY Tuesday morning, anxious to get started. He cooked a few eggs, scrambled them with American cheese, then topped them off with a dollop of salsa. A strong need tugged at him. He craved a good dose of gardening to make up for socializing with all of those boring people.

Well, they hadn't *all* been boring. Some had been reasonably entertaining. But the most fun he had was playing with Evan and Timmy.

He finished his eggs, downed a large glass of orange juice and took his pills. After rinsing the dishes, he put them in the dishwasher, grabbed his back strap and denim shirt, and briskly walked outside. He'd meant to get the pool opened by Memorial Day, but hadn't managed. He was determined to get it started today, because the weatherman predicted a heat wave by Thursday.

It was wonderfully cool outside. Heavy dew covered the grass and leaves. The orange plastic wheelbarrow leaned against the black walnut tree where he'd left it. He grabbed the handles and steered it toward the driveway. Two bags of sand and chemicals waited in the back of the SUV. He hefted the bags into the wheelbarrow, carefully nestled the chemicals on the side, and headed for the pool.

First, the pool cover needed to come off. It was dark green poly, new last year. A deep layer of rainwater and leaves brewed on top. Deeper than Sam realized, it was almost ten inches in the center. The cover stretched taut at the rim due to the weight of the water.

Sam walked back to the barn. He grabbed the blue submersible pump and a fifty-foot length of yellow garden hose. Walking back to the pool, he connected the hose to the outlet of the pump, set the pump on top of the cover in the deepest part, and plugged it in. Instantly, it chugged and sucked water. A steady stream of brownish liquid spurted out the end of the hose. Sam walked the hose all the way past the cherry tree and over to the knotweed colony. He looked at the tall, dry stalks that towered above. Determination flooded through him.

I'm knocking down a bunch today. Maybe the whole damn patch.

He eyed the knotweed, then his mind rushed again.

I need to start the fire pit. And I really ought to mow again. And trim around the gully. And fill the birdfeeders. And plant those nasturtiums. And cut that dead tree limb that's still hanging off the beech tree. And...

He stopped himself, took a deep breath, and focused.

One thing at a time. Slow down there, soldier.

While the pump worked to lower the water level on the cover, he decided to attack the knotweed. It wouldn't require any mechanical means, and wouldn't wake the neighbors. His rule of thumb was no motorized equipment until at least eight o'clock in the morning. He emptied the wheelbarrow by the pool, and pushed it over to the knotweed patch.

He started on the nearest tall patch, pulling thick stalks toward him and twisting until their brittle stems snapped. Hollow and dry, they sported ridges every few feet that resembled bamboo, but were thinner and not as tough. The stands stretched ten to twelve feet high. He broke off stalks and stuck them under his arm in a loose bundle. When he had stuffed about two-dozen beneath his arm, he went to the circular stone fire pit and laid them over the pile of dry twigs and branches. The weeds he'd pulled days earlier had started to dry and would burn just fine.

After pulling off the pool cover and starting the hose to bring the water back up to the right level, Sam made headway in the jungle. He worked for an hour, clearing a rectangular section eight-by-twelve feet. The wheelbarrow stood half-full of rocks that he'd cleared to make rototilling easier. He looked at the tall burn pile with deep satisfaction, stopped and stretched, then massaged his sore back.

It was time to start the fire. He walked into the barn and pulled three paper towels from the roll he kept on top of the freezer that held last year's tomatoes and several frozen turkeys. Unscrewing the top of the lighter fluid, he squirted it onto the paper towels. Sam walked back to the fire pit and stuffed the paper towels underneath the bottom twigs. He left them sticking out a little, so that when he dropped the burning match they'd catch. He hoped.

He backed up a few steps, looked around to make sure Rachel wouldn't see what he was doing, struck a match on the side of the box, and dropped it.

The match went out and fizzled.

On the second try, the towel whooshed with a foot-high flame. Sam repeated the action on the other two towels, and the inferno rose high about his head. He nodded in satisfaction and went back for more fuel.

By noon, Sam had added the pool chemicals and hooked up the filter. The water wasn't exactly sparkling, but in a week or so it would clear up. His work in the knotweed had also been productive: he'd uncovered a great deal of the patch. The soil beneath the old, dead stalks looked soft and dark. After raking the stones and debris, he'd be able to till it in no time.

By mid-afternoon, he'd had his fill of clearing land, and decided to hop on the lawn tractor to remow the front and tackle the lush side sections that he never got to a few days ago. He hoped to finish it by suppertime.

The drone of the lawn mower was almost cathartic. Sam wrenched the wheel around and around, circling the white lilacs. He edged the white garden and looped around the blue spruce in the front yard. He'd set the deck level at two inches this time, down a half-inch from last week when he had barely been able to mow through the heavy, thick meadow in his front yard.

"Saaaaaaaaaaam."

Sam was startled out of his grass mowing stupor by what sounded like someone calling his name. He stopped the mower for a minute, lowered the throttle, and looked toward the house, half expecting Rachel to be at the door.

She wasn't.

He shook his head, then pushed the throttle and kept going.

When he circled the ancient cedar tree with the blue bachelor buttons growing at its base, he heard it again.

"Saaaaaaaaaaam."

He wondered if it was somehow the mechanical whining of the engine that sounded like someone calling his name. It seemed farfetched.

"Saaaaaaaaaaam."

This time it was unmistakable. The voice was clearer, and he knew to whom it belonged.

It's Billy.

Billy called Sam in the same melodious voice he had used fifty years ago. Sam drove the tractor to the barn and stopped. The voice stopped as well, but a warm glow pulsed in his pocket. He dismounted and headed out to the glider in the fenced garden. Completely hidden from the house or road, he lowered himself slowly and reached for the green marble.

Billy was calling.

Chapter Thirteen

THE TRANSPORT TO THE PAST was swift this time, whisking Sam back to his childhood the instant his hand wrapped around the marble.

They sat in the back of the Oldsmobile station wagon on sticky plastic seat covers. There were no seatbelts. Sam perched between Bruce and Billy, holding his bat and glove. He tried to hold back scalding tears that threatened. Clenching and unclenching his fingers around his glove, he couldn't stop the parade of humiliating images that marched across his mind's eye.

He'd lost the game. Everyone had been there, even his teacher. Sam had swung wide, missed the pitch, and sealed his fate. He wanted to die.

Billy sat beside him, his quiet presence comforting. Billy felt his embarrassment, understood his shame. They exchanged soulful glances when they got in the car. There was no need for words.

Bruce sat with them in the back seat. He pushed his thick glasses onto the bridge of his nose and uttered a petulant sigh.

"The pitch was bad. He almost hit you with that ball!"

Sam tried to control his irritation. His father looked at him from the rear view mirror and smiled sympathetically.

"No." Sam said. "The pitch was good. I just missed it."

Bruce turned to him, angry this time. He raised his voice to a tinny whine.

"I saw it. He almost hit you! It wasn't fair. We should have won."

Bruce didn't get to play often; he was usually benched.

Sam's mother turned to look at Bruce.

"Now, Bruce," she said in her company voice, "it was only a game. Let's not get worked up over it, okay?"

She said it with a smile, but meant business. Her tight voice precisely enunciated each word.

Bruce ducked his head. "Okay. Sorry, Mrs. Moore."

"That's okay. Well now, who wants ice cream?"

Sam instantly forgot about baseball and shot his hand in the air with Billy and Bruce.

"We do!"

His father took a left turn down Oak Street. He pulled into the Pleasant Valley ice cream stand. Dozens of cars filled the gravel parking lot. Families packed the area, waiting in line at two windows, sprawled over picnic tables, and chatting beside their cars. His father pulled in beside a black Chevy Bellaire with red fins. They got out, stood in line, and discussed the flavors. Sam chose orange sherbet, Billy asked for chocolate chip, and Bruce ordered chocolate butter almond. His mother had a strawberry shake, and his father had his usual, pistachio.

With cones in hand, the boys ran ahead to find a table. Bruce tripped over nothing, flew in the air, and landed hard on his right knee. The cone spiraled out of his reach and splattered in a sandy patch of dirt under a pine tree.

His face scrunched in pain and he bent over his knee. Blood trickled from his fingers.

"Are you okay?" Billy asked when he reached Bruce first and helped him up.

Bruce held back the tears and nodded.

"I guess so."

Sam pulled a red handkerchief from his back pocket and handed it to Bruce. He dabbed it on his knee, wincing. The ragged tear in his uniform revealed a small cut. Billy picked up the dirtied cone and tossed it into an open receptacle.

"You can have mine," Billy offered, holding it out to Bruce.

Bruce shook his head,

"No. It's okay. You eat it."

His mother reached them seconds later.

"You're bleeding," she said, examining Bruce's knee.

Bruce actually smiled. He savored the attention, even if it was for something like this.

"I'm okay, Mrs. M."

His father appeared a moment later with another cone in his hand.

"Here ya go, big guy."

Bruce got up, accepted the ice cream gratefully, and hobbled over to a picnic table.

Sam took Billy aside and put his arm around him. He ruffled his hair affectionately.

"That was nice of you, termite."

Billy looked at his brother, who towered over him by four full inches. They were only a year apart, but Sam had been through a recent growth spurt.

"Well, I felt bad for him. Things like this are always happening to him."

They looked at Bruce, who basked in glory between their parents, then back at each other.

"Yeah, I know." Sam lapped his dripping cone. "He's kinda accident prone."

He and Billy shared a quick smile, and headed for the picnic table to rejoin their parents.

Chapter Fourteen

SAM WOKE SLOWLY, slumped against the glider. He opened his eyes, rubbed his neck, and stretched out his legs. Rising like a dizzy prizefighter, he glanced at the position of the sun, then at his watch. He'd been out for over an hour. He put the marble away and took a few unsteady steps.

Stopping in his tracks, he licked his lips.

Tastes like orange sherbet.

Shivering, he walked back to the glider and sat down. He touched his fingers to his lips, tentatively.

They feel sticky.

A feeling of vertigo overcame him, as if he were fluctuating between two realms. The cottonwood trees moved in and out of focus, closing in on him and then zooming away. The sound of children playing in the Pleasant Valley picnic area echoed and bounced around the edges of his brain.

It's time for him to die.

The voice shouted in his brain, strident and harsh. Sam held his head in his hands, shook it to dispel the feelings of nausea and disorientation, and sat still.

I must be imagining it.

The starlings warbled about him, swooping down to the feeder and back to the dilapidated eaves of the barn. A car whooshed past. Lila meowed and rubbed against his legs.

He leaned down and absentmindedly stroked her back. She stood on her hind legs and pushed her nose against the palm of his hand. Sam looked down at her and smiled.

"Good girl. Good kitty."

He sighed, pushed the thoughts of Billy and the nameless hellish voice out of his head, and stood up, feeling sturdier now. Lila rubbed around his ankles and purred loudly. He picked her up. She climbed onto his shoulders with alacrity and suddenly purred into his ear. Sam let her balance there for a few moments, stroked her back, and gently put her down. She trotted off to the house.

He finished mowing the lawn, then started up the tiller and walked it to the cleared section of the knotweed patch. With a great sense of satisfaction, he began to churn the dirt. He stopped, lowered the throttle, and leaned down to grab the debris that rose to the surface. Pieces of broken bottles, aluminum cans, foil, old metal springs, and even TV dinner trays surfaced. He continued to stir up the soil and expose the garbage that someone had once assumed would never be disturbed.

Had it been his parents who buried the trash? He tried to remember, but could only summon pictures of the old incinerator they burned from time to time. Everything that could be burned was thrown in the barrel. The vegetable matter was composted. The rest went to the dump.

Sam pressed on. He tossed the garbage in the wheelbarrow and continued to work the patch. When he was about halfway through, the tiller hit something, and stalled. Sam tried to tilt it back, and grimaced when it wouldn't move.

The tines were stuck hard on something.

He yanked on it again, pulling it from side-to-side. Finally, it broke free. He lifted the tiller again, this time it rose slowly. He knelt down and looked, leaning over to brush off some of the dirt. Reeling, he fell to the ground and scurried backwards.

One tine of the tiller protruded through the eye socket of a small human skull.

Chapter Fifteen

Rachel placed a cool cloth over Sam's eyes. He slumped in the recliner, mumbling under his breath.

"Billy. I know it's Billy. He's been out there all this time."

Sam's insides rolled with grief. Rachel gently shushed him.

"You don't know that. Let's wait for the police to do their job. Then you'll know for sure."

The local police lieutenant stood outside with several officers from Conaroga, the state police, and the county coroner. They also called in federal agents, who were expected the next day. Sam wasn't sure why they were summoned.

He sat up slowly and looked out the window at the men who streamed over his property.

"Look at 'em all." He loosed a low whistle.

Neighbors and curious onlookers had gathered on the roadside. Manfred Healey, Doug and Cindy Smythe, and Harvey Allen gaped at the skeleton lying unearthed, dusted free of dirt and debris. Everyone thought it was Billy. Sam was sure of it. Sure as he knew his own name.

It's Billy.

Billy had called him to the site through the marble. He meant for Sam to find him.

Officer Ned Olsen walked up to the kitchen door and poked his head inside.

"Sam?"

Rachel wheeled over to Ned and whispered something that Sam assumed was a protective, mother-hen comment.

"I'm fine, Rachel. Come on in, Ned."

Ned looked apologetic. He ran his bony hand through short gray hair, then drew a handkerchief from his pocket and mopped at his forehead.

"Damned hot out there."

Sam had known the lieutenant for years. He'd treated all of Ned's children, helped Ned's wife survive breast cancer, and sang with him in the church choir. Ned had a fine baritone voice.

"Come on in, Ned," Sam said.

Ned headed for the couch. "Thanks."

Rachel wheeled up behind him. "Cold drink, Ned?"

Ned mopped the perspiration from his brow with a wrinkled white handkerchief and nodded.

"Yes, please, Rachel. Got any lemonade?"

"You bet. Comin' right up."

Sam looked hard at Ned, who didn't flinch. Ned collapsed on the couch and fanned himself with a copy of the Stokes seed catalog that Sam had been reading the day before.

"So? Is it him?" Sam asked.

Ned grimaced.

"Billy?"

Sam nodded. The lump in his throat clogged his airways. His pulse pounded hard in his ears. Ned scrubbed his hand over a patch of stubble on his chin. The clock on the mantle ticked loudly.

"Officially, I can't say a word until the coroner is through. But these bones look like a younger child. Maybe six or seven. Billy was eleven, right?"

Sam nodded and spoke in a hoarse voice. "Just turned eleven the day he disappeared. Rode off on his new bike and never came back."

Ned was silent for a minute. A drop of perspiration rolled down his temple.

"This one might match a cold case that's been open for years. Young boy from Livonia went missing on a summer evening about fifty-five years ago. Name was Tommy Donahue. Five years before Billy disappeared. The number one suspect was the boy's uncle, who killed himself shortly after being accused. Years later, it was discovered he couldn't have been in the vicinity at the time the boy was taken. Apparently the uncle was unstable to begin with, and the stress of the accusation sent him right over the edge. Poor fella." He sighed.

Sam was almost afraid to let the relief flood his body. What if they were wrong?

"So what happens now? Is the case re-opened?" Sam asked.

Ned nodded.

"I think so. Haven't ever had to deal with this sort of thing before. But the Feds will know. They've been tracking this and other related murders from various states in the northeast. Scuttlebutt is that a boy's been taken every five years for the past fifty-five."

Rachel wheeled back into the room with a tray on her chair.

"What? Oh, Ned, that's horrible. Do they think this poor child was one of them?" She pointed toward the backyard where skeleton had been found.

"Could be. They're investigating all murdered children. Problem is, we're in the sixtieth year now. This is the year they're afraid the thirteenth murder will be committed. Assuming the bastard is still alive."

Sam looked thoughtfully at Ned.

"So, he'd have to be at least my age, or older, right? I'm sixty-two." He looked at the ceiling while he did the math in his head. "The first abduction would have been when I was seven. Hmmm. I see what you mean. He could have passed away."

Rachel spoke up.

"Let's hope so, gentlemen."

Both men nodded. Sam sighed, still shaken. He'd been so sure the bones belonged to his little brother. He didn't know whether to be relieved or disappointed. As upset as it first made him, it would have been good to know, after all these years.

"Ned?" Sam asked. "Have they ever tried to match the prison releases dates of Manfred Healey with that killer's five-year pattern?"

"I doubt it. Manfred was suspected in Billy's disappearance, but there was no evidence, and nothing connected him to the other cases."

"Might be a good thing to look into," Sam said softly. "Especially since he's out again."

Ned laced his fingers beneath his chin.

"I'll suggest it to the Feds. I'm sure he's on one of their lists, anyway, with his history."

Sam stood.

"Good. I still think he was the one."

Ned pressed his lips together.

"I know, Sam. I know."

Chapter Sixteen

ON WEDNESDAY MORNING, Sam drove along Bruce's winding driveway, avoiding the potholes dotting the pavement. Around the last curve the mansion came into view, sitting regally amidst a weed-infested lawn. Fronted with Doric columns, the majestic three-story home was topped with a widow's walk. A few black peeling shutters hung crooked from windows and the front storm door swung on one hinge. As Sam approached, the true condition of the old place became clearer. It looked shabbier than he remembered. Windows were smeared with grime, old wooden clapboards were rotting, leaves from the previous fall littered the porch floorboards, and on the north side of the house the ivy grew so thick it obscured four windows.

Bruce's limo was parked out front, beside a dark blue sedan and an electrician's van.

The arborvitae flanking the front door tipped inward from both sides, seriously overgrown. It would have to come down. And the trumpet vine that raged up the side of the portico climbed out of control. Sam would suggest a heavy pruning.

He passed the van and observed the cracked fountains, overgrown flower gardens, a sad-looking orchard, and a seedy lawn that appeared to have been attacked by a rusty fungus and overtaken by masses of dandelions.

Bruce waved to Sam from the barn on the north side of the property. The estate had once boasted showcase stables. All that remained of the former elegance were acres of faded post and board fencing badly in need of whitewashing.

Sam waved back. A white haired man hurried away from Bruce, heading for the sedan. Sam watched him drive away, then greeted Bruce beside the watering trough.

"Hey! You made it!"

Sam smiled.

"It's only a few miles."

"I know. Right around the corner. We'll almost be neighbors again, huh? Anyway, thanks for coming. I appreciate it."

Sam grunted and smiled. "No problem. I'm retired now, remember? I have time on my hands. And it's kind of nice to get away from all the ruckus at my place."

Bruce squinted in the sunlight, hung his hammer on the fence, and motioned for Sam to follow him.

"They're still crawling all over, huh?"

Sam rolled his eyes. He'd explained about the skeleton to Bruce on the phone earlier.

"Yeah. It's unbelievable. They're trying to identify the bones to see if they fit with the serial killer. Pretty creepy."

"That guy who just left was looking for your place. He got turned around, I guess. Remember him?"

Sam shook his head. "Didn't look familiar. Who was he?"

"His family bought old lady Graymore's house long ago. When he was in fourth grade. He was two years behind us in school."

Sam looked up. He had a vague recollection of the quiet, nondescript boy who had lived in the Graymore house.

"What was their name? Sullivan? Scranton? I can't remember. It started with S, though, didn't it?"

Bruce nodded.

"Stewart. It's funny. He went to Everdale, my high school, then on to Harvard. I used to tease him, told him to quit following me. It was our running joke. He's been in the Bureau since he graduated from Harvard. A real star, so I hear."

Sam reached down and picked up a dried branch that lay across the path.

"So he's part of the investigation? Was he looking for me?"

Bruce ducked under a low hanging branch.

"No, no. He's just interested in the crime scene. Said he's been chasing this maniac since the beginning. Knows the most about the case. I gave him directions. Said he hadn't been back in town in a long time and got all turned around on these country roads. I hope you don't mind, Sam."

Sam shook his head.

"I vaguely remember him. Anyway, what's one more agent? If that murderer really did kill the boy in my backyard, I hope they catch him before he does it again. Sick bastard."

Bruce sobered.

"It's horrible." He paused. "Let's try to forget about that creep for a while and take a tour."

Sam nodded and gestured ahead.

"Okay. Lead on."

They walked around the back of the barn, turning toward the orchard.

"Do you ever think about him, Bruce?" Sam asked, pushing through the long grass.

Bruce stopped. The perpetual smile on his face softened, faded. He grimaced, and sat on a boulder, making room for Sam, who sank down beside him. The strong June sun beat on their backs.

"About Billy? Sure. Sure I do."

An overwhelming wave of sorrow washed over him. Bruce was one of the few people left who had really known Billy.

"Why didn't you guys ever talk about him after it happened? You never said a word when I came back from the hospital. It was strange. Like he never existed. My folks were the same way. As if they came up with a pact *not* to talk about him."

Bruce's smile faltered.

"I know. We were so afraid you'd lose it again; we decided it was best to talk about other stuff. Baseball, girls, cars… anything but Billy. You scared the hell out of us, Sam, when you had that breakdown. And then, when they took you away, well, it was like you disappeared, too."

Sam turned to Bruce. There was a catch in Bruce's voice when he spoke the last words. Sam searched his eyes, and recognized his old friend, but without the thick glasses.

"It must have been tough on you. Billy and I were all you had back then. Your folks sure weren't around much."

Bruce's face dropped.

"It was the worst time of my life. You and Billy were my only real family, Sam. You know that. My parents, bless their souls, weren't cut out for children. After I was born, my mother swore she'd never have another. I was an annoyance, nothing more. That's why I hung around you and Billy so much. And your folks. God, I still miss them."

Sam smiled sadly.

"They were the best." He sighed and looked off into the distance. "It'll be ten years in August, you know."

"I know. I still remember the day I heard about the crash. I was in Washington, campaigning. I wanted to come home to see you. I felt horrible about it, but was afraid to face it. I remember thinking up some lame excuse why I couldn't make it back home for the funeral. But I stalled until it was too late. I'm still ashamed of that."

They sat quietly for a few minutes. Sam leaned forward and flicked a blade of wet grass from his boot. A robin chirped nearby, breaking the silence as she hopped over the grass searching for worms.

"We all do things we regret. It was a tough time. I know you loved my folks. But you know, eventually I accepted their passing. Because *I knew what happened.* It wasn't like with Billy. You know, the constant questions. The never-ending blasted questions."

Sam's face fell. He ran his fingers along the rough surface of the boulder, flaking off some mica that winked in the sun. He wanted to talk about the marble with Bruce, but couldn't muster the courage.

He'll think I'm nuts again, Sam thought. *Just like when Billy disappeared. Hell, maybe I am nuts.*

"It still upsets you, doesn't it?" Bruce asked.

Sam's eyes shifted down. He wasn't sure how honest he could be with Bruce. He ran his fingers through his wavy gray hair.

"Yeah. Tell you the truth, it haunts me. Every damned day."

Bruce lifted a hand to Sam's shoulder and squeezed.

"I'm so sorry, my friend," he said in a hoarse whisper. "I'm so very sorry."

Sam looked up. Bruce seemed sincere. It touched him.

"I just wish I could talk to him, you know? Find out what happened. Even if he is dead, which I know is most likely the case, I just want to know *what the hell happened.*"

Bruce's expression froze for a moment. He closed his eyes, seemed about to say something, and shook his head imperceptibly. He stood up.

"I know. But it's been fifty years, Sam. You really have to try to let it go. Look to the future, and all that. Now, what say we continue the tour? Let's head over to the perennial gardens and take a look."

The topic was closed. Sam sensed Bruce's mood shift. Was it impatience? Or was he just uncomfortable discussing something so painful?

They walked through the old orchard toward the house.

Sam shelved his feelings and focused on the trees. He ran his hands over their gnarled trunks and examined their branches, breaking off twigs to look for green growth. "You can probably reclaim these apple trees. You'll need to prune them hard, and give them some decent fertilizer. Dig the grass out from around their trunks; open up the soil a bit. You might actually get them to produce again."

Bruce looked through the thick, crisscrossed branches and smiled. "Really? That would be nice. I love apples."

They meandered toward the house, passing through an overgrown patch of elderberry bushes, along a cracked walkway that snaked through the thickly populated backyard. Statues of angels, small wishing wells, and ceramic squirrels and rabbits met them around each bend. The plants encircling them grew untidy and oversized. Sam recognized most of the perennials, although the flower buds were still tightly closed.

"You've got a nice clump of Rudbeckia there," he said, pointing behind the wishing well.

"A clump of *what?*" Bruce asked.

"Rudbeckia. More commonly known as black-eyed Susan."

Bruce smiled. "Nice. What else do we have?"

Sam listed dozens of plants until Bruce's eyes glazed over. He stopped and put his hand on Bruce's arm.

"You really aren't interested in the plants, are you?"

Bruce lowered his eyes.

"I'm sorry. I guess I just wanted an excuse to see you, Sam."

"Why?"

Bruce hesitated. "I miss our friendship. The older I get, the more I think about our childhood and the comfortable relationship we had. The people I've been dealing with for the past few years have been abominable. They try so hard to please me, but they don't even know me. Frankly, I'm sick to death of them, and I'm sick to death of the person I've become when I'm around them."

"Is that why you moved back here?" Sam asked quietly.

Bruce stopped, ran his hands over the cement head of a cherub, and nodded.

"I just wanted to come home."

A rush of affection warmed Sam. He smiled at his old friend; relieved he hadn't completely gone to the dogs.

"I'm glad you're back, Bruce. You've got your work cut out for you with this property, though. Come on. Let's get busy."

Chapter Seventeen

THE FBI SPENT TWO WEEKS on Sam's property, sifting through the dirt. Sam visited Bruce several times and helped him clear some of the undergrowth from the orchard, sick of the commotion on his land and glad to get away from it for a while. The only positive result of the FBI invasion was the bulldozing of the jungle to search for clues. The knotweed was practically gone, leaving a broad bare patch of smooth earth. They filtered through the refuse buried around and above the body. Each sardine can and piece of tin foil was scrutinized. Sam planned to rake the soil when they were gone before scattering grass seed. The new sprigs of red-leafed knotweed would probably grow among the blades of grass, sprouting from the bits of shredded vegetation and remaining roots. He would mow it until, starved of nutrients, it shriveled and died. At least that's what he hoped.

On Wednesday, Sam watched the excavation from his roadside garden, which had grown and blossomed in the past few weeks. It spread eighty feet from the woods to the barn. The perennials grew seven-feet deep along the stretch. Red hollyhocks, rose and gold honeysuckle vines, brilliant orange-red roses, red and pink Monarda, vibrant pink and purple beard's tongue, "paprika" yarrow, and various other assorted flowers sprawled along the long bed. The indigo blossoms of the Baptisia plants were just starting to bloom; red Geum flowers clamored for attention beneath them.

He knelt beside a patch of gladiolas he'd planted a month earlier and pulled out the dandelions growing through the mulch. He was anxious to hold the marble again, but hadn't been alone in weeks. Outside, he was always in the proximity of the federal investigators. Inside, Rachel hovered, sensing his unease.

He felt the pull of the smooth green glass. The draw of unheard voices was strong. It troubled him that he couldn't respond to the summons.

With green stained hands and dusty jeans, he moved another few feet, tackling the next patch of weeds. The weeds had to go. He was as persistent with them as he would be chasing Billy's killer.

Sam pondered the significance of the bizarre events that took place over the past few weeks. Had he not been obsessed with clearing the land, he wouldn't have uncovered the marble. Had he missed its reflection in the soil, he wouldn't have flown back to his childhood. Was the experience truly being orchestrated from beyond? Were the vignettes in which he was thrust real, or the imaginings of a brain gone mad? No. He remembered these events. They'd been real.

But what did Billy want?

"I've got it!"

The voice came from the federal investigator closest to him. Sam moved slowly. He rose, lifted the wheelbarrow full of weeds, and walked it toward them. The men huddled together over something. Sam worked his way closer, turned the corner around the fence, and dumped the weeds into the burn pile. Their backs were turned to him. He stepped closer. They ignored him, as they had for the past two weeks.

"Is it intact?" the white-haired agent asked. He looked like the man who had been at Bruce's two week's earlier.

The young agent held something in his hands.

"Yeah. It's like the others."

"Silver, or bronze?"

The young man held it to the sky after dusting if off.

"It's silver. Looks like another World War II medal. I can make out some words on it. Looks like 'valor' and 'honor.'"

"Same as the Baltimore murder?"

The younger man answered.

"Same as all ten murders. All except the second one, if there *was* one. Year five. Who knows if that one will turn up?"

Suddenly the senior agent turned and stared at Sam. His piercing gray eyes bored into Sam's.

"What are *you* doing?" he asked.

Sam sensed the man's irritation. A fleeting feeling of guilt washed through him, quickly replaced by indignation.

"What am *I* doing? I'm on *my own property*. I'm gardening. And I overheard you. I'm wondering who the heck this boy was who's buried on *my* land?"

He looked back at the agent with unwavering determination. The man capitulated and held out his hand.

"Mac Stewart. We used to go to school together."

Sam shook his hand. The agent motioned to the bench in the shade. He took the medal from the younger man and walked with Sam. Sam figured Mac must be sixty; probably getting close to retirement.

"I hear you're the one who found the skeleton."

Sam crossed his legs and leaned back. "I did. Hell of a shock."

"I'll bet." Mac took out a toothpick and started to chew on it.

"I thought it was going to be my brother."

Mac shot a look at him. "Billy, right? I remember. He was a year ahead of me in school."

Sam massaged his forehead with one hand. "Yeah. When I tilled up that skull, I thought for sure…"

Mac finished his sentence. "That it was him?"

Sam nodded and looked off into the woods. "Yeah."

"I'm sorry. I remember it well. I've always considered Billy's case part of this investigation. Even if we never found his–" Mac stopped.

"It's okay." Sam's voice grew hoarse. "His body. You never found his body."

Mac turned the grimy medal over and over again in his fingers.

"Aren't you worried about disturbing the prints?" Sam asked.

Mac shook his head. "No. After fifty years we've never been able to lift a set from any of the medals we've recovered buried in the dirt."

"So that's his modus operandi, huh?" Sam asked.

"Yeah. I shouldn't be telling you this, but to tell you the truth, I'm damned tired. Tired of the department. Tired of the searching. Tired of being so tight-lipped about it. I told them to use the newspapers and the Internet. Maybe they'd find out more, you know?" He leaned forward and massaged his temples with one splayed hand, then sat up again and locked eyes with Sam. "I'm tired of searching for years for a monster who has eluded us ten times. Eleven young boys, for God's sake."

"Twelve, if you count my brother," Sam said.

"Well, we don't know that for sure."

Sam smacked his right hand with a balled fist. "It *has* to be. This boy was killed in our backyard. My brother disappeared five years later. The next boy was killed five years after that. It's too coincidental."

Sam hated to think about it. To imagine some freak killing his brother. It was too hard to swallow. But he couldn't ignore the coincidence. "Where was the third boy found?"

Mac looked at him and sighed.

"Like I said, I shouldn't tell you this."

He glanced at the other agents and then back at Sam.

"It was Boston. Cambridge, to be exact."

"That far away?"

Mac nodded.

"Yeah. Same kind of metal was attached to the boy's shirt. That one was discovered not too long after he was killed. Buried near a cemetery. Name was Alan. Alan Krupner. It was my first case."

Mac's expression soured as if he were remembering the gruesome discovery.

"Awful way to start your career, Mac."

"Yeah, but that's the business I'm in. Made a lasting impression on me. Kept thinking about that poor boy. What he must've gone through. What his folks went through. I can't stop until I find him. I can't let him do it again."

Sam listened to him discuss the deeds, but wondered about his sincerity. He said the right words, but almost seemed to get a thrill out of the conversation. He wondered what kind of a person would go into this field in the first place. How could they stand it? Looking at dead bodies, fighting against monster child-killers? He shrugged, pushed the unkind thought out of his mind, and realized he was glad there were such brave souls in the world. Who else would protect the kids?

"What's the theory behind the war medals pinned on the boys? Is the killer a guy who's anti-military? Thinks too many young boys died in the war?"

Mac chewed on his toothpick for a while.

"The psychologists think maybe his father was in World War II. He was abused, or witnessed some horrific act by his father. The murders could be his way of getting back at him."

"But why the five-year cycle?"

"A ritualistic frequency? Hard to tell what causes the patterns. Maybe we'll find out, if we ever catch him."

Sam repeated the same question that he'd been asking Ned.

"What about Manfred Healey? He grew up right over there, not far from my backyard where we found the bones. I always thought he was the one who killed Billy. Creepy guy, really nasty. Seems to thrive on other people's pain and discomfort. He always hated my brother and me."

"Oh, he's a real winner." Mac shook his head and almost smiled. "I remember him. He used to drive around in hot rods, terrorizing the neighborhood."

"That's him."

"We're checking his record. Ned suggested we match the murders against Healey's prison release dates. He does fit the profile. Had a rotten father, rotten family. Lots of problems growing up. Apparently he's drifted around the east coast, New York, Boston. Yeah. I'll keep an eye on him. If he's the one, and if the pattern continues, he's getting ready to go after his thirteenth victim."

After a thoughtful pause, Mac stood and started to pace, his arms waving at his sides. "You know what? We're going public. I don't care if they call me on the carpet for it. I'm ready to retire, anyway. I'm phoning the papers when I get back to the hotel. It's his anniversary this year. Maybe we can flush him out."

Mac stopped and stared into the woods, as if Healey lurked there, watching us.

"Good." Sam shifted on the bench and tried to ignore the warm sensation of the green marble glowing against the fabric of his pockets. Echoes of the eerie demonic voice that spewed words of hate, that talked of it "being time for him to die," kept repeating in his head. He took a deep breath and braved the words. "I have a gut feeling the bastard's getting ready to do it again."

Mac tossed Sam a quizzical look.

"Oh?"

Sam felt his face grow red. He knew he sounded nuts.

"I'm not claiming to be psychic or anything. It's just some... some recurring dreams I've been having. Pretty weird stuff. I heard a man's voice say, 'It's time for him to die.'"

A polite expression of disbelief washed over Mac's face. Sam knew he'd lost him.

"Forget it. It was just a stupid dream."

He stood and shook the agent's hand. Mac gripped his fingers for a long time, slowly pumping up and down while he scrutinized Sam's face. *Probably looking for signs of dementia*, Sam thought. His face felt wooden and an overwhelming desire to pull weeds hit him. Anything to get away from the narrowed eyes that glittered with what almost looked like amusement.

"Thanks for filling me in, anyway," Sam said.

"If you have any more premonitions, let me know. Meanwhile, I've got some calls to make."

Chapter Eighteen

THURSDAY MORNING, Sam walked to the mailbox to get the paper. The story had been all over the television news. He flipped the paper open and read the headlines.

Serial Killer, linked to Upstate. Medal of Honor Murders. Five-Year Psycho, Ready to Strike Again?

Pictures of the murdered boys flashed over the morning shows and Internet. Photos of the skeleton in the knotweed patch, thankfully without Sam's address, were shown in addition to close-ups of the medals, laid out on a neat square of black velvet. Experts were interviewed. The medals had all come from World War II, but analysts believed the chance of all ten medals being awarded to one soldier was slim. They'd probably been purchased at places such as pawnshops or Ebay.

The front page of the paper displayed photos of the boys and the medals. The second square was blacked out, with a small insert ballooned to the side with a photo of Billy. The caption read: *Billy Moore, second victim?*

Sam's heart twisted when he saw his brother's face smiling at him from the paper. The marble warmed against his leg. Insistent. Urging him to cooperate.

He headed toward the back of the barn to sit on the bench and read some more. A chart filled the center of the page.

Year	Victim #	Name
0	1	Tommy Donahue - Livonia, NY
5	2	?
10	3	Alan Krupner - Cambridge, MA
15	4	Mike Shaw - Cambridge, MA
20	5	Duncan Meyer - Trenton, NJ
25	6	Phil Broughder - Long Island, NY
30	7	Norman Silverstein - Oakland, Maine
35	8	Barry Waldman - Washington, D.C.

40	9	Frankie Peabody – Manhattan, NY
45	10	Bobby Reece – Manhattan, NY
50	11	Jason Freedman – Baltimore, MD
55	12	Mackenzie Ryder – Virginia Beach

Sam studied the list and longed to compare it with Manfred Healey's imprisonment record. Ned Olsen had promised to call him tonight with the results. He looked in the direction of Healey's house. Through the woods, it was about a ten-minute hike, slightly uphill. If the man truly was a threat, or planning another murder, maybe someone should be watching him.

He glanced toward his own house, watching the men wrap up the work in the broad patch of dirt that used to be the knotweed jungle. An idea began to form.

The last investigator tossed his equipment into his car and skidded out the driveway with a brief wave of his hand. The bulldozer operator finished leveling the ground, and loaded the rig onto a trailer. With a belch of black smoke, the transport truck slowly rolled down the road, leaving Sam's grounds quiet for the first time since his rototiller had unearthed its grisly prize.

Sam headed for the back porch, stepped into the kitchen, and grabbed the binoculars from the peg on the wall beside the door. He slung them over his shoulder and wandered into the living room where Rachel sat weaving the cane seat of an antique chair.

"Thought I'd do some bird watching today." Sam shuffled his feet and looked toward the window. He knew Rachel would disapprove of his clandestine intentions. The guilt churned in his stomach. He shot a quick glance at her, toying with the binoculars strap.

Rachel didn't look up from her work. She'd been taking in chairs to re-cane for twenty years. This particular chair belonged to the church and would be done for free. She'd finished setting up the strands and had begun to weave across them.

"Really? Oh, honey, that's a great idea. It'll get you away from all this for a while." She gestured toward the television set. The volume had been muted, but the same photos of the victims that Sam had studied on the front page of the paper paraded across the screen.

"Yeah. I need a break." He leaned down and brushed his lips over her forehead. She smiled up at him.

She wheeled back from her work. "You'll need a lunch and some bug repellent. Go douse yourself and I'll throw a sandwich in a bag for you."

Sam ducked into the laundry room to get the bug spray on the shelf over the washing machine. He squirted the repellent all over his clothing, concentrating on his socks and pant legs. It was a bit early for ticks, but he didn't want to take a chance.

"Don't forget sunscreen," Rachel called from the kitchen.

He rummaged behind the bleach and other bottles of chemicals to find the sunscreen, slathering it onto his face, neck, and arms. When he was done, he strode back to the kitchen, picked up his lunch sack, leaned down to kiss Rachel, and headed for the woods.

Chapter Nineteen

SAM LAY ON HIS STOMACH on the incline below Manfred Healey's house. Lush grass created a soft green bed for him, hidden behind a cluster of bushes. He peered through the binoculars at the dilapidated structure and the seedy grounds.

Shutters hung crooked from many of the windows. Some had fallen off and lay against the foundation in high grass. The lawn had turned to a field decades ago, with patchy grass a foot high, full of weeds. *How odd that both this old place and the mansion are in similar states of disrepair.* But the mansion's grounds weren't littered with a defunct washing machine, a rusty swing set, dozens of tires, an old yellow school bus, a rotting couch, several storm doors with broken glass, and a chaise lounge on which Manfred Healey snoozed.

The old man was thin with scraggly gray hair. He sprawled on the chaise lounge with eyes closed and mouth open. His taped glasses had fallen down his nose.

Beside him were a shovel, a bucket, and an empty bottle of whisky. Sam studied the shovel with the field glasses. Dirt clung to the steel blade. *Fresh dirt.*

Sam's skin crawled.

What had Manfred buried?

He shivered.

Or whom?

He studied the area behind the house, searching for patches of upturned soil. Slowly raking the glasses back and forth over the property, he stopped when a rabbit hopped into his field of vision, twitched his whiskers, and scuttled beneath the bus.

The marble warmed in Sam's pocket. It called to him with its insistent glow, its unrelenting tug. He nearly reached down to take it out, but was arrested by something fluttering in the breeze beside the school bus. The dirt was not turned, nor was the tall grass disturbed. Nevertheless, Sam zoomed in on a bicycle handle protruding four inches above the ground. Long grass lay flat beside it, where the rabbit had been sleeping in the shade. The red rubber handles had disintegrated over the years, but the white plastic streamers remained intact.

Sam's heart pounded hard. His pulse raced. And he stared at the handle of Billy's birthday bicycle.

The marble burned the skin on his thigh. He glanced down at his pocket. It glowed, shining through the fabric of his jeans. He couldn't stand the heat. Taking it out, he cupped it in his hand.

Green fire seared through his palm. Sam plummeted through the void. Jade streaks swirled behind his eyelids. He moved rapidly through time, internally blinded for a millisecond, then whooshed into the dining room of his childhood.

༄༅

A blue flashbulb exploded and nearly blinded him.

"Good one! Okay, now one more of you two boys together, okay?" His father replaced the burnt flashbulb and motioned for the boys to move closer together.

Sam leaned nearer to Billy and slung his arm around his shoulder.

"Say cheese!" his mother said.

The boys obeyed. "Cheese."

The flash sparked again. Fluorescent green dots danced about the room wherever Sam looked. Billy rubbed his eyes and grinned. His birthday cake dripped with white, fluffy frosting, covered in split strawberries. "Happy Birthday Billy" scrawled across the top in red icing. A yellow candy "11" stood in the center of the top layer. His mother leaned over the cake and lit twelve candles. Eleven for Billy's age, and one to grow on. His father set the camera on the sideboard, drew the drapes, and turned off the dining room light. The candles on the cake shimmered and flickered in the darkened room.

"Happy birthday to you, happy birthday to you, happy birthday dear Billy, happy birthday to you."

The voices intertwined in different keys, sounding ridiculously mismatched, yet wonderful to Sam's ears. Billy took a deep breath and blew. The candles wavered in the breeze and snuffed out, curling into wisps of smoke. His father turned up the lights, opened the drapes, and they clapped and cheered.

His mother sliced the cake into generous pieces and placed them on small blue plates. Sam wolfed down his piece, licked his lips, and watched his father walk into the kitchen. Billy's present waited behind the door: a brand new bike wrapped in red ribbons, with a bell, streamers, and reflectors. Sam exchanged excited smiles with his mother and held his breath while his dad rolled the bike into the dining room.

Billy jumped from his seat and sputtered.

"Holy Cow! I don't believe it. It's so keen, Dad. Mom. It's *brand new!* Oh, Sam, look! It has streamers. It's so neat!"

Billy leapt onto the bike and rode it around the dining room table.

"Not so fast, son. Not in the house. Take it outside, please," his father said with a smile.

"Come on, Sam. Let's go for a ride!"

Billy pleaded with arched eyebrows and such an enthused expression that Sam couldn't say no. "Okay, buddy. I'll go for a ride with you."

The black phone on the desk trilled. His mother picked it up.

"Sam? Why, yes. Sam's right here."

Sam looked at the phone curiously.

"For me? Who is it?"

His mother shrugged, smiled shyly, and handed him the receiver. He accepted it as if it were an alien. Nobody ever called him. All communication was made on the street, with bunches of kids on bikes or combing the woods together. The guys rarely used the telephone to talk.

"I'll be out in a sec, Billy."

Billy waved to him, then jumped off his new bike and pushed it through the kitchen door.

Sam lifted the receiver to his ear. "Hello?"

"Hi, Sam. It's Renée."

Sam's heart flew into his mouth.

Renée! Renée Snell is calling ME.

He couldn't speak. His knees knocked. Visions of her creamy skin and flaxen hair swam before his eyes.

"Sam? Are you there?"

Sam stuttered, then squeaked in a ridiculously hormone-laced voice.

"Yes. I'm h…here."

His father raised one eyebrow and glanced at his wife. He mouthed the words, "A girl?" and received an answering nod from his wife.

Sam turned his back to them and spoke for a long time to the girl who made his legs wobble and his heart hammer. He'd catch up with Billy later.

Chapter Twenty

THE MAN SAT IN HIS CAR and ruminated about the past. About the boys. All the boys he stopped on their eleventh birthday. The year it happened to him. The year his family had fallen apart. The year they'd forgotten about him. Their own child. Cast aside like an unwanted kitten.

His mind switched gears to the kid he'd been following. He stared at the boy through the telephoto lens on his camera. This one looked so much like Billy, it was uncanny.

The little bastard has to go.

I've waited so long. Too damned long. The years of elaborate plotting had been delicious, but the act would be so much sweeter. And when it was over, the perfect plan will have come to a lovely, voluptuous, raging head.

Look at the kid. Always the center of attention, so damned goodlooking and bright. They love bright. They don't like awkward, plain, and unloveable.

I'll show him.

Once the kid is gone, *he'll* suffer. They'll be sure he did it; there'll be no doubt about it. He'll suffer like I do. Every single day. Suffer real bad.

He glanced down at the newspaper folded to the front page on seat beside him. His illustrious history, laid out for the world to admire. Those boys were innocent. Happy. Cute as buttons.

Except after he strangled them. Then they were real quiet. Real sorry they'd been such a pain in the butt.

He shifted on the leather seat and sighed.

It's almost time.

Chapter Twenty-one

SOMEONE KICKED SAM in the ribs.

He looked up, momentarily blinded by the sun. The marble had rolled out of his hand and lay on the grass beside him. A man stood silhouetted in the sunlight overhead. Sam sat up and rubbed his side. Healey leered toward him, reeking of whiskey.

"What the hell are you doing in my backyard, you snooping shon-of-a-bitch? Spying on me, huh?"

Healey booted him again. Sam scooted backwards and held up his hands.

"Wait a minute! Just hold on."

The next blow was harder, knocking Sam onto his back.

"Can't give me a minute's peace, can you?"

Sam scrambled to his feet and backed away. He ducked as the drunk swung at him. Healey stepped toward him, pulled his arm back, and landed a solid blow on Sam's jaw.

Sam reeled, cradled one hand over his aching jaw, and sprinted away from his attacker, toward Healey's house. Healey followed close behind, stooping to pick up a metal pipe that he swung in wide arcs over his head.

Sam ran as fast as his sixty-two-year-old legs would take him.

Healey swung the pipe against Sam's back and connected. Hard. Sam went down near the lawn chair at the back of the house. He got up, but Healey shoved him before he could recover. He tripped over the shovel with the fresh dirt on the blade and knocked over the bucket. A pile of worms and dirt spilled onto the ground. Sam saw the fishing pole that leaned against the house and scrambled over the bucket to regain his footing. Realization flooded his brain.

Healey's going fishing. He dug for worms, not bodies.

Sam began to run again, this time back toward the woods. The binoculars swung heavily against his neck. His breath rasped in his throat and he paused to catch his breath. He turned to see the old man stumble.

Healey screamed when the gap between them lengthened. "Vermin! Swine!"

Sam stopped at the spot where he'd flattened the turf spying on Healey. On his knees, he combed his fingers frantically through the grass.

Where is it?

Healey grew closer, slurring his words. "Wait up, you shon of a bitch."

Sam raked his fingers over the ground until Healey was nearly upon him. When he thought he'd lost the marble for good, his fingers finally closed around it. He shoved it in his pocket and bolted. Healey grabbed at his shirt, but missed. Sam kept moving. His knees hurt, his chest heaved, and his head felt as if it would explode. He moved faster than he had in years, leaping over fallen trees like a young boy.

Healey's voice faded. Sam stopped and looked back. The drunk had fallen again. His bloodied face trickled red from a gash on his forehead.

Sam hesitated, thinking more like a doctor than a scared kid now. Should he help him?

Healey began to wail.

"Mommy! It hurts. It hurts real bad. Mommy!"

Sam's eyes widened.

Healey got to his knees, wobbled a bit, then lurched after him again.

Sam spun around and took off. He bolted down the path that twisted and turned through the woods. Branches slapped at his face, the binoculars rapped against his chest. His breathing was tight; his vision strained.

Healey's voice started to grow hoarse. "Pig! Vermin!"

Sam kept running, but his strength was running out.

"Wait!" Healey's voice cracked and a loud wail filled the woods. He fell to his knees, sobbing. Sam paused, wondering if it was over. The old man collapsed amidst a volley of tears and profanity.

His voice turned whiny. "Daddy, why did you kill my Mommy? Why did you make me bury her in the woods? I want my Mommy!" Abruptly, Healey's voice deepened and steadied. "Shut up, prissy boy. Or you'll follow her to the grave."

Sam dropped to the ground and laid his face against the wet leaves while he caught his breath. It smelled of ripe mushrooms and fetid algae. Listening to Healey spew the insanity chilled him.

Healey stared at Sam, then screamed long and shrill, huddling in a whimpering mass, his arms wrapped around his knees. Rocking and crying, he seemed encapsulated in the self-comforting ritual. While Sam watched, the old man flopped sideways, popped his thumb in his mouth, and cried himself to sleep curled in a fetal ball.

Sweat ran down Sam's temples and back. His shirt stuck to his body and his breathing was still labored. The side of his hand stung where he'd ripped it against the thorns of a blackberry bush. He raised it to his mouth and licked the salty blood. He waited five minutes until his respiration steadied, never taking his eyes from the sleeping demon.

That's the man who killed my little brother.

He got up and walked closer to him, staring.

I could smash a rock against his skull. Take him out forever.

Instead, Sam took one last look, felt an awkward, overwhelming sense of pity for the man, and flipped open his cell phone to call MacStewart.

Chapter Twenty-two

THE FBI AND SEVERAL MEMBERS of the local police department searched Healey's property that afternoon, unearthing the bicycle in minutes. Much to Sam's embarrassment, it wasn't Billy's. It was an older model, possibly old enough to match the bike Tommy Donahue had ridden. There also was the distinct possibility that it had belonged to Healey when he'd been a child. There were remnants of silver paint on it, not red. It had been crushed by something heavy, maybe a car. Sam studied it, strangely disappointed. He wanted closure. He *needed* closure.

He stared at the baseball cap that had been uncovered beside the bike. It had almost fallen apart, shredded into nothingness. It made him sick to see it sitting on the investigator's table, bagged and tagged like a fabric cadaver. He felt sick to the stomach and sick at heart. Had the little boy whose skeleton he found in the knotweed patch worn this hat? Had it belonged to Tommy Donahue?

Although Sam hadn't received the confirmation he expected, he was pretty sure Billy was dead. He'd sensed it for years. It was a sinking, low-lying, uncomfortable feeling. It had lurked in his heart, prodded at his subconscious, and given him unbearably sad nightmares. The certainty was there. But he usually pushed it away and tried to maintain the fantasies that gave him hope.

And now, now as he looked at this rotten piece of fabric that might have belonged to another murdered child, buried beside the rusty bicycle, he heard a voice in his head. This time it didn't belong to a deranged killer. Instead, it was the voice of dry-eyed logic.

Your brother is gone. Give it up. He's dead.

The faint hope he occasionally fostered about abduction faded. The delusion about the sixty-one-year-old brother who had lived his life in another city and who would someday come home, be reunited with him, vanished. Like an air-bound fish, the fantasy flopped and died on the pier.

Sam's spirit collapsed. The agents roamed around him, murmuring important phrases, busying themselves with analysis. A large tow truck arrived to drag the dilapidated school bus away. The same bulldozers raked and dug at the earth here, as they had in the knotweed patch. They attacked the ground ravenously, as if hungry for more bones. More skeletons. More boys.

Sam idly wondered if they'd search the woods next for Healey's mother's bones. He'd have to remember to tell Mac about that later. So many bones. So many deaths.

The world grew dim. He steadied himself on the chaise lounge that Healey sat in earlier. He let himself drop deeper into it, unable to take his eyes away from the bicycle and remnants of the cap. If they belonged to Tommy Donahue, then Healey was surely the killer. If he killed Tommy, then he had probably killed Billy, too.

Billy? Are you buried here? Right next door to me, all along? My neighbor? An underground tenant, guest of the monster who murdered you and buried you outside like an unwanted piece of trash?

Mac Stewart sat down on an overturned plastic bucket beside Sam. Ned Olsen joined them, standing close behind Mac and looking a bit sheepish. Mac cleared his throat. Sam tried to ignore him. He studied his hands and steadied his breathing.

Mac leaned forward. "Listen. We're not so sure about the bike. Problem is—" he paused until Sam met his gaze. "We've got some new information. Healey's incarceration timeline doesn't match the murders. Maybe he did kill Tommy or Billy, or maybe his old man did it, or one of his hooligan friends. But he couldn't be the serial killer."

Sam looked at them with glazed eyes. He didn't really care whether Healey matched the profile. He felt dead inside.

Ned shuffled his feet and swept a hand over his hair, looked at the school bus. "We'll keep looking, Sam. We'll figure it out."

Sam sighed and looked away again, unwilling to believe he'd ever learn of Billy's fate.

Mac touched Sam's sleeve. "Ned's right. We'll test the bike and cap to determine a date. But get this. Healey claims they were his when he was a kid. Says they buried the bike with the rest of the trash after his father ran over it with his truck."

Sam's jaw dropped. "What? It's not Tommy Donahue's bike?"

Mac looked at the police car in which Healey sat, shackled, with his scraggly gray hair partially hiding his face. A white bandage covered the wound on his forehead.

"He could be lying. We'll try to link the bike to the Donahue boy. But unless we do, I can't hold him."

Sam persisted. "But Mac, I just *know* it was him. Even if that isn't Billy's bike. I just know it. Maybe Billy's buried here. They have to keep digging!" He realized his voice had taken on a desperate quality, and tried to steady himself. "You know what I'm saying, don't you?"

Mac chewed on his toothpick and shook his head.

"The records say they searched this property a hundred times over when Billy first disappeared. Isn't that right?"

Ned nodded. "I remember the search. My father was part of the investigation. They didn't find anything."

Sam leaned back and summoned the memory. The police had searched the Healey's house first. They'd looked for freshly dug earth. They'd found nothing. Not a hint of impropriety. And Manfred Healey supposedly had an alibi. Sam hadn't bought it, though. Anyone could buy a lie. For the right price.

Ned looked liked he had something to say, but didn't want to say it.

Sam shot him a look. "What? What else did you find?"

"I've been digging through the old records again. Checking out Healey's original alibi."

Sam's voice trembled. "What was it? My parents never told me."

The truth hovered in the air, toying with him. Taunting him.

Ned shuffled his feet and looked at Sam with pity. "Healy was in court the whole day, Sam. It was his first trial, for boosting old lady Walgrove's Chevy. He went kind of crazy and screamed at the judge, so they kept him in prison overnight, for contempt of court."

"What?" Sam's head began to pound. Healey had a solid alibi on the day of Billy's disappearance? Why hadn't anyone ever told him?

Mac stood up and gestured toward Healey. "Looks like you'll have to give up on this one."

The realization settled in his gut.

Healey is innocent.

Innocent.

After all the years of blaming Healey, Sam felt the bottom of his stomach fall away, as if he was riding the Tilt-a-Whirl and his car just wrenched off the base of the platform. He was in free-fall. As he tried to assimilate the new knowledge, Ned was called away and Mac's expression turned contemplative. He looked back at the bus on the trailer and the disturbed earth, then at Sam.

"You know, Sam, if I didn't have good instincts about people, I'd have to consider you."

Sam's eyes remained dull.

"What?"

"Yeah. Tommy Donahue's remains are found on your property. You're the one who was always with Billy. Maybe there was an accident. You panicked. You hid the body somewhere, afraid you'd be blamed. And you're the one who has it in for Healey. You stalked him, for God's sake. Maybe it's all an elaborate, fifty-year-old scam to divert the blame away from yourself."

Sam shrugged and expelled a loud breath. He looked at Mac as if he were crazy.

"Sure. I killed some kid from the next town over, who I never met. Next, I killed my own brother. Then, I uncovered and reported finding the first boy, Tommy Donahue, right in my own backyard. Makes complete sense to me, Mac."

Mac smiled.

"I know. But I do have to cover all angles."

The marble glowed hot against Sam's leg. He fought the impulse to give in to it. He couldn't, not with all these people around. One of the agents called for Mac.

"Mac, they need you over there."

A tinkling sound filled his ears, followed by a roar. Certain of the source, Sam heard the babble of children on the school bus. It penetrated the present, insistent in its loud clamor. He felt the chair beneath him, saw the agents swarming over the yard, and heard the twitter of birds in the trees. And yet, somehow, the voices of the kids were clear and loud.

"Sam!" Billy called.

Sam swayed. He grabbed the chair handles to steady himself, and saw a flash-vision of Billy in the school bus with his childhood chums. They displayed their baseball cards proudly, comparing collections and trading for favorites. The chatter was loud.

Sam forced himself to stay in the present. He dragged himself back, studying the details of the yard around him. Fishing pole. Pail of worms. Old man in the police car.

He looked at the ground beside his feet and did a double take. A tattered baseball card—Babe Ruth, Billy's favorite—appeared beside his shoe.

Sam picked it up and stared, suspended in a state of disbelief.

I'm definitely going nuts.

He watched the agents roaming around the property and sensed veiled looks in his direction.

He felt foolish, regretting his overactive imagination that led him to stalk Manfred Healey.

Why did I do this to that pitiful old man?

No evidence could convict him fifty years ago, and no evidence would convict him now.

Sam picked himself up. He pocketed Billy's baseball card and headed home in a daze.

Chapter Twenty-three

SAM FOLLOWED THE SAME TRAIL he'd raced over earlier. There, in a flattened area of dirt and leaves, was the spot where Manfred had fallen and sobbed like a child.

Did Mr. Healey really kill his wife and bury her in the woods?

Sam had forgotten about that part when Mac interviewed him earlier. He vaguely remembered Mrs. Healey vanishing long ago. Rumors had abounded about her leaving to live with her sister in Minnesota. But no one had ever known for sure. And no one had blamed her, if she had. Mr. Healey was known all over the county for his cruelty.

Hell. Maybe she had left. Maybe Manfred Healey had imagined her death to justify being abandoned by his own mother. Maybe he was as crazy as Sam felt.

Nevertheless, he'd have to bring it up to Ned or Mac later. Just in case.

But why had Billy shown him the birthday scene with his new bicycle, just when Sam saw the streamers on the buried bike, especially since the bike wasn't Billy's? Why had he shared the school bus vignette with the kids and their baseball cards? Why had he "given" Sam one of his cards?

There *had* to be something there. Something important that would help explain Billy's disappearance.

Unless Sam was self-inducing hallucinations.

Is it possible?

He tried to remember the few psychiatric classes he'd taken years ago in med school. Since then, he'd done lots of reading in medical journals. But he never heard about a case like this, where a patient was seemingly clear headed most of the time, yet completely knocked out while hallucinations of time travel raged in his mind. With a grimace, he imagined the articles and theories his situation would spawn in the medical world today.

The woods seemed quieter than usual. Were the birds resting?

The chipmunks sleeping? Even the leaves lay quiet in the trees. No rustling. No stirring.

The loudest noise seemed to be the thoughts that raced through Sam's mind and the sound of his feet scuffing along the path.

He picked up the pace, and within minutes, saw the roofline of his house and barn.

When Sam reached the back of the barn, he stopped and stared. A container of Lincoln Logs sat on the bench. He walked over and inspected it.

"Billy Moore" was scribbled on the side of the box with an indelible marker.

It looked old. The penmanship was unmistakably Billy's.

Did this toy manifest itself from the past? Like the card in my pocket?

Sam remembered playing with the Lincoln Logs with his little brother for hours on end when they were kids. He shook his head and snorted.

No. This is real. Somebody put this here for me to see. To drive me crazy.

Or crazier.

❧☙

"He's playing with us," Mac said.

They sat in the kitchen drinking Rachel's strong coffee. She looked back and forth between Sam and Mac, who studied the container of Lincoln logs on the table. Sam had called Mac, and the agent had abandoned his investigation at Healey's to hurry to the Moore's house.

"If he's 'playing with us,' does it mean he was involved in Billy's disappearance?" Sam asked. He almost said "murder," but couldn't quite get the distasteful word to roll off his tongue.

"Not necessarily. He could be some maniac who has a grudge against you. Maybe taunting you is his primary goal. Or he could be the serial killer; possibly the one who killed Billy. At this point, it's impossible to know."

Sam grunted. "We still don't know if Billy's really dead. There's no evidence."

Rachel covered his hand with hers and squeezed.

Mac shot Sam a look of disbelief.

"You still think he's alive out there somewhere?"

Sam sat silent. The conflicting thoughts within him raged. His eyes fell.

"I don't know." He scraped his chair back and slammed both hands on the table. "But who the hell *is* he? Healey couldn't have put the toy on the bench. I was watching him the whole time."

Mac furrowed his brow. "You have to forget about Healey."

Sam got up and stood by the window, staring at the knotweed patch, uneasy with the thoughts that jumbled through his mind. Still shaken, he leaned against the sink, reached for a clean glass, and filled it with sweet well water from the tap. He downed it and returned to the table. Rachel wheeled over to him and stroked his arm until he put up his hand to stop her.

"I'm okay, honey."

He wasn't okay. She knew it. He knew she knew. Her saddened eyes smiled when she backed up, wheeling over to her usual spot at the table. She took a sip of coffee and emitted a small sigh. Sam felt guilty, but couldn't quell the crazy thoughts that tumbled through his brain like a brood of unruly pups.

Mac got up and began to pace, his eyes wild. "He's here. I can sense it. He's watching us. He's taking delight in confusing us. Probably thrilled that you found the first victim. All the attention. The papers. The resurrection of the case. And this," he pointed to the Lincoln logs. "This looks authentic."

Sam's eyes closed.

"It is. It's Billy's writing. I remember the day he wrote it. But I can't imagine how he got it. Unless he took it when we were kids and kept it all this time? Seems crazy. Most of Billy's old things have been boxed and stored in my attic. I never threw away any of his toys. I just couldn't."

Mac squinted and chewed on his toothpick.

"You'd better check. Let's see if he got up there."

Sam looked up in surprise. Rachel inhaled sharply.

"Sam?" she asked. "You don't think..."

Sam bounded up the stairs, down the hallway, and burst up the narrow stairs leading to the attic. Breathing hard, he stood at the top of the landing, making his way past boxes and trunks toward the far corner. His lips parted; he stood rooted to the spot. Mac appeared behind him.

Boxes were scattered everywhere, overturned and gutted. The toys that remained were strewn about the floor.

"When the hell did he..." Sam asked.

Mac leaned down to right a few of the boxes, inspected them.

"When's the last time you two were both out of the house?"

Sam thought, chewed his lip for a moment, and returned Mac's intense stare.

"Memorial Day. We were at the parade for almost two hours."

Mac nodded grimly.

Sam squatted to examine the remaining toys.

"He took a lot of stuff. The Tonka trucks are gone."

Sam spent a few more melancholy moments, lamenting the missing items, then followed Mac back to the kitchen.

Mac said, "We'll have to dust for prints here, Sam. There is a chance that he left us a calling card."

Sam nodded slowly. Seeing Billy's toys, especially in such a state of disarray, unsettled him.

"Okay. Whatever you think."

They reached the kitchen. Sam gave Rachel the bad news.

"They broke into our home?" Rachel's voice cracked and her eyes filled with tears.

Sam nodded. "But they didn't really break in, honey. We never lock up."

Mac sputtered, rolled his eyes, and ran one hand through his short-cropped white hair.

"Not wise. I would suggest locking up at all times. At least until we catch this guy."

Rachel grabbed Sam's hand and looked at him in silent alarm.

The phone rang. Sam picked it up; Mac stood and nodded goodbye. He slipped out the kitchen door.

"Hello?"

"Dad? What time do you want the boys to come over?" Andy's voice sounded natural and calm. Sam felt reassured by the normalcy of it.

But he'd forgotten about tonight's sleepover. Forcing himself to relax, he realized that no one would try to break into a house full of people. Anyway, the thief had already stolen exactly what he wanted. He tried to speak in a normal voice.

"Sure, son. Bring them over any time. Your mother baked a lasagna and I've got fixings for hot fudge sundaes."

Andy agreed to deliver the boys in an hour. Sam hung up and hurried up the stairs to check on the bedroom for Evan and Timmy. Ominous, unbidden thoughts crawled across his brain.

Billy's dead. And his killer's been rummaging through my attic.

Reaching the top of the stairs, he paused on the landing to stare at the light that streamed through the stained glass window at the end of the hall. Now in the late afternoon, the ruby glass shone on the wooden floorboards with hues of pale golden rose. The marble in his pocket was cool. Quiet.

Another thought bolted through him.

If Manfred Healey was really in court that day—then, who the hell killed Billy?

Chapter Twenty-four

HOURS LATER, in the boy's bedroom, Sam leaned back in the overstuffed rocker with Timmy on his lap. The baby laid his head against Sam's chest and sucked his thumb. Evan typed at the computer set up on Rachel's old desk in the corner.

Sailing ships and dolphins covered Evan's twin bed, tucked into one corner of the room. A light blue and red braided rug spread between the twin bed and the crib set against the far wall. Pale blue sheets and a fluffy white blanket decorated the crib.

Over the crib, a unique selection of oil paintings featuring colorful balloons and clowns hung on the wall, mounted high enough so little hands couldn't reach them. The fuzzy sheep on the mobile faced the mattress. Timmy was too old for it now, but Rachel didn't want to take it down.

Nineteen months old. Sam soaked in the comfort brought by the close contact with Timmy. He rocked back and forth, talked about silly nothings, and stroked the boy's silken hair, still curled from his bath.

Timmy popped his head up and stared into Sam's eyes.

"Eat? Hungry!"

"Are you hungry, buddy?" Sam asked. "How about a bite of my peach?"

Sam had brought up two peaches and a small dish of sunflower seeds. He also had Timmy's Sippy cup ready, filled with milk.

Timmy nodded, held out his hands for the peach, and took a big juicy bite.

"Bite it," he said with his mouth full. "Peach."

Sam smiled, wiped the nectar from the boy's chin.

"Yup. Peach. That's right, buddy. May I have it back now?"

Timmy slid onto the floor, backed up a few steps, and looked at Sam mischievously.

"Mine."

"What? Are you taking my peach, little guy?"

Evan chuckled.

"He's always doing that, Grandpa. He takes everybody's food."

Evan didn't move his eyes from the screen and his fingers still flew over the keyboard.

"Is that so?" Sam said. "Well, I'm prepared. I've got another one."

Sam took a bite of the second peach and then slid the dish of sunflower seeds closer. He dipped in for a small handful and tossed them back in his mouth, enjoying their salty crunchiness.

"Some?" Timmy said, sidling up to Sam.

Sam looked at Timmy's innocent face and expectant eyes. Was it okay to give him sunflower seeds? They were small, and easily chewed. Not like nuts. He decided to let him try a few.

He held the dish at Timmy's level.

"Just take a few, now. Just a little."

Timmy looked at the dish, and immediately plunged his chubby hand into it.

"Little," Timmy said.

He scooped a giant handful of seeds out of the dish before Sam could stop him. With his hand flattened against his face, he mashed the seeds into his mouth. Most of them fell onto the ground. He handled the influx of seeds well, chewing them carefully. Sam laughed out loud. Evan turned around to watch.

"Here, let me help you," Sam said.

He put a few seeds on his own hand, and offered them palm up. He expected Timmy to pluck them from his hand. Instead, Timmy lowered his head to Sam's outstretched palm and lapped the seeds off of his skin like a pony taking a sugar cube.

"Taste good," Timmy said. His eyes sparkled.

Sam and Evan burst into laughter. Timmy grinned, basking in the attention.

"More?"

Rachel rolled into the bedroom. Sam had helped her upstairs earlier. He was able to hold one arm while she grabbed the stair railing and hobbled one step at a time. Carrying the wheelchair wasn't so easy. He realized that a second chair and a stair lift would be the best solution, and vowed to get it taken care of in the coming weeks.

She held a book of fairytales on her lap. Timmy's face lit up. He toddled over to her and pulled both flip-flops off her feet.

"Timmy!" she chuckled, "what are you doing with Grandma's shoes?"

Timmy giggled, put the sandals on the floor, and inserted his little feet into them, with the divider placed between his toes. He scuffed forward, with his tiny feet in Rachel's size six sandals.

"Shoes," he beamed. He spied some errant sunflower seeds on the rug and hobbled toward them, almost beating Sam.

"No, no. Dirty. Let Papa get you some more, okay?"

Sam gave Timmy another small handful of seeds, and sat him on Rachel's lap for the story. While Rachel read to the boy in her singsong voice, Sam wandered over to the computer. Evan seemed entranced.

The boy's fingers flew over the keyboard. He straightened and stared intently at the monitor.

"Talking to friends?" Sam asked.

Evan shook his head.

"No. I'm searching for a murderer."

Sam looked askance at his grandson. Was he playing some kind of mystery game online?

"What?"

Evan gazed at the screen. A smile stole over his face. He pointed to the monitor.

"There. That's the guy. Screen name is Commando1070. He's been bidding on World War II medals all day long."

"Evan? Are you talking about the serial killer?"

Rachel looked up in alarm.

Evan nodded.

"Well, yeah. Didn't you read the papers, Grandpa? My friends and I have been talking about it for days. There were eleven, in all.

Each one was buried with a medal. We came up with the idea of tracking the online auction bids, thinking maybe he bought them that way. This guy really likes his medals. He's bid on twenty-four separate auctions today."

Rachel spoke up, her face white with concern.

"Honey? I think maybe it's time for bed now. And you don't want to go digging into a police investigation, do you? They might get cross with you, sweetheart. Why don't you just let them handle it?"

Evan shrugged, signed off, and took a long drink from his pouch of cherry juice. "Okay. But someone should tell the cops to watch this guy. He might be the one."

Sam put a hand on Evan's shoulder.

"I'll take care of it, son. You get ready for bed."

Evan nodded, grabbed his pajamas, and headed for the bathroom to change.

Rachel closed the storybook and handed Timmy to Sam, who lifted the sleepy boy, gave him his pacifier and his stuffed rabbit, laid him in the crib, and covered him with the blanket. Rachel's eyes followed him around the room.

"Sam?" she asked. "What if…"

"I'll take care of it, Rachel. I'll take care of it. It was probably just an avid collector, you know."

Inside, his heart was pounding. If Evan was right, the murderer was anxious to procure another medal. Another medal to pin on the chest of his next victim.

Chapter Twenty-five

THE CRIES CAME in the middle of the night. Sam woke instantly. *Billy's crying!*

He fumbled to his feet and listened.

Rachel raised her head from the pillow. "What's wrong with Timmy?"

Shaking himself from the heavy cocoon of dreams, Sam finally remembered.

Right. The boys are sleeping over.

The cry came again, this time worse, in the form of a scream. He raced to their room, stumbling over the edge of Rachel's wheelchair on the way. He hopped on one foot for a brief second, then limped along the hallway to the boys' room.

Timmy stood in his crib in a full-fledged wail. Tears streamed down his red cheeks. Sam glanced toward Evan's bed on the way to Timmy's outstretched arms.

Empty.

Panic seized him. He hurried to Timmy, picked him up, and searched the room.

"Evan?" he called. Fear bubbled into his throat. Images of serial killers, ripe with evil intentions filled his imagination. "Evan, where *are* you?"

A sudden noise surprised him. Evan shuffled into the room, his eyes half shut.

"Right here."

"Where were you?" Sam asked. His heart still beat too fast.

"I had to go," he mumbled, flopping back into bed. He pulled the blankets up to his chin. His eyes closed immediately.

Sam collapsed in relief on the edge of the bed. He shifted Timmy to one knee and smoothed the blankets around Evan's body, covering one leg that stuck out over the edge.

He's so young. So vulnerable.

Timmy's face crumpled again and he began to wail, muttering one word over and over again. Sam couldn't make it out.

"You want a drink?" he asked.

He wailed louder. "No! Want my...grbluginky!"

Sam panicked.

What in the world is he saying?

Evan murmured thickly, "Binky. He needs his Binky."

Timmy collapsed against his chest, shaking and whimpering. Sam wrapped his arms around the boy and kissed his cheek. He searched for pacifier in the rumpled blankets, found it, and popped it into Timmy's mouth. The boy started sucking on it, but his chest still heaved from crying.

"It's okay, little guy," Sam whispered. "You wanna come in with Grandma and me?"

Timmy lifted his tear-stained face to Sam and nodded, still half-asleep. Sam leaned down to kiss Evan's forehead and carried Timmy into his bedroom. He placed him gently in the center of the bed, and slid in beside him, drawing up the red corduroy comforter. Timmy's eyes were open now, bright brown buttons that peeked out from the covers. He flashed a little smile at Sam from behind the pacifier. It moved in rhythm with his lips and made tiny sucking sounds. Sam snuggled beside him.

"Piwwow."

Sam looked at Timmy, then realized what he was saying.

"Oh, you need your pillow, is that it?"

The baby nodded.

"Piwwow."

Sam got up again, placed his own pillow on his side of the bed so Timmy wouldn't roll out, and padded down the hall to grab Timmy's small, fringed pillow from the crib. The boy didn't go anywhere without it. Sam trotted back to his room and gave the pillow to the baby.

Timmy hugged it close to his cheek. He combed the fringe with his fingers, over and over again. After a few moments, he flopped the pillow onto Rachel, and back onto the bed again.

Sam took it, positioned it between his and Rachel's pillows, and whispered in Timmy's ear.

"Okay, buddy. Time to sleep. Night night."

At five in the morning, dawn broke and the birds sang outside Sam's window. Timmy looked outside with curiosity as if to question the wisdom of Sam's statement. Sam drew the window shades.

"Time to sleep, buddy."

He could still see Timmy's face from the hall light. The baby shifted and sat up. He moved his pillow to his side, and wiggled his legs.

"Piwwow."

Sam rubbed the back of his hand over the child's soft cheeks. So innocent, so endearing. His heart twisted with affection. Timmy wiggled again, taking his legs out from under the covers and flopping them on top.

"No bwankie," he said firmly.

The room was chilly.

"Are you sure, little guy? Aren't you cold?"

Sam felt his chubby little legs. He wore a pair of knit shorts and a tee shirt. The skin was warm.

"Papa," the boy said, pointing to Sam's face.

"That's right, honey."

"Rachel," he said, squirming onto his side and looking at his grandmother.

"Yes, but you call her grandma, right?"

"Honey pot pie," Timmy said, still looking at his grandmother.

"That's right, Timmy. That's what grandma calls you, isn't it?"

"Honey pot pie," he said again. Looking back at Sam, he smiled and said, "Papa pot pie."

Sam laughed out loud. "Papa pot pie?"

Timmy sounded as if he were mimicking Sam's laugh.

"Ha, ha, ha!" he squealed. "Papa pot pie!"

They both lost it, and started to belly laugh together. The connection was strong, immediate. Sam felt closer to the boy than ever before. They lay in the bed and looked into each other's eyes.

"Will you two pipe down? It's the middle of the night!" Rachel said without turning over.

"Sorry, love," Sam whispered. He put his finger to his lips. "Shhhh, we have to be quiet."

Timmy's voice echoed off the walls. "Quiet!"

Sam rolled his eyes good-naturedly. He pulled the covers back over Timmy's legs. They felt cold now. Timmy yawned and rubbed his eyes. He wiggled some more and dug his elbows into Sam's side. Flinging his pillow onto Sam, he stood up and flopped on top of the pillow on Sam's stomach. Sam maneuvered around until he got the blanket over the boy and pillow. Rachel began to snore softly. Sam smiled.

"Papa, quiet," he said in a loud voice. "Gramma seepin'. Gramma coughin'."

"I guess you could call it that," Sam chuckled. "Go to sleep, buddy. Night, night."

Timmy's eyes fluttered. He ran his fingers through the fringe on the pillow in a self-comforting ritual. The action slowed and his breathing steadied. His eyes closed, then opened, then closed again. Finally, he drifted off to sleep on top of Sam. Sam lay there for the next hour, watching Timmy's little lips as they puckered around the pacifier. Affection swelled in him and he offered a silent prayer to thank God for the blessing of grandchildren.

Chapter Twenty-six

The next one will be special. Probably my last.

Atonal music blasted, providing him strange comfort. He scribbled furiously in the notebook on the desk. He felt safe, because it was night. No one would bother him now.

He'd chosen the day. Now he just needed to plan, sketch, and get the details down.

But where? This type of event would require a locale with significance.

He tapped his pencil against the keyboard, then scribbled for a few minutes more.

With deep satisfaction, he closed the notebook and glanced at the Purple Heart medal sitting on his desk. He'd bought it for a steal at a yard sale last week.

This will be the ultimate kill.

The ache in his stomach was bad tonight. The cancer had spread. Oddly enough, when he looked in the mirror, he saw no difference, except maybe a mad brightness, tightness around his mouth when the pain surged.

No one can know.

He'd wait 'til he couldn't take it anymore, then maybe, just maybe, end it all.

After my last kill.

He opened the book and wrote again, tapping his foot to the music. When he'd drawn a plan of the victim's house, he stood and opened his closet. Pushing and pulling at suitcases, he freed a cardboard box, dragged it out, and emptied the contents.

Before him sat a velveteen rabbit, missing one eye. Beside it lay a metal harmonica, a blue wooden top, a yellow glow-in-the-dark yo-yo, a turquoise Tonka truck, and a white metal horse trailer. All from Sam's attic.

It was so brilliant. He'd watched them at the parade, drove like mad to their house, and walked right into the kitchen. They hadn't even locked their doors.

Idiots.

The boy whose toys he fondled had been stopped at eleven. Stopped dead in his tracks. Just like the others. The double ones. Snake eyes. A great age to die.

Chapter Twenty-seven

On Saturday morning, Sam stirred scrambled eggs with a plastic spatula. He flipped them and added two slices of American cheese, then covered the pan and turned down the heat.

Rachel and the boys still slept upstairs. He listened at the bottom of the stairs, heard nothing, and returned to the kitchen to drop fat slices of bacon into a hot cast iron skillet.

This'll wake 'em up.

He chuckled at his own thought and carefully laid the strips in the pan.

The smell of bacon always wakes...

The phone trilled. Sam checked the clock on the wall. *Almost eight.* He wiped off the grease on a paper towel and scooped the receiver into his hand.

"Hello?"

Pinning it between his ear and shoulder, he stretched the cord and returned to the stove to nudge the spitting bacon.

"Sam? Mac, here. Hey, I got the message you left last night about the Ebay auctions."

Sam turned off the burner, repositioned the phone, and slid onto a kitchen chair.

"Yeah. Evan surprised me all right."

"Amazing kid. He tagged the guy we've been watching."

"What?"

"Commando1070. He's the buyer who's bidding on all of our listings."

"Your listings?" Sam asked.

"Yeah. We posted most of the metals up there. Fake listings, you know, to draw out the bastard."

The light dawned. "You mean Evan was watching auctions the Bureau set up to catch the guy?"

"Yup. We're pressuring Ebay right now to release Commando's information. They're stalling, you know, 'protecting their client,' but by nightfall we'll have a court order. We're close on his tail, Sam."

A shiver of hope swept through Sam. He shifted the phone to the opposite ear and leaned forward.

"Really? You think you'll nail the bastard?"

Mac laughed. "Oh, yeah. We're gonna nail him. Soon."

Sam stood, switching the burner on again.

"Good. Let me know if you hear anything."

"You got it. Hang in there."

※※

At ten-thirty, Andy arrived to pick up the boys. With a familiar pang of sadness, Sam hugged them goodbye and watched the van disappear down the road.

He turned toward the gardens and looked across the grounds with longing. They'd have to wait. He'd promised to help Bruce today. He kissed Rachel, hopped in the car, and drove to Bruce's house, parking between Harvey's truck and Doug's sports car.

When the senator called his old childhood pals, they'd agreed to help spruce up the barn in preparation for the arrival of Bruce's new horses. For three hours, they cleaned, swept, reattached stall doors, and repaired fences. After a fancy lunch served by a dour man in a butler's uniform, they returned to the barn to clean the hayloft.

They'd been at it for almost an hour when Sam leaned on his broom and swiped at the perspiration on his brow.

"What time did you say they're coming, Bruce?"

He swept side-by-side with Bruce in the hayloft, pushing the pile toward the open door on the side of the barn. Pieces of hay and straw floated in a dusty, dizzying circle onto the bed of the tractor wagon parked below.

"About four," Bruce said, pulling the red bandana away from his mouth.

Bruce's curly steel gray hair remained neatly in place after working and sweating all afternoon. Sam idly wondered if he used some kind of gel or hairspray. His own hair felt wildly disheveled and dusty. He smoothed it self-consciously and shouted to Doug who sat on the tractor in the yard below.

"Okay, that's the last of it. We're ready for the new hay as soon as you are."

Doug started the tractor and headed for the edge of the property where Sam had erected a fence to hold the hay, grass clippings, and leaves gathered from the barn and paddock. It would be the start of a wonderful mulch pile, especially after the horses began to donate their own fertilizer to the mix.

After pitching the last of the old hay into the compost pile, Doug circled back to the barn with the tractor. He and Harvey lifted the hay elevator to the open door in the loft. After hooking it up, they loaded long, green bales of alfalfa and timothy from a wagon onto the metal conveyor belt.

Sam and Bruce took turns catching bales and stacking them under the eaves. The sweet scent of hay soon filled the air. When they'd stacked forty bales in a neat, rectangular block, they climbed down the ladder to the first floor.

Bruce had recently whitewashed the rough-hewn plank walls of the barn. He'd spent the last week preparing the property for the horses he admittedly purchased on a whim. The main aisles separating the stalls were swept clean, new black rubber water buckets hung on the walls, red plastic grain bins were mounted in the corners of two stalls, and fresh oat straw covered the floors.

Harvey carried a hundred-pound bag of grain into the barn on his shoulder.

"Where do you want this?" He struggled with the heavy load, wobbling a little under the weight.

Bruce ran beside him and opened the lid on a metal barrel beside the water spigot in the far corner.

"Right here. That's it. Just lean it halfway over the edge so I can open it."

Bruce struggled with the string seam woven into the top of the bag.

"Anybody have a pocket knife?"

Sam stepped forward, bringing out his old pearl-handled jackknife.

"I'll do it. Step aside, Senator."

Bruce smiled while Sam deftly slid the blade of the knife under one stitch and ripped it open. The contents of the bag spilled into the bin. Sam inhaled the aroma of the molasses, corn, and cracked oats. It brought back pleasant memories of his barn before they'd given up the horses.

"Mmm. Smells good."

Bruce laughed.

"I hope the horses agree." He closed the lid and folded the bag. "Hey, isn't that your old pocketknife, Sam? Man, you've kept it all these years?"

Doug and Harvey crowded around to look. Sam held it open on his palm.

"Yeah. It's the one my father gave me when I had my tonsils out. Remember?"

Harvey laughed. "Oh my God. I forgot about that. We had them out the same week that year. Man, was that awful. But I sure loved the ginger ale and ice cream diet. What a sweet deal that was."

Sam laughed. "Yeah. And then two weeks later we all got the chicken pox. Remember?"

The men flopped onto three bales of straw in the aisle.

Doug laughed. "Oh, the itching... I'll *never* forget. My mother practically tied my hands together to stop me from scratching." He rubbed his sleeve over his weathered, red face.

Doug's rusty hair had turned reddish gray, and hung limp and thin around the large bald spot on the back of his head. Of the four men, he was the only one who had started to lose his hair. He usually wore a cap to cover it.

Harvey pushed back a thick lock of pure white hair and chuckled. "Billy got it the worst. Remember? He was *really* covered."

His smile faded when Doug and Bruce glared at him.

"Oh. I'm sorry, Sam. I didn't mean to…"

Sam's heart lurched, then he recovered and smiled at Harvey. He remembered his brother's chicken pox well. The poor kid had suffered a severe case.

"It's okay, guys. We can talk about him. It's not like I'm going to lose my marbles."

Doug and Bruce both looked disapprovingly at Harvey again.

"I…" Harvey started to speak, but he lost courage and his voice trailed off into nothingness.

"Really, guys. It's okay," Sam said, wishing they'd stop tiptoeing around him. They'd avoided talking about Billy for fifty years. He was tired of being treated like a fragile nutcase. He stood and faced them.

"Listen, guys. I loved my brother. He was a great kid. And yes, I still miss him. But he's gone. And it's okay to talk about him."

Doug averted his close-set pale blue eyes, busying himself with a strand of straw. He stuck it between his teeth and chewed. Harvey sat silently beside Sam, his mouth partially open and his puppy dog eyes wide. He looked from Bruce to Doug. Doug finally spoke up.

"So, you still think about him a lot?" he asked.

Sam breathed a sigh of relief. It would be good to talk about it. He started to pace.

"Yes. I think about him all the time. Some days are worse than others. Like now. Finding that boy's bones in my garden kinda knocked me for a loop." He paused to make contact with his friends' eyes. Each one looked down, avoiding his glance. "And knowing there's a guy out there who might be Billy's murderer, who is probably stalking some other poor kid…"

Harvey looked at Sam in surprise.

"But you don't know that Billy was murdered, Sam. Do you?" he asked.

Doug elbowed Harvey in the side.

"Harvey! That's enough. Let's not bring up the gory details, for God's sake."

"Well, he doesn't know that for sure," Harvey added defensively. "He might have been kidnapped or something."

Sam looked at the three men.

"It's okay," he said evenly. "It's really okay."

Bruce stood up abruptly as the sound of tires crunching on gravel came from the driveway.

"Can we finish this later, Sam? The horses are here."

Sam nodded and pushed the thoughts away. "Of course."

Bruce flashed a politician's smile. "Come on, men. Let's greet my new guests."

Doug jumped to his feet and lurched toward the entrance with Bruce. Sam held back. He put a hand on Harvey's arm to detain him.

"Harv. Wait a minute."

Harvey's eyes filled with concern. He turned toward Sam. His eyes dropped and he fidgeted with his watch. Dust motes danced in the aisle between them.

"You're right. I don't know if Billy was murdered. There's never been a shred of evidence to prove anything, one way or the other. But I'm sure he's dead, or he would have contacted me. Even if he'd had to wait for decades, he would have found a way."

Harvey rubbed a meaty hand over his eyes, and stared at his shoes. His thick white locks hung over bushy black eyebrows.

"I feel so stupid. I never know what to say, Sam."

Sam put his arm around Harvey's broad shoulders.

"It's okay. I wish we could talk about him more, to tell you the truth. I was just saying that to Bruce the other day. I think I *need* to talk about it, or I'll go bonkers. Sometimes I think I already have." He smiled at Harvey. "Come on. Let's go see those expensive horses."

They walked out of the barn and watched Bruce unload the first of his prized equines. The golden palomino shone with health and vigor. He tossed his curly blond mane and backed out of the trailer, looking around with nostrils flared. Snorting, he pivoted in a tight circle, then lowered his head to rip the grass on the lawn with his teeth.

Doug walked him toward one of the stalls. Sam helped Bruce back the white mare out of the trailer. She was petite and pretty.

"Is this one for your wife?" Harvey asked. They led the well-behaved animal into the barn.

"Yeah. She's the quiet one. Kim's never ridden before."

Sam wondered if Kimberly would step one dainty fashionable foot in the barn. He exchanged doubtful glances with Harvey and smiled. "So, you didn't tell her yet?"

Bruce shook his head. "Nope. When she comes up from the city this weekend, I plan to surprise her."

Doug whispered under his breath, "She'll be surprised all right."

Bruce laughed.

"Oh, stop. I know she's a bit of a prissy miss, but maybe she'll take to it. It's better than shopping on Park Avenue. Breathing in all those fumes. Dodging the traffic. A lot healthier."

Doug passed Sam and whispered under his breath. "And a lot better than screwing around with that judge."

Sam ignored the tasteless comment, shrugged his shoulders, and locked the mare into her stall. Bruce tossed a few flakes of hay over the stall walls. The horses munched with their heads low and eyes half closed. Sam stroked the mare's nose and she pushed her head toward him. In some bizarre way, she reminded him of his cat, Lila. Sleek, white, and trim, Sam liked her immediately and suddenly yearned for the days when he and Rachel would take off across the fields on their own horses.

"Bruce?" Harvey asked. "What happens if you really *do* get elected President? Will you sell this place?"

Bruce looked at him in surprise. They hadn't talked about this subject, either.

"Well, Harv, I'd keep it as my weekend retreat. It would be a nice place to escape to when things get crazy, you know?"

Harvey nodded amicably and Doug rolled his eyes. The four men ambled outside. The truck and trailer had just disappeared around the curve in the driveway.

"Thank you, men. I truly appreciate your help."

They shuffled their feet and murmured responses.

Bruce put his arm around Harvey's shoulder. "You know I could have hired someone to do this."

Doug snorted and brushed hay from his sleeve. Apparently the same thought had occurred to him.

Bruce narrowed his eyes in Doug's direction. "But I didn't, because I wanted to see my old pals again. Seemed like a nice excuse."

Doug looked sheepish.

"Uh. Yeah. It was nice, Bruce. Sorry."

As the others chatted about old times, Sam looked at the mansion on the hill. It had begun to take on the majesty it possessed years ago and was really coming along.

Some retreat, he chuckled to himself. He said his goodbyes and headed home to Rachel.

Chapter Twenty-eight

SAM ROSE EARLY Sunday morning, pulled on jeans and a tee shirt, and headed outside.

Almost the whole day to catch up.

Today he planned to collect the dead wood blown down from his trees, trim rotten branches from the beech and peach trees, and remove one massive limb from a sugar maple that loomed over the young cherry trees. He needed to let more sun into the area to encourage the trees to produce fruit.

He walked into the barn, picked up his clippers and limb saw, and laid them in the wheelbarrow. The tools clattered in the basin when he walked it toward his cherry trees.

Something flashed in the woods.

Sam glanced toward the trees, searching the area. All was still, except the cardinal who chirped from a nearby pine.

He rolled the wheelbarrow forward a few more steps and glanced at the trees again.

Had he seen the flicker of a deer's tail? The flight of a pheasant? Lila, chasing a bird?

He shook his head and dismissed the thought, then went to work on the branches. He rolled the wheelbarrow over the lawn, gathering dead sticks scattered below the trees. After a half hour, the pile of sticks had grown until the wheelbarrow nearly toppled. He rolled it to the fire pit, dumped them, and started a blaze.

The marble warmed in his pocket. Billy's face swam before his eyes. He understood the process now, and knew it would be counterproductive to resist. The distant sound of splashing water entered his brain when he palmed the marble and sat firmly on the bench, letting himself rocket back to his childhood.

ಬಀ

A multicolored mist swirled and receded into the rainbow glistening over the falls. Sam looked around in surprise, recognizing the spot in the woods located about halfway between his house and Manfred Healey's. Soft earth cushioned his bare feet and drops of moisture floated in the air, wetting his skin and clothes. He looked down at his supple hands, turning them in the light.

I'm twelve again.

A feeling of euphoria swept through him as he glanced at the pond and waterfall. The whole gang was there, gathered at the water's edge. Harvey, Doug, Bruce, Billy, and Renée.

"I'll go first," Harvey said.

Harvey started across the log spanning the stream below the falls with arms held out straight, teetering back and forth. With a physique mature for a twelve-year-old, his young muscles rippled in the sunlight.

Sam watched his friends through his boyhood eyes. Memories began to flood back to him.

I'm remembering more, now.

Harvey's favorite class was gym. He struggled academically. His dad was in the service, somewhere overseas.

Sam catalogued the facts from long ago and watched Harvey maneuver across the log. His thick blond hair spilled over his eyes, giving him the impression of a goofy, lovable sheepdog. He made it to the other side and beckoned to Renée.

"Come on," he shouted. "It's easy!"

The falls roared twenty-five feet above the ground. Water dashed over the edge of the cliff in a gushing stream, splashing into the silken pool below. The slippery log stretched twelve feet above the pool of water. Droplets sparkled in the air and moistened Sam's hair, face, and arms.

Harvey flexed his muscles in a mock wrestling pose.

"Come on! You can do it."

Renée plunged ahead. In her orange pedal pushers and an orange-and-white striped tank top, her slim arms and legs waltzed rapidly along the log. She leapt to the shore with glee.

"I did it!" she squealed. "I did it!"

Long blond pigtails flew up and down; she clapped her hands and jumped in circles. Sam felt himself inexplicably drawn to her face, her hair, her eyes. Infatuation overwhelmed him, filling him with adoration.

Billy was next. His face looked drawn, tense.

"Sam?" he pleaded with wide eyes.

Sam saw his brother's fear. He felt afraid, too.

"You don't have to, Billy. No biggie. We can just walk down the bank to the pool. We'll go swimming."

Billy's expression changed. He looked across the expanse, then behind him at Doug and Bruce who waited in line. His eyes became determined, his mouth set.

"I can do it."

Sam nodded and eased past him.

"Okay. But let me go first, okay? Don't look down. Keep your arms out, like this."

He stretched his arms like an airplane and started across the log. Billy followed right behind him. They made it safely across and fell onto the ground with relief when they reached the shore. Doug and Bruce stood on the other side, hesitating. Doug, the youngest of the group, always too young to play with the older kids, had insisted on tagging along. He ran his fingers through his red hair and pouted.

Bruce poked Doug between the shoulder blades.

"Come on. Don't be a baby. Go!"

Doug stalled. He scuffed his feet.

"I can't," he moaned. "Sam! Help me?"

Sam sighed and rolled his eyes, gritted his teeth, and crossed back to fetch Doug.

"Okay. Follow me."

Doug grabbed Sam's shirttail and followed behind. He screamed when he started to lose his balance, nearly pulling Sam off the log. Sam swiveled and caught him before he fell. Steadying him, Sam took a deep breath, and slowly helped him cross to the other side.

Bruce crossed last. He pushed his glasses up his nose, hitched his shorts, and screwed up his face. He started across the log, but halfway over, tripped on a shoelace. He flew up and out, and landed with a massive belly flop in the pool below.

Sam and Harvey raced to the water's edge.

"Bruce! Are you okay?"

The boy surfaced and splashed awkwardly toward the shore. His glasses skewed across his nose and hair plastered his forehead.

"I'm okay." He sputtered and pulled himself out of the water.

Wet clothes stuck to his scrawny body. Harvey helped him up.

"It's okay, pal."

Renée and Doug laughed at him. Together, they could be cruel.

"Ha, ha, you fell in!" they taunted.

Sam frowned, disappointed particularly in Renée. She should know better.

"Cut it out, you two! Act your age, for goodness sakes."

He pushed past them and ruffled Bruce's hair.

"Come on, buddy. You can use my towel."

Bruce looked at him gratefully. A strong thought passed from Bruce to Sam.

Sam's like the brother I never had. My best friend.

The vision grew distorted and smoky. It faded as Sam drifted into a green void and spiraled back to the present.

Chapter Twenty-nine

SAM AWOKE TO FIND THE FIRE IN EMBERS. He rubbed his gritty eyes and glanced down at the bench on which he slumped.

Billy's Tonka truck.

He closed and reopened his eyes. The truck was still there. He picked it up. It was Billy's truck, all right.

Turning it around, he examined it closer: a turquoise metal body, with a few scratches and a little rust on the white truck bed. There was a tiny hitch that used to pull the white horse trailer. He turned it over, and saw the marks he'd inscribed in the bottom fifty years ago for Billy.

W. Moore.

Sam shook himself. Someone was really trying to mess with his mind. This truck had come out of the box in the attic. It was real, from this century, and was put there to scare the hell out of him.

He looked around nervously, aware that someone must have been watching him. Spying on him. Waiting for him to nod off.

How else could they have made the truck seem to appear out of nowhere? Did they know I was time traveling? Or did they think I'd fallen asleep?

Just thinking the words made him uncomfortable.

Time travel? Is that what it really is?

He shook his head in disbelief. He was a man of science, of facts. Studying medicine had groomed him in the art of analysis and common sense.

The faint sound of splashing water still lingered in the air.

This whole experience flies in the face of logic.

Before he could question his sanity further, a rustling sounded from the woods, as if something or someone had scurried away. Sam looked up and imagined the spirit of his little brother. He could have left the toy there, as a sign of some sort. He stood and shook the ridiculous thoughts out of his head.

I'm going insane.

He leaned down and grabbed the marble. It rolled cool between his fingers as he held it to the light.

"What are you trying to tell me?" The green glass flashed in the sunlight. Mute, it remained cool and unresponsive.

He pocketed it and looked toward the woods. More rustling from the trees. He checked his watch. Eleven. He still had an hour until Rachel would call him for lunch. Scanning the woods, he walked toward a path that curved beneath the maple and beech trees. Something on the ground flickered in the light. He leaned down to examine it.

Billy's harmonica.

Sam picked it up in disbelief. The smooth metal felt warm to the touch. Someone, or something, had just dropped it.

"What the h—"

The scuffling came again, followed by footsteps. Sliding the harmonica into his pocket, he studied his hands.

Are they young or old?

They were large, capable, sturdy, and browned by the sun. He was sixty-two. No question about it.

"Billy?" Sam called; shocked he said it out loud.

A flash of red and blue flitted in the distance.

Someone in a baseball cap?

Sam began to chase the apparition.

It has to be human. It has to be real.

As he ran, he was hit by the double sensation again—a back and forth perception of moving from one dimension to another. It vibrated faint, but persistent.

His knees ached, but he followed the path toward the falls. Breathing hard, he stopped and listened. The babble of water called to him, pulling him, luring him as if each splash was of great consequence.

The stream had overgrown considerably since the last time he'd visited. The log still spanned the pool overhead, although it was covered in moss.. The sun sparkled from the water flowing in a steady stream over the rocky edge of the cliff.

The dream had been so immediate, so real. And the voices of his playmates and little brother still echoed in his brain.

Billy had looked so frightened and small.

Sam looked at the water. The pool beneath the log swirled in eddies caused by the roiling water that churned from the falls twenty feet upstream. He stared at the pool, and took a few tentative steps onto the log. It seemed as if it might hold him.

"Saaaaaaaaaaam."

He jumped. The voice faded. He mentally shook himself, then lowered himself onto the log. Sitting in the bright sunlight, Sam felt the mist of the falls carry the moisture on the air. A cloud moved across the sun, changing the reflection of the water below. Something moved in the current, beneath the water, about three feet from the edge of the pool. It was white, and spindly. It floated back and forth, back and forth.

Sam froze. The cloud passed and the sun once again brightened the reflection. He stared hard at the water, trying to make it out.

What is it?

Rising, he balanced with his arms outstretched and carefully walked across to the opposite side. He climbed down the bank, bending down to get a closer look. Something definitely floated beneath the water. Something white. Something thin. Several somethings.

He removed his shoes and socks, rolled his pants to his knees, and waded into the water. After staring at the swaying skeletal thing beneath the surface, he still couldn't make it out. Taking a deep breath, he reached down for it. His hands closed around what felt like bones as he yanked it from the pool.

Sam closed his eyes for a minute, unable to look. After a few heart-pounding seconds, he opened them.

He held the decaying blanched branches of a tree limb. Drift wood. White, brittle, skeletal. Not bones.

Not his brother's bones.

Sam chided himself once more and backed out of the pool. He sat on the grassy bank and held his head in his hands for a long time. He felt like sobbing. The childlike feelings of grief and loss poured over him, sapping his strength.

Billy. Where are you?

A few cumulus clouds stirred across the sky, tumbling in the breeze, providing a cotton background for the cowbirds who swooped and sang overhead. Their calls sounded like water. Water. Water everywhere.

He lay back on the bank, studying the sky. With determination now, he focused on regulating his breathing. After two steady breaths, his heart hitched again.

What's happening to me?

He waited until it stopped pounding, then sat up. Pulling himself together, he put his socks and shoes on and rolled down his jeans.

What was Billy trying to tell him? Why had he lured him to the falls?

"Saaaaaaaaaaam."

This time, Sam knew the voice was real. It sounded like a man's voice, singing in falsetto tones. Singsong. Like Hollywood ghosts calling to people in movies.

Anger flared inside him.

Someone's playing with me. Someone in this lifetime.

He stood and looked around. The flash of red and blue came again, this time in the lane that led to their old fort in Healey's Cave. Sam started to run.

"Who are you?" he shouted. "I know you're there!"

He ran along the track to the cave, recognizing overgrown landmarks as he went. The dead pine tree that spanned the track seemed to have shrunk in size. It was bleached now, and hardened like petrified wood. He stepped over it and continued. The gray boulders marking the opening of Healey's Cave were still there, but were covered in low growing ivy and nearly hidden by honeysuckle bushes. The massive oak tree split in half by lightning years ago still stood crooked on the hill looming above the cavernous hole. The opening was high, but not as vast as he remembered.

A shuffling sound came from within.

Sam stopped short, just shy of the entrance. He moved inside, in spite of the whisper of fear trickling down his spine.

Chapter Thirty

SAM HESITATED INSIDE THE YAWNING CAVE and realized he had no flashlight or matches. Whoever was in there was trying to lure him deeper into the darkness. It would be suicidal to plunge into the cavern.

Despite the voice screaming in his head, telling him call the cops, he stepped into the dim interior.

"Saaaaaaaaaaam."

It resonated from deep inside the cave. He inched forward. The holes in the ceiling resembled skylights that dappled the sandy floor. He'd forgotten how bright Healey's Cave could be inside. It started to come back to him—climbing overhead as a youth, crawling over the knobby rock formations, and having to be extra careful not to fall through the random fissures that let the sunlight through to the floor below.

"Saaaaaaaaaaam."

Sam continued toward the deep end of the cave. They'd played there as children, near the little stream that trickled out of the wall and flowed to the floor, meandering through the cavern and out a side shaft.

The light dimmed.

And the marble heated up.

"Saaaaaaaaaaam."

He fingered the warm glass and removed it from his pocket. It glowed softly. An eerie, green circle of light surrounded him. He felt protected as he approached the form sitting on the outcropping of rocks near the back wall.

"Step into the light," he said to the figure. The boy wore a baseball cap.

Sam moved closer, unable to see the motionless face. Drawn back in time, the double phenomenon whirled within him and he wobbled back and forth across dimensions. He heard the sound of a yo-yo sliding up and down on its string. Up and down, up and down, the yo-yo whirred and spun.

A younger version of Sam wavered through a green gelatinous screen. His younger self sat on the rocky outcropping, like the figure before him, spinning the yellow glow-in-the-dark yo-yo. His friends gathered around and told stories. In seconds, he flew into young Sam's brain and the screen dissolved.

"Sammy?" Doug whined, "Can I pleeeease try it?"

Doug stood before him, puny, with a pinched expression on his face.

"Sorry, Doug. Billy's next. Then Harvey. Then Bruce. Then you. We already decided, remember?"

The yo-yo glowed. Sam loved the way it slid on the string. He moved the small loop of string on his index finger as he commanded the toy to rise and drop. The group of boys raised and lowered their heads as they watched in awe and envy.

Doug whined again.

"Why am I always last?" He kicked the sandy soil with his black hi-top sneaker. "I'm *always* last!"

Bruce was the first to snap.

"Geez, Doug. Why are you such a baby? Why don't you go home and ask your momma for a bottle? You're too little to hang out with us, anyway."

Doug's eyes filled with tears.

"I am not!" He stomped his foot.

"Are, too!" Bruce said, shoving Doug. "Go on. Go home and play with the other babies."

Doug fell on the ground. His covered his face with his hands.

"Aw, leave him alone," Sam said. He helped Doug up. "Come on, Dougie. Come sit by me and you can watch how I 'walk the dog.'"

Doug sniffled and wiped his eyes. He stuck his tongue out at Bruce, pushed past Billy, and walked toward Sam, hopping onto the ledge.

Billy sat cross-legged against the wall, watching the whole thing. He smiled at his older brother, and seemed proud of Sam for standing up for the little guy.

Bruce snorted, kicked the dirt, and motioned for Harvey to follow.

"Let's get out of here. These guys are BORRRRING."

Harvey seemed conflicted. He hated fights, as much as he loved talking about war. His obsession with warfare was crushing. Yet the minute a spat broke out among his friends, he was the peacemaker. He radiated gentleness with kind brown eyes.

"Let's just hang out here. I want my turn with the yo-yo."

Bruce shot him a dirty look. His mouth tightened and fists curled. He stood to his full height, but remained a foot shorter than Harvey. Turning on his heels, Bruce stomped out of sight.

"He'll be back," Billy said. "He always comes back."

"Yeah," Harvey said, warming to the idea. "He'll be back."

A green flash washed over Sam, rippling and undulating in the dark cave. He felt sand on his face, and heard the trickle of the stream where it spewed from the cave wall.

He woke, face down on the ground. The stream had soaked his shirt and pants. It trickled past his arms and legs; sending icy shivers down his spine. He spit sand and sat up. His head hurt. He reached around and felt something warm and wet on his hair, then studied his hand.

Blood.

A baseball bat lay discarded nearby. He crawled to it and touched the wet end. More blood. *His* blood.

Sam scanned the cavern. The figure sat on the rock, unmoving. The sun had arced overhead, brightening the cave. He studied it again and realized it was posed. Moving closer, Sam touched the hand of a mannequin. The young boy wore a red and blue baseball cap, and clothes similar to those Billy wore the day he died. Suspended below his outstretched plaster hand hung a yellow yo-yo.

Sam spun around. His vision swam as someone or something scuttled away from him. Footsteps and faint laughter echoed in the cave. He took a step forward, ready to give chase, but an overwhelming sense of vertigo floored him. He rested on the ground and breathed slowly. Spots of green light danced behind his eyelids. Finally, he felt grounded again, rooted firmly in the present. Hunting around for the marble, he pocketed it, grabbed the yo-yo, and headed home.

Chapter Thirty-one

THE KILLER LAY IN BED with sweet thoughts coursing through his mind.

It was luscious...

The titillating excitement of the chase, luring Sam into the cave, dropping Billy's toys while Sam lay knocked out on the ground, had been more satisfying than he ever imagined. Sam seemed afraid, almost hypnotized. It was a little eerie when the thing in his hand glowed green, but he figured it was one of those glow sticks.

I don't think I hit him too hard. He woke up eventually. He seemed kinda dizzy. But that was good. It gave me time to slip away before he recognized me.

He just wanted to scare him, shake him up a bit. He needed to build some fear, some anxiety in Sam's eyes. It would add to the pleasure when he stood at the funeral of Sam's grandson and pretended to mourn with all the others.

The last of the eleven-year-old innocents.

He toyed with the idea of killing Sam, too. The thought thrilled him. Standing at the funeral of both grandfather and grandson had a unique appeal.

Think of the headlines.

It would probably get national coverage and create a hell of a stir.

The first boy who died years ago was interesting. Tommy Donahue. He'd watched Manfred Healey and his inebriated friends chase the boy on his bike with their car. After swerving down the road and terrorizing him, they accidentally struck him. The tires of the white Belair had crunched over the boy. He saw it happen from his vantage point on his front porch late that night when he couldn't sleep. His father had been brutal, screaming drunken words at his mother and crashing around their bedroom earlier in the evening. No matter how hard he tried, he'd been unable to sleep.

He shook off the memory of his father and tried to remember the good part of that night.

Ever so carefully, he'd followed them when they dragged the body away and buried it in the woods behind Sam's house. He thought about it for years afterward and had been to the burial site many times. He left little trinkets on the unmarked grave, including his father's war medal. But no one discovered the boy beneath the ground until Sam rototilled the skull. It had been so easy for Manfred to hide the kill. And he'd literally gotten away with murder.

He often wondered about Tommy.

Why had he been riding on their street at that hour, anyway? Had his parents known he was out?

He thought Tommy had probably run away from home and been drifting through the streets of Conaroga when the drunken teens spotted him. There hadn't been anything about it in the papers. They just reported that he'd gone off on his bike and had never come home. Just like Billy.

There was something about the stealth, the thrill of almost being discovered, the sound of the shovels as they bit into the dirt, that pleased him. He remembered the details for years. He recounted the events, imagined doing it himself. The boy's face had been obliterated from his memory. He wished he remembered it. He especially loved knowing what happened, keeping it secret all these years. That was his favorite part.

He sighed and rolled over in bed as his mood shifted, remembering *her.* So delicate. So lovely. So innocent.

She had liked him at first. They'd gone to the movies, kissed in the back row, and shared a jumbo box of popcorn. He remembered the way she had tasted. Salt and butter kisses. Soft lips. Curls that shone in the flickering lights of the theater. He'd been mesmerized by her, absorbed with her every movement. *Obsessed with her.*

He'd floated in a state of constant bliss for weeks, soared over the pavement from pure joy. His feet had skipped along the schoolyard, he'd whizzed through his homework, and had raced to her house every day after school. It had been perfect. Until he introduced her to *him.*

The rage burned in his chest and spiraled to the sick cancer in his belly. Nausea plagued him. He imagined the cancer spreading, sending its bloated, filthy cells throughout his body. He needed to get even soon. Very soon. Before the cancer finished him off. He had to get even for the brutal way the bastard had treated his sweet love.

The prick had seduced her, enticed her to his bed, and had defiled her innocent young flesh. His beloved had been sullied forever. And when she was later rejected by the big jerk who ruined her, it had been too much for her to handle.

He rolled onto his back, plumped his pillows and stifled his own scream.

Shut up. Just shut up! Forget about him for now.

Revenge will be sweet and complete. The vile attack perpetrated on his beloved would soon be avenged.

Think about something else. Someone else. Someone like—Evan.

The boy looked so much like Billy it was almost comical. Perfect. The perfect end to an illustrious, brilliant killing career.

No one would ever find out. They never did.

The clock is ticking.

It's almost time.

Chapter Thirty-two

WHEN SAM RETURNED HOME he called Ned Olsen and explained what happened in the cave.

"Are you sure he hit you on the head? Are you sure you didn't just fall and bump it when you blacked out?" Ned asked.

Sam sighed. It was so hard to explain what happened without revealing the truth about the marble.

"Yes. I'm certain. There was a baseball bat with my blood on it right next to me."

Ned grunted. "Okay. I'm heading out there now to investigate. Wait for me before you go back there. And for God's sake, don't touch anything."

"Don't worry. I'm not going anywhere. My head's killing me."

"Sorry." Ned hesitated as if rethinking his plans. "Listen. I'm calling Mac Stewart. I think I'll bring him with me."

"Good idea. It could be dangerous for you, too."

After the phone call, Sam and Rachel sat on the couch together, holding each other. He refused to go for stitches, but took some heavy-duty painkillers leftover from last year when he'd thrown his back out.

"Honey?" Rachel patted his shirtfront gently.

"Hmm?"

He was falling asleep sitting beside her, nodding from the drugs.

"Who hates you enough to do this to you?"

Sam opened his eyes and stared at her.

"What?"

She straightened and stared at him, her worried eyes boring into his.

"Someone has it in for you, Sam. Someone who knows about your childhood toys, and the cave. Who in the world would *do* such a thing?"

"I don't know," he said slowly. "It's sick. Stealing Billy's toys. Taunting me with them. Luring me into the cave. And for what?"

Rachel squeezed his hand.

"Do you think he was trying to kill you? When he hit you on the head?"

A chill ran down Sam's spine.

"I don't know. I hadn't considered that." He noticed the frightened flash in her eyes. "But I don't really think so. I think he just wanted to get out of there anonymously. Anyway, my head's too hard. It would take more than that to do me in."

Rachel slapped his arm.

"Oh, Sam. This is serious, honey. A monster is out there, and if it's the same one who killed those little boys…"

"Rachel," Sam said. "Don't let your imagination run wild. There's no reason to think it's the same guy. This is probably someone's idea of a sick—"

Rachel gave him a disapproving look.

"Joke? No. I'm not buying it. Maybe the toys popping up everywhere could be an elaborate, hurtful prank. But no one would have bashed you on the head for a laugh. He was serious."

Sam gave up trying to dispel her fears. She was right. But he couldn't force himself to examine the possibilities. After all, the only people who knew about Healey's Cave and the games they played there were his best friends and Billy.

He helped Rachel up the stairs. After getting her settled for the night, he flopped into a drugged sleep.

ಐಡ

In his dream, Sam slumped on the brown couch in the lounge of the Sweet Briar Home. He wore pajamas, a robe, and slippers.

An odd assortment of people circled him. Nurses, filled with the appropriate mixture of vigor and compassion, reached for him. Their clown faces turned down in sympathy, but their brisk voices made him realize they'd never understand the deep, dark feelings that strangled him. He couldn't speak. Crushed, blackened, and nearly numb, a tidal wave of depression washed over him, equal in intensity to the fresh feelings of grief he'd experienced when they locked him up. Sam turned away from the nurses and faced his parents, their faces misshapen and concerned.

Betrayed, lost, and abandoned, he sobbed inside, but no sounds erupted from his parched lips.

They left him in that awful place when he needed them the most.

The surging, overwhelming melancholy draped him like a shroud. His body, heavy and sluggish, moved in slow motion.

Doctors passed, whispering in conference, judging him, pronouncing him catatonic, and schizophrenic, and other equally frightening and foreign names. He shrank back from them and floated out to the gardens. The grounds seemed peaceful and serene, but were actually prison yards that held him captive. Threatened, he wandered about the gloomy yard.

The dream progressed as it always did.

He sat on a bench, feeling acutely alone. A troll-like patient rode past him, leered in his direction, and wobbled back and forth on Billy's bike.

Billy's bike.

As always in this part of the dream, Sam sat on the bench with his heart hammering. And he screamed.

Billy!

Then came the tears. Hot, scalding tears sheeted down his cheeks. And then, without warning, they stopped.

There he was! Billy sat beside him. His freshly scrubbed skin shone and his hair lay neatly combed, parted on the left. He wore his usual checkered shirt and blue jeans. And of course, the red and blue baseball cap. He smiled at Sam and spoke, although his lips remained still.

"Don't be sad, Sam. I'm okay."

The pall of despondency lifted from Sam's heart like a basket of doves released in the air. He smiled back at the watery image of his little brother, feeling at peace as Billy slowly evaporated.

The dream changed.

Now Evan sat beside him. His eyes widened in fear. He mouthed the word "Gramps?"

Sam startled awake, his pillow soaked. Rachel thankfully slept on, drugged by the sleep-inducing drugs that were part of her regimen.

Evan's face haunted him. He'd taken Billy's place on the bench. *Billy's place.*

Sam sat bolt upright in bed. He realized what Billy had been trying to tell him all along.

Evan is the next target. The thirteenth victim.

Although it was only 3:50 in the morning, Sam jumped out of bed and hurried down to the kitchen. He turned on the light, grabbed a pad of paper and a pencil, and went to work.

Chapter Thirty-three

Number One. The killer was one of my boyhood friends.
Number Two. He knows Billy's toys are kept in our attic.
Number Three. He's twisted. Evil. And getting worse.
Number Four. He was in Conaroga when Billy disappeared, then Cambridge for the next ten years. After that, it was New Jersey, Long Island, Maine, and Washington D.C. For the past twenty years, the murders had revolved around New York City.

Sam stared at the piece of paper.

It has to be. It has to be him.

He made the call.

Chapter Thirty-four

MAC STEWART AND NED OLSEN sat in Sam's living room early Monday morning. Sam went over the details, one by one. He finished with the bizarre scene played out in Healey's cave. Of course, he omitted the part about the marble and his dream.

"You want us to do *what?*" Mac asked.

"I want you to arrest Senator Bruce McDonald for murder. I want you to get him off the street before he kills my grandson."

Mac and Ned exchanged dubious looks.

Sam persisted. He laid out the timeline of the serial killings that was published in the papers.

"See? They all match Bruce's history. He was at Harvard for ten years. Did his apprenticeship in New York City. Long Island and New Jersey are just minutes away. I even found this old post card that Bruce sent me from his summer vacation in Maine. It was the same year the seventh victim was found. The rest of the murders match Bruce's career. He was stationed in Washington for a term, then in New York City after being elected Senator."

Mac picked up the post card. Ned pursed his lips.

Mac tossed the post card on the table. "You want me to arrest a United States Senator for the murders of those boys? For which we have not one shred of evidence, aside from the fact that he happened to be in the same city each time one occurred?"

Mac shook his head and continued.

"I see why you suspect him, Sam, but we need more evidence to bring him in."

Ned spoke up.

"I checked out Healey's Cave before I came here, Sam. It was empty."

Sam shot him a surprised look.

"Nothing? Damn." After a moment, he shrugged. "Figures. He knew I'd call you."

Mac, Ned, and Sam sat silently at the table. The clock on the microwave clicked over to 10:00. Suddenly, Sam brightened.

"Wait a minute. I still have the yo-yo, harmonica and the truck. My prints will be on them, but maybe you could check them anyway?"

Mac nodded.

"Okay. We'll take a look. But this killer is not that sloppy. The guy who killed these boys left nothing. Never a print. Not a shred of evidence. Except the medals. And we've run up against a brick wall with the online auction."

Sam shot Mac a questioning glance.

"Why?"

"He's getting really bold. Commando1070 registered under your name, Sam. Used your full name and address."

"What?" Sam jumped to his feet.

"I'm afraid so. I don't know where he would have had the medals sent, had the web hosts not spooked him. Probably a P.O. box. But he's getting cocky now. Thinks he's quite clever."

Sam pinched the bridge of his nose. "Whoever it is, he's trying to drive me nuts. But why? Why is he bringing back Billy's toys, strewing them around me, and trying to upset me? What's he got against me?"

Mac chewed on his lip for a minute and ran his hand over his cropped white hair.

"Well, let's step back a moment. We still don't know that the guy who's after you *is* the murderer, Sam. He might be one of your boyhood buddies who's gotten off on the whole story and is keying in on Billy. On the other hand, if he *is* the murderer, then we have to consider all possibilities." He paused for a moment and continued in a more somber tone. "It doesn't take much to turn a young mind that has the propensity for being warped. An unkind word, jealousy, rivalry, an imagined slight." Mac sighed as if he'd seen it all. "Anything of that nature can turn a kid. He probably obsesses about the offending event all the time. Blows it way out of proportion. And somehow, Sam, you and Billy were involved."

Ned said, "Can't you remember anything, Sam? Anything that might have turned one of them against you?"

Sam struggled. He sat again and fingered the cup of coffee that had cooled long ago.

He had clear memories of his childhood. Childish spats were common. Doug, Bruce, and Harvey were always scrapping.

"It's possible the kids were jealous of Billy. I loved my brother, and always put him first. There was no arguing about that. Billy was my first priority."

Mac and Ned nodded, listening and waiting for more. Sam thought for a while longer.

"Bruce always wanted to be part of our family. After Billy disappeared, that stopped. I lost it for a few months, then when I came out of the institution, I was changed. I felt dead, discarded. I didn't hang out with any of the kids that year, or any time after that."

Ned spoke up.

"So maybe he felt rejected, huh? Kind of pushed away?"

Sam nodded.

"It's possible. But of course, the others might have felt the same way. We all used to be real close."

Mac looked at the list again.

"What about the other kids? What about the Marine? Any feelings about him?"

Sam put one hand out as if to stop Mac's words in flight.

"No way. Harvey is one of the good guys. I couldn't picture him harming an innocent child."

"The girl? What about her?"

Sam shook his head again.

"Renée wouldn't kill anyone. Besides, she only hung out with us once in a while. As soon as she matured, it all stopped. She liked an older kid. Basketball player."

"That leaves the computer nerd. What's his name? Doug?" Mac asked.

Sam nodded.

"Yeah. Little Doug. He was the smallest of the bunch, a year younger than Billy. Always tagging along, always too little to do stuff." Sam hesitated, thinking back. "He used to kind of idolize me. And then I drifted away from all of them."

Ned stood up and accepted the yo-yo, harmonica, and truck from Sam. He had bagged them in plastic and held them carefully.

"Well, let's get these prints run. Maybe we'll catch a break this time, gentlemen."

Chapter Thirty-five

THE PHONE RANG at ten past noon. Rachel and Sam had just finished bowls of pasta sautéed in olive oil with sugar snap peas and garlic cloves. He picked it up.

"Hello?"

"Sam? Ned, here."

Sam shifted the receiver to his other ear and leaned against the counter.

"What's up?"

"We just got a call from the lab. They checked for prints on the toys."

Sam tensed. "And?"

"And nothing. They were wiped clean before you handled them."

Sam's face fell.

"Sam?"

"Yeah?"

"I'm sorry."

"It's okay. I guess I was hoping for a real, live culprit. Someone to point a finger at so I could dispel these idiotic thoughts that keep running through my head."

"Like what?" Ned asked.

Sam hesitated.

"You'll think I'm nuts. Heck, *I* think I'm nuts."

"Maybe talking about it will help."

Sam sighed, then, against his better judgment, shared his preposterous ideas.

"All right. I know it's absurd, but at first I hoped it was Billy who was leaving the toys around. I've been thinking about him so much lately that I'm kind of losing it. I hate to admit it, but since they never found Billy's body, I always had hopeful theories rattling around in my brain. Kidnapping was the favorite. Someone wanted a kid and just took him. That's the least upsetting possibility."

"Actually, that's quite natural, Sam. A lot of people who lose loved ones will concoct elaborate theories to keep hope alive. To be honest, I don't think you should hold out much hope after fifty years. I don't mean to upset you, but it's not likely. Even if Billy had been kidnapped, once he became an adult he would have found you. By this time, anyway. He was old enough to remember his family name, address, and the neighborhood. And I can't imagine him torturing his big brother like that, you know, strategically placing those toys around your yard. Doesn't make any sense, does it?"

Sam looked off into the distance, continuing with the outlandish train of thought.

"Unless he got hit on the head or something, Ned. You know, amnesia. Like in the movies. Made his way home, sensing that it was important to him, but not knowing why. Fascinated by me, drawn to his old toys. But frightened, so he kept out of sight."

Ned sighed.

"I don't think so, buddy."

"I know. I know. It's just…"

"What?"

"It's just that I still miss him, Ned. After all these years. I miss him so damned much."

Rachel rolled into the room, stopped beside Sam's chair, and reached up rub her hand on his back. He looked at her compassionate face, her tender smile, and took her hand. She squeezed. He squeezed back. He mouthed the words, "I love you," and turned his attention back to the phone.

Ned mumbled sympathetically, then changed the subject.

"There is hope, though, Sam. We were able to lift some prints from the paint on the doorjamb in your attic. And a couple from the metal box that held the baseball cards. We'll need you and Rachel to give us your prints so we can sort it out. And we'll need your friends to come down to the station for printing. If we tell them what happened, get them all together to talk about it; I'm sure they'll agree to get fingerprinted. If anyone hesitates, it could be an indication of guilt."

Sam picked at a loose thread on his shirt. "Good idea. I've been thinking of trying to get those guys together, anyway, to see if I could sense anything. See how they react to what I tell them."

"Well, be careful, Sam. We'll probably want to keep an eye on this little get together, you know."

"Sure thing. I'll let you know when it's set up. And you know what?" Sam twirled the phone cord around his hand and looked off into the distance.

"What's that?"

"I'm really getting mad. I want to find out who this bastard is and watch him squirm when I narrow in on him."

Ned chuckled. "Don't blame you there, buddy. But keep your eyes open. He's tried to hurt you before. Be vigilant."

"Will do, Ned. Will do."

Chapter Thirty-six

THE KILLER HAD BEEN SURPRISED when Sam called to discuss the campout. Surprised, and excited to hear everyone would be there.

He would be there. The monster. The one who had defiled his lovely Olivia. He pushed down the persistent rage that rolled in his belly.

Relax. Just breathe. There's plenty of time for revenge. "Patience is a virtue."

He heard his grandmother's voice in his head, low and gravelly. It calmed him. She was the only one who understood him, who really cared. And yet, she did nothing to extract him from the clutches of his father, did she? The drunken rampages went on for years.

A cold sense of pleasure pooled in his cancer-filled stomach. His plan—five decades in the making—was about to be culminated.

Excitement mingled with angst. The old group would be together under the stars. He pictured their faces reflected in the light of the campfire. Visions of their young features melded with their weathered, older faces.

There would be one major difference, this time.

Billy won't be there.

Sitting on the edge of his bed, he stopped dead, looking out the window in a contemplative daze. A sick smile spread across his lips.

Or would he?

Chapter Thirty-seven

ON FRIDAY NIGHT, the stage was set.

Sam scanned the area around the campfire. Each of his boyhood pals sat on a canvas chair circling the fire pit. Bruce McDonald, Doug Smythe, and Harvey Allen. Renée had declined. Since she was such a negligible part of the group anyway, he really didn't care. In a way, he was pleased. It would be just the guys tonight.

Rachel invited their daughter, Beth, for their own girls' sleepover party. Beth had flown in from New York City earlier that day. After Sam picked her up at the Jet Blue terminal and brought her overnight bag upstairs, he'd kissed both of his girls goodbye and headed outdoors.

Using the tractor and cart, he made three trips to the campsite with coolers of meat, drinks, and assorted foods. He lugged his sleeping bag and air mattress, paper plates, napkins and various other cooking utensils, and plenty of ice.

The campfire blazed beside the pile of wood Sam had stacked. There would be enough to keep the fire roaring through the night. Sparks shot into the air; the wood crackled and spat.

At seven o'clock, it was still daylight, but the horizon muted the bright hue of the sky into a darker, more somber cobalt. A few streaks of orange darted across the black hills in the distance.

He chose the same spot where they camped years ago, the one too close to the Healeys' property line, that Sam later discovered actually belonged to his own family, not the Healey's.

Bruce smiled at Sam and lifted the red ale he brought to impress his buddies. The microbrewery had opened last year in Rochester, and he'd reported that he made a special trip to purchase a case for tonight. Or maybe one of his lackeys had gone on the errand for him. Sam wasn't sure.

"Here's to old times, gentlemen."

Sam raised his iced green tea in response, wondering how Bruce had dodged his bodyguard, Rufus.

Or had he?

There'd been a rustling in the woods before they all arrived to set up their bedrolls. It distracted Sam a few times.

Was it Rufus? Or was it Ned Olsen?

Sam knew that Ned and probably Mac would be on watch tonight. But he doubted they would be so close or so clumsy as to make loud rustling noises in the brush. He pictured Mac and Ned watching Rufus, and Rufus watching the men around the campfire. He almost smiled. Talk about bizarre.

"Here, here." Harvey swept his heavy white locks away from his bushy dark eyebrows.

He lifted a can of local brew, graciously rejecting the designer beer Bruce tried to push on him. He wore a red and black plaid jacket, faded jeans, and scuffed work boots. Sam smiled at him, thinking of him as the last of the good old boys. Solid. Reliable. Decent. Brave. He'd forgotten how much he enjoyed Harvey's company.

Doug arrived last and placed his laptop carefully on his bedroll amidst raised eyebrows from the men.

"What?" he challenged. "I'm working on a great piece based on childhood. I wanna read it to you guys later tonight."

Harvey and Bruce exchanged surprised looks with Sam. No one knew Doug dabbled in writing.

Doug stuck out his legs in front of him with a pleased expression on his face. Adjusting the purple cap that covered his bald spot, he studied his old friends. He raised a bottle of hard lemonade in the air.

"And I, being the youngest, would like to propose a toast to all you old farts who let me hang out with you when I was an annoying, bratty kid," Doug said.

He tipped his bottle and knocked back half of it.

"You're still annoying, Doug," Bruce laughed.

The others shifted uneasily. Sam didn't want the night to start like this.

"Oh, come on, Doug was always a good sport," Sam said.

Harvey lifted his can of beer and agreed.

"No problem," Doug said with a smile. "And thank you, Sam. But actually, I rather enjoy the teasing. Reminds me of my youth. And it's good fodder for my story."

Harvey took the bait.

"Okay, Mr. Computer Genius. Tell us about this story. What's it about?"

Doug sat up, clearly energized. He spoke rapid-fire, as if he had been waiting for this moment for a very long time.

"I don't want to read it yet. Not 'til after we eat. But I'll tell you a little bit about it now."

He looked self-important, almost preening.

"It's a short story about a group of kids who hung out one long, hot summer. How they played around the falls, swam in the pool, and fought with each other like weasels over a dead chicken."

Bruce's eyebrow raised a fraction of an inch. Harvey looked surprised. Sam just listened. The image was distasteful, but intriguing.

"Am I in it?" Bruce asked.

Doug snorted.

"Of course not, stupid. They're all made up. But I didn't tell you the best part yet."

Silence ensued. Surprised that Doug would refer to the Senator in such a tone, coupled with curiosity about the story, Sam prodded Doug with a sense of foreboding.

"So, Doug, what's the best part?"

Doug leaned forward, clasped his hands over his knees, and looked intently around the circle.

"The best part is… that two of the kids are murdered."

Sam's heart skipped a beat. A fleeting expression of bold madness flickered beneath Doug's heavy lids. They narrowed to slits as he looked from one man to the next, gauging their reactions.

Could Doug be the one?

He sat back in his seat and forced himself to relax. He needed to stay vigilant, like Ned had advised. His eyes flickered from Doug, to Bruce, to Harvey, then back again to Doug. If Doug wasn't the murderer, then the others might react oddly to the idea of a fictitious murder set in their childhood. He watched and waited.

Chapter Thirty-eight

BRUCE SHIFTED UNCOMFORTABLY in his chair and Harvey looked at Sam with a worried, puppy dog expression.

"Murdered?" Harvey repeated.

A mischievous smile stole over Doug's face.

"Yeah. Isn't it a great idea? I think it would make a super movie, too."

Bruce interrupted.

"Is anyone else hungry? I'm starving."

Doug shot him a nasty look, apparently irritated that he'd lost his moment in the spotlight. "I guess I could eat."

Harvey rose and nodded. "I'm ready. I haven't eaten since noon."

Sam jumped up and lifted the cover on the first cooler.

"Right here, gentlemen. Steak, baked beans, corn on the cob, and Rachel's potato salad. Let's get that grate over there on top of the fire. I'll start the steaks. Doug and Harvey, why don't you husk the corn and wrap it in aluminum foil? Bruce can help me with the meat."

Doug and Harvey went to work on the corn. They tossed the cornhusks onto the fire. The leaves curled and sizzled, disappearing almost instantly. Bruce whispered to Sam when they carried the heavy cooler to the fire.

"I thought you said you had something important to tell us tonight."

Sam nodded. They set the cooler down, and Sam answered him under his breath.

"Later. After we've eaten and Doug's told his story. It can wait."

"Okay. Just didn't want you upstaged by Doug."

Sam chuckled and tossed Bruce a smile. "Thanks."

Sam grilled the steaks to perfection. He handed the A1 sauce to Harvey, who cast him a look of approval. Sam loaded the sturdy paper plates with corn roasted in tinfoil jackets, beans heated in a can on the coals, cold potato salad, and the steaks. He doled out the plates, and finally sat down to eat.

They ate fast, gobbling the meal as if they'd been on a two-week fast. No one spoke, except to exclaim over the juicy the steaks or tangy potato salad. Finally, when their hunger was almost sated, Sam broke out Rachel's chocolate chip cookies. Large and chewy, they boasted big chunks of nuts. The men groaned in pleasure and finished off the entire batch.

Bruce patted his stomach and belched.

"Ah. Felt good to do that with no journalists around to document it."

The men laughed.

"Must be hard, sometimes," Sam said.

Bruce barked a laugh.

"It is. Sure, I was lucky to win the seat, but sometimes being in the public eye can be overwhelming. I get sick of being so damned proper, you know?"

Harvey belched in agreement and all four men burst out laughing. Sam rose and began to collect the paper plates and the silverware.

Harvey held out a hand to stop him. "No, Sam. You sit and talk. I'll do the cleanup."

"It's okay. I like to keep busy."

Harvey collected the empty recyclable bottles and cans. Between the two of them, they finished quickly. When they sat down again, Doug and Bruce were already in a conversation. Bruce's eyes looked glazed over. Doug was droning on in one of his monologues.

"So, anyway, when they transferred me to Virginia Beach, of course, I got this sweet apartment on the waterfront. It was a steal. Got it for a quarter its value. That's the year I got my Corvette, too. A classic sixty-three. Just beautiful, that machine. Four on the floor and leather seats. Man. What a vehicle she was. I looked so good behind that wheel! Lost her, though, in a nasty crash on the Thruway. Almost died. Did you hear about that?"

Bruce shook his head, looking numb.

"Really? Nope. Sorry, Doug. Never heard."

Doug continued. "Oh, yeah, I was in traction and everything. That was before I met my wife. And those nurses. Wooeee, did they love me. They'd bring me donuts and all sorts of contraband when I asked. Guess it's all just part of the Smythe charm, huh?"

Bruce stood and turned toward Sam. He flashed a look of pleading and mouthed, "Help!"

Sam recognized his plight. Doug kept talking. Bruce stretched his arms high over his head and covered a yawn.

Sam interrupted Doug's flow when he took a breath.

"Doug! It's story time, buddy. Come on. Boot up that laptop of yours and let's hear it."

Doug's pale eyes flashed with anticipation. He scooted over to his bedroll to grab the computer.

"Okay. Come on, guys. Hey, Harvey, would you grab me another bottle of my brew? That's it, thanks."

The blue screen reflected Doug's glasses. Mesmerized, he waited for the laptop to complete its startup routine. Finally, Doug sighed in satisfaction and opened the file.

Harvey settled down with his third can of beer and mashed a mosquito against his forearm. Sam tossed him the bug spray.

Bruce listened attentively. Sam threw another four logs onto the fire, and settled down between Harvey and Bruce.

The story was awful, the writing stilted. Doug's prose displayed no sense of motion, no flow, no purity. After the first paragraph, Sam's brain tuned out. His eyes raked over the three men, looking for telling clues.

Doug had developed a beer belly and a ruddy complexion. His eyes—pale watery blue—were small and close set above his beak-like nose. As he spoke, he spit a little. He took off the baseball cap and ran his fingers through thinning hair. Strands of gray laced the longish red hair nearly covering his ears.

Sam found it hard not to imagine him as the knobby-kneed, clinging little boy who looked up to him for approval. It was as if time had frozen that fateful summer. The paunchy adult across from him bore no resemblance at all to the Doug in Sam's mind.

Harvey had weathered the years well. He'd broadened as he matured and stood well over six feet. His white hair grew shaggy, completely opposite from the brush cut he'd worn as a Marine. He stayed in shape and had a muscular chest and arms. Usually, Sam saw him dressed in white pants, tee shirt, and a white apron when he cooked behind the counter in his restaurant. The Harvey of the past had merged with the man Sam saw regularly around town. Harvey still remained actively involved in veterans' affairs. He'd been the simple, good soldier who followed orders, exhibited extraordinary bravery, and cared deeply for the friends he made and lost in the war. He still volunteered at the VA hospital, and had petitioned Bruce for legislative aid in the past.

Bruce had changed the most. The skinny, awkward little boy had transformed over the years, and had been groomed into a sleek, trim man. His curly steel-gray hair was perfectly sculpted. Sam looked at him again, wondering for the first time if he wore a toupee. He stood at five-feet-ten and had remained in excellent shape due to the merciless vigor of a personal trainer. Bruce's clothes were tailored, his sneakers trendy, his contacts tinted to bring out that blue in his eyes, and his teeth capped. Sam thought he looked too packaged and a bit unreal. He even wondered about his chin.

Was it that pronounced when we were kids?

Sam had a hard time relating the senator to the little pal of his boyhood.

Doug was almost finished. His eyes shone. He continued with the horrific prose while Sam, Bruce, and Harvey tried to look engrossed. Sam sat forward, clasped his hands before him, and looked at Doug with simulated interest.

"And then, the little fat kid held the rock over the bratty one named Saul and crashed it down over his head. Saul rolled over when it missed and he yelled at the fat kid named Rick and then it happened again. But suddenly they both stopped as a gunshot came from the woods and killed them both."

Doug paused, scanned his audience, and announced, "The End."

They applauded politely.

Sam was disappointed. He had been hoping for some kind of clue, some minor intimation that Doug was *the one*. There was nothing of the sort. Nothing to go on.

"Wow. That was really something," Sam said honestly. "How long have you been working on the story?"

Doug shut down the laptop, shimmered with self-satisfaction, and snapped the cover shut.

"Over a year now. It came to me when I was training some guys down in New York. I was missing the country, you know, and I got to thinking about our childhood. We had some pretty good times, hey, guys?"

The men shifted in their seats, grateful the torture was over.

Harvey started. "Yeah. Remember the time we saw the fawn?"

Sam brightened. He'd forgotten. They'd been traipsing through woods that opened into a meadow. A spotted fawn, just weeks old, had stood beside her mother in the field. The boys froze, and so did the deer. In that magical moment, the warm breeze lifted their hair and the smell of honeysuckle drifted across the field. It came back to him in a flash, in a palpable rush of sensation. He almost felt as if he would cross over, and felt his pocket to assure himself the marble wasn't glowing. It wasn't. It remained cool.

Bruce spoke up.

"Those were good times, men. Good times." He stretched and turned to Sam. "Sam? Weren't you going to tell us something important tonight?"

Sam imagined Ned and Mac sitting up and taking notice in their clandestine positions in the woods. They'd placed high tech listening devices around the campfire and probably recorded the entire evening's trivial remarks.

"Yeah. I guess I do want to discuss something with you guys. Let me just throw another few logs on the fire and put some coffee on."

Chapter Thirty-nine

SAM LOOKED AT HIS OLD FRIENDS and sighed. It was time. He gathered his courage.

"Okay. Here's the deal, guys."

The three men stared at Sam with unabashed curiosity. Harvey picked at his teeth with a fingernail. Doug set his feet on the warm rocks circling the fire. Bruce crossed one leg over the other.

"First of all, I want to talk about Billy."

Harvey's mouth dropped open. Doug drew in his breath. Bruce's eyes widened.

"Billy?" Bruce said.

Sam nodded.

"Yes. I want to say I'm sorry I turned away from you guys when it happened. It knocked me for a loop, and I just collapsed into myself. When Billy never came back, I imagined the most horrible things. After a while, I was completely empty inside. Just plain numb."

Sam watched his childhood friends. A strange rush of affection washed over him. "Anyway, I'm really sorry."

They murmured appropriate words of comfort, dismissing his concerns. Sam took a deep breath.

"The second thing I want to tell you is that someone..." He stopped and swallowed hard. "Someone is out to get me."

Each man sat up, staring at Sam. Harvey spoke first.

"What do you mean, 'out to get you'? Do you mean *kill* you?"

Sam hesitated.

"Possibly. But whoever it is, he's certainly trying to scare me. Or drive me nuts. And he knows a lot about me. About us. And Billy."

Bruce's face changed to a scowl of disbelief. He mouthed the word, "What?" to the others.

Harvey shook his head, shaking his long white hair so it rippled like the fibers of a soft paintbrush.

Doug asked, "What do you mean, about *us? The four of us?*"

Sam watched Doug's face. His skin grew pale. His eyes widened in what seemed genuine concern.

Sam answered somberly. "Yes. And I mean *all* about us. This will sound even weirder, but he's got Billy's toys."

Harvey sat up.

"What? What the hell?"

Sam calmed his pounding chest.

They all seem surprised. Sam scratched his chin and squinted into the firelight. *Somebody's a damn good actor.*

"Yeah. Billy's old Tonka trucks, the horse trailer, his harmonica, and who knows what else. He stole them from my attic. He's been watching me. Stalking me, I guess. I dropped off for a nap, and woke up with Billy's truck beside me. Then someone called me from the woods. The voice was eerie, singsong. Like he was trying to spook me." Bruce shivered. Harvey's mouth dropped open. Doug's eyes narrowed.

Sam shifted on his campstool. "It was these woods, actually. He left Billy's harmonica on the ground for me to find. Just over there."

Bruce sat straighter, his mouth set tight.

"That's really sick." His brows knitted together.

Doug leaned forward. His jaw dropped.

"Frigging unbelievable."

Harvey nudged Sam. "There's more, isn't there."

Sam swiped a hand across his lips.

"Yeah. He lured me into our old fort in Healey's Cave just before he bashed me over the head and left me unconscious. And he set up a mannequin, a dummy of a little boy, with clothes that looked just like Billy's. With this old yo-yo. Anyone remember this?"

Sam held up the glow-in-the-dark yo-yo.

The three men gawked at it. Sam put the string on his finger and began to spin it up and down. The sound of the whirring mingled with the crackle of the logs that shifted and sparked on the fire.

"He knocked me out cold, on the floor of that cave. And Ned—Ned thinks only one of us would know everything he knew."

Harvey looked shocked.

"Wait a minute. He thinks it's one of us?"

Sam nodded slowly.

"I'm afraid so."

Chapter Forty

Doug rolled onto his side on top of his sleeping bag. He rested his chin on his hand. "Sam? When did that guy in the cave knock you out? Maybe it wasn't one of us. We might have alibis. It could be someone we talked to about our childhood, you know? Someone who listened really close and just got weird about it. He might be trying to scare you, to get something from you."

Sam shrugged. "Like what? What could anyone get from me? The only money I have is earmarked for Rachel, Beth, and Andy. Even if they kill me, they wouldn't get that. Anyway, to answer your question, it was the day before yesterday. About four in the afternoon."

Bruce spoke slowly.

"Thursday? Four o'clock? Let me see. I guess I was driving back from an interview with that gal on Channel 13. She was pretty tough interviewer, pushed me hard up against the wall on a few issues."

He stopped, seemed to realize he was being self-centered, and turned to Harvey.

"What about you, big guy?"

Harvey answered quickly, without hesitation.

"Working. As usual. We're open until seven every night. You all know that."

Bruce nodded.

"Right. The whole town knows where to find you." He turned to Doug. "How about you, Doug? Last Thursday at four?"

Doug gazed into the distant darkness.

"Let me think. Oh, right. Reinstalling an operating system in Henrietta. College kid downloaded a bad virus. Wiped out his whole hard drive."

Sam looked at them. They all seemed genuine, natural. None of the men looked flustered or defensive. And each one could have been lying, or at least have ducked out from their purported activities for an hour or so. He'd have to see if Ned or Mac could corroborate the statements. Maybe Bruce's interview really ended at two? Maybe he never went? Maybe Harvey left work for an "appointment." Maybe Doug never went to Henrietta.

A wave of exhaustion rolled over him. He looked back and forth between the men. It was time to ask.

"Okay, guys. I knew it couldn't have been any of you. I felt stupid asking, but Ned insisted. I guess you won't mind getting fingerprinted, then, huh? Ned wants you all to go down to the station tomorrow. Just for the record."

There was a long silence. Harvey broke it.

"Wow. That's so weird."

The others nodded in agreement.

"Bizarre, is what it is," Doug said softly.

"So, you'll go?" Sam asked gently.

They all nodded and murmured their consent.

"Thanks." He stretched and covered a yawn. "Guess we'd better turn in."

A cloud of unease stole over the group. With awkward glances at each other, they shuffled their belongings, wiggled into their sleeping bags, and started snoring. Sam fell asleep last.

Chapter Forty-one

SAM WOKE FEELING COLD. The fire had died to glowing embers. He shivered, and glanced at the three occupied sleeping bags. Unzipping his flannel-lined bag, he scurried over to the woodpile. He stirred the embers with a long piece of black walnut, and pushed them around until a small flame erupted. Next, he crisscrossed three long logs over the pit. The flames began to lick hungrily around the dry wood. After a few minutes, he added two more heavy logs to the pile. The blaze leapt into the dark night, shedding sparks into the blackness.

Satisfied, Sam almost went back to bed, but realized at the last minute he needed to tend to nature's call. He walked past the lane into the woods. A breeze ruffled his hair and he startled.

Is someone watching me?

He spun around. Were Ned and Mac still out there?

Sam found a thicket of spruce trees. When he re-zipped his jeans, he heard something.

"Saaaaaaaaaaam."

It was the same voice. The same plaintive, wailing, taunting voice from the cave. He looked into the hills, wondering if Ned or Mac had heard it. Were they still listening? Were they asleep?

"Who is it?" Sam answered in a normal tone of voice. He didn't want to sound afraid.

"Saaaaaaaaaam. It's me. Billy."

Sam's blood chilled. With adrenaline pumping, he turned around and searched for the source.

"Billy? Where are you, buddy? I've missed you."

Sam answered in a loud voice, hoping the others would hear him.

"Come on, Billy. It's been so long. I want to see you."

Silence ensued. Crickets peeped loudly. An owl hooted. And the sound of boots scraping across the ground came from the thicket on his right.

Sam bolted toward the noise. A skittering erupted from the pine trees beyond. He ran toward it into the dark pine grove. He stopped and listened hard. On the far side of the thicket, eyes glittered. The pale moon reflected in the corneas of the man or creature hiding in the shadows. Before Sam could speak, he tossed something onto the ground by Sam's feet. Sam hesitated, then reached down to pick up Billy's blue and yellow twirling top.

A voice whispered, but this time, it sounded exactly like Billy. "Sam. Look out!"

Sam stared down the barrel of a gun. The marble in his pocket seared the flesh on his thigh. He dropped to the ground when the revolver flashed. His spirit tumbled through time entwined in a swirling wreath of blue smoke ivy.

Chapter Forty-two

S AM SHIVERED UNDER THE COVERS. His twelve-year-old arms, legs, and torso itched with maddening persistence. Chicken pox erupted in school last week and half the students were home with it.

"Sam?"

Billy stood over his bed.

"D-don't get too close. You'll catch it, Billy."

"It's okay. Mom says I should try to catch it so I can get it over with. Says she's gonna bring the television in here so we can watch Howdy Doody and The Lone Ranger." Billy's freckled face pulled down in concern. "You look awful."

Sam shivered again. He reached for the calamine lotion on the bedside table and smeared some of it on his right forearm.

"Does that stuff help?" Billy asked.

Sam nodded.

"A little."

"Smells awful."

"I know."

"Want me to read to you?" Billy asked.

Sam looked at his little brother's earnest expression.

"Okay."

Billy picked up the Hardy Boys book that lay open at the foot of the bed. Mrs. Moore had been reading it to Sam earlier in the morning. Billy struggled with some of the words, but managed to finish three chapters before Mrs. Moore came into the room with a tray full of food.

"Okay, Sammie. Tomato soup made with milk, grilled cheese on rye, and a dish of custard for dessert."

Billy looked enviously at the tray.

"D-don't worry, buddy." Sam stuttered and shook with the fever. "She'll make you the same stuff when you g-get it."

Billy smiled, scooted over to make room for the bed tray, and closed the book. Mrs. Moore straightened Sam's covers and plumped Sam's pillow. She turned to Billy and ruffled his hair.

"Come on, little guy, I have some for you in the kitchen."

☯☯

Sam woke on the cold ground, tasting tomato soup on his lips. Billy's voice roared inside Sam's head.

"Get up, Sam!"

The flashback must have been mere seconds this time. Sam's side burned, but this time it wasn't from a long lost sphere of green glass seeking his attention. He'd been hit near his ribs. The bullet had ripped into his jacket and torn along his midriff.

The pine needles stuck to his cheek when he moaned and tried to move. With a Herculean effort, he got up. Another bullet zinged past his head.

He lowered his head and scrambled away from the shooter.

"Come on, Sam," the voice whined. "Hold still."

Another shot whizzed past his ear.

Sam stumbled from the thicket. The path headed away from the campsite and through the woods. He took it, cursing his luck. If he'd exited the thicket on the other side, he could have easily made his way back to the campsite, and roused his friends.

Would Mac or Ned see him? Hear him? He shouted, hoping to attract their attention.

"Ned! Mac! He's here!"

He panted and tried to concentrate on moving away from his pursuer. The pain in his side throbbed. He lurched and fumbled in the cold woods. Holding an arm tight beneath his ribs, he followed the dirt path. The shadows of leaves and branches dappled the silver moonlit track. Thudding footsteps crashed behind him. Another bullet cracked in the night and embedded itself in a nearby tree. He tripped, lunged forward, and caught himself on a birch tree. Hanging onto it, he spun and looked for his attacker.

The silhouetted figure stood against the purple-black sky. Sam tried to make out his features, but it was impossible. Motionless, he pointed the gun at Sam. He squeezed the trigger again, but this time, the hammer jammed. Sam bolted in the opposite direction. As he rounded a corner, he heard the gun go off again. He fell to the ground as a ripping tear seared along his shoulder blade.

Sam rolled over and stared while his attacker escaped in the opposite direction. His vision clouded and he fell into a black void as Billy's face flashed before his eyes.

☙☾

Someone called his name. Someone from this world.

"Sam!"

Ned Olsen and Mac Stewart found him. Ned sat him up and rolled him over.

"He's been shot!" Ned yelled. "Mac. Get an ambulance down here, now."

The next few minutes passed in a blur. Sam held Billy's top in his hands while strong arms carried him back to the campfire. His friends surrounded him, looking worried and concerned. All three offered to help. Sam gritted his teeth when his wounds were exposed and something pressed hard against them. He forced himself to think of other things, but could focus only on the killer, and how close he was to him at that moment. The man who held all the secrets about Billy's demise had stood right beside him. The man who killed his little brother ate steak from his grill, drank his coffee, and ate Rachel's cookies with good humor and laughter.

Didn't he?

But which one was it? Which one had stuffed his own sleeping bag to make it look occupied?

He was no closer than before, and had no strong suspicions about anyone in particular. The killer remained obscured behind the concerned mask of friendship. He was good, Sam thought, trying to ignore the smoldering pain in his side and shoulder. *Too damned good.*

Chapter Forty-three

ANDY STOOD BESIDE HIS FATHER'S BED in the Rochester Memorial Hospital recovery room.

"Mom's going nuts, Dad. She really wants to be here."

Sam mumbled through an anesthesia-induced stupor.

"No. Make her stay home. I'll be released tomorrow. Tell Beth to stay with her."

Andy shuffled from foot-to-foot. This type of vigil usually went to his sister, Beth, or his wife Maryellen. Maryellen stayed home with the boys, who both had bad colds, and Beth stayed with Rachel, who had suffered through a bad day with her MS even before she heard about Sam. Her spells were like seizures, caused by the lesions on nerve bundles in her brain. After an attack, which often lasted an hour and could occur frequently within the day, she was left weak for hours, with shaky legs that refused to cooperate.

"The doc said you'd be fine in a few weeks. One bullet chipped a rib, but went straight through your side. They stitched it up. And the one that hit you near your shoulder blade grazed the skin, but it should heal on its own. You were lucky, Dad."

"It was the marble," Sam mumbled.

"What?"

Sam reached for his son's hand. Young and strong, the skin was smooth and brown from the sun. He pressed it to his chest, above the bandages. He couldn't tell him about Billy's marble scorching his skin just as the gun fired. Of course, that was why he'd dropped to the ground and avoided a potentially fatal shot. Billy had saved him.

"Nothing, son. I love you. You know that."

Andy flushed and looked down.

"I know, Dad. I love you, too."

"How are the boys? Are they upset?"

Andy relaxed. This was comfortable territory.

"I didn't tell them. I didn't want them to worry. They're okay. They both have that awful summer cold, but Evan won his track meet last week and Timmy's learning his colors."

"That's for the best," Sam said. "I'll be out of here tomorrow, anyway. I'll be fine by the weekend, I'm sure, so count me in."

"You mean you still want to watch the boys next week?"

Andy scratched his head and looked at his father with disbelief. He served in the National Guard and had just been notified that he'd be shipping out next week. The entire family was shaken, including Sam, who found out as he was getting prepped for surgery. Maryellen had promised to be with her own father in St. Louis, scheduled for heart surgery on the following Monday. Sam and Rachel agreed to take the boys for the week.

"Dad, that's crazy. You've just been shot, for Heaven's sake."

"No. I don't want any strangers watching my grandsons. Your mom will be better by then, and I'll be walking around in no time. I insist." Sam tried for a forceful look, but his energy sagged and his face fell.

"Well, we'll see how you are by Saturday. Fair enough?"

Sam nodded. The tug of sleep melted his resolve.

"Okay, son. You'll see, though, I'll be…"

His eyes closed as he fought the drowsiness.

"I'll be…"

Andy finished his sentence as a nurse came in to shoo him away.

"You'll be fine, Dad. I know."

He patted his father's hand, kissed him on the forehead, and headed home.

Chapter Forty-four

Behind Andrew and Maryellen Moore's house, the killer lay on his stomach in a soft patch of pine needles. He refocused his binoculars. The boy had eaten a bowl of soup and had gone through a half box of tissues before rolling over with his back to the window. That was twenty minutes ago.

He scowled.

Maybe the kid went to sleep. Turn over, damn it! I wanna see your face.

He was about to lower his binoculars to clear his vision when the boy flipped as if on command.

He smiled and peered through the lenses.

Good boy.

He stared some more, raking the glasses over the boy's face.

He has the same freckles, the same sandy hair.

He laughed out loud, feeling ridiculously giddy and sick at the same time. It came to him in a flash. A realization so enormous that it rocked him with its enormity.

It's Billy.

Smiling now, he chuckled in anticipation.

Billy. Welcome back. We all missed you, kid.

There was no television in the boy's bedroom. He thought it was strange in this day and age, when it seemed everyone had a computer, television, Playstation, X-Box, and DVD player in each room of the house. He liked Andy and Maryellen. They were good parents.

Too bad he intended to kill their firstborn.

The crease in his brow smoothed.

They'll still have one kid.

He adjusted the focus of the binoculars again.

I'm not completely heartless.

He formed the plan carefully. Savoring the details, he thought them through and studied the house, the family's habits, and their schedules.

The boy kicked his blankets off.

He looks sweaty, probably has a fever. Too bad he has to be sick the last week of his life. Those are the breaks, kid. Maybe I'll bring you a toy.

Would they suspect him if he came bearing gifts? Would it seem odd?

He couldn't risk it. The only contact would have to be at Sam's house, or at the hospital. Maybe the boy would be there tomorrow, visiting his grandfather.

When he'd called Rachel to find out how Sam was doing, the girl had answered. Beth. That was her name. Kind of stuck-up, a big-city girl returned to the provincial country. He smiled as he thought of putting her in her place, but reconsidered.

I need to control myself. Dammit. I'll blow the whole ball of wax.

He couldn't give in to urges like that just now. Just boys. No girls allowed. One more kill. The *pièce de resistance*.

All of the agents would be disappointed when it was over. No more mystery. No more wondering at night about the identity of the wicked serial killer. They'd be let down, depressed. He was sure of it.

Too bad. He'd been a decent adversary. The murders had been brilliant. Clever. Carefully contrived, beautifully choreographed. Right down to the war metals.

I really am gifted.

He floated for a few minutes in self-glorification. His heart swelled with pride as he recounted the episodes of precision and brilliance.

Maryellen interrupted his reverie, marching into the room with a tray and a smile. She placed it on the night table and headed for the window. He almost dropped the binoculars.

Did she see me?

No. Everything's okay. She was just opening the window. She pulled the curtains back so the boy would get more sun.

He zoomed in on the bowl of ice cream and cookies. Refocusing, he thought they looked like chocolate chip. A chill filled his heart.

Little bastard.

The boy sat up and began to eat. He looked happy. Really happy.

The killer's face pulled down in a frown, reddening. Jealousy flooded him. *His* mother had been a bitch. She *never* did stuff like that. *Never.*

He pounded the ground beside him. Over and over again. Harder and harder, until his hand hurt.

It's not fair!

The thoughts consumed him, ate away at him like locusts chewing on a field of beans and like the cancer cells streaming through his body. He cried out, but muffled the sound against his wet sleeve. Sobs wracked his body as he screamed inside, writhing in agony on the pine needles beneath him.

He needed to exact his revenge again, and soon. Before the cancer stopped him.

Chapter Forty-five

"DAD!" ANDY SOUNDED ANNOYED. He held Sam's suitcase by the hospital room door and rolled his eyes. "What in the world are you doing?"

Sam hunkered on his hands and knees beneath the hospital bed, wishing his son would go away for just a few minutes.

"Looking for something," he mumbled.

"Geez, Dad. Get off the floor. I'll help you. What did you lose?"

Sam backed out from under the bed, flustered. He held onto the side of the bedrail for a moment and grimaced in pain.

"My marble."

Andy's mouth dropped open.

"You lost your marbles?"

Sam shook his head and laughed.

"No, son. I haven't lost those yet. But I did lose one little green marble. It's a talisman of sorts. A good luck charm."

Sam's nurse hurried into the room. She rummaged in the drawer by his bed. Biting her lower lip, she reached way back. Finally, with a triumphant flourish, she held up the marble.

"Is this it, Dr. Moore?"

Sam smiled and accepted it with relief.

"That's it, all right. Thank you, Betty."

Her face blossomed into a satisfied smile. Sam's heart warmed.

"You wanted it several times during your stay. It seemed to comfort you, Dr. Moore."

He nodded and squeezed Betty's hand.

"Thank you. You are a superb nurse, my dear."

Betty flushed and looked at her white shoes.

"Why, thank you, Dr. Moore. It was my pleasure."

Sam flashed a weak smile. Beaming, Betty turned on her heels and left the room. He took Andy's arm and followed him to the wheelchair.

"I don't need this chair. I told you. I'm fine."

Andy looked at his father with affection.

"I know, Dad. But it's hospital rules. Come on, now. We'll have you back in your garden in no time."

Sam lowered himself into the chair, favoring his ribs and shoulder.

"I hope so. Those weeds will have taken over if I don't get out there. Did you have a chance to run the rototiller or mow, son?"

Andy pushed the wheelchair carefully down the hall.

"Yes, Dad. I tilled between all the rows, and mowed down that awful stuff that's growing in the new area that you cleared. My God, it must have grown ten inches in a week. What is it? It comes up with little pink nubs, then those reddish leaves poke through, and it starts to grow like mad. The stalks are so thick and almost—juicy. What the heck is that stuff?"

Sam turned around to look up at his son.

"It's the knotweed, Andy. Japanese knotweed. One of the most pervasive weeds in the world. It's so bad they even have an alliance against it in the UK. Can you believe it?"

Andy laughed, rolling his father into the elevator.

"Yes. I can. They should figure out a way to harvest it, or use it somehow. It grows like a…"

Sam looked at him again. Andy pushed the button for the ground level.

"Don't." Sam said.

"Sorry, Dad. It's just too good. That stuff grows like a weed."

Sam shook his head.

"Son. That was really corny."

The elevator reached the ground floor. Andy pushed Sam out to the lobby.

"I know, Dad. I get it from you."

Sam laughed out loud, drawing a few stares from the passersby.

"Yeah. I guess you do."

Sam fingered the marble in his pocket and closed his eyes. It was warm. He needed to get home.

"Okay, son. Let's get out of here."

Chapter Forty-six

He hadn't meant to kill Sam. The bullets that whizzed past Sam in the dark forest had been calculated to frighten him, heighten the tension, and scare him into accusing the others. He'd been surprised when Sam dropped to the ground.

He fingered his blue-black revolver; it glinted in the yellow rays of the streetlight. It felt cold, smooth, and solid in his grip. He aimed it at the house a few times, picking out targets. He imagined blowing apart the stone lions flanking the front porch steps or sending a bullet through the bedroom window with the orange fire safety stickers. That room must be the other side of Evan's or Timmy's rooms. He'd stared into it from the pine grove at the back of the property all week. This was a new angle.

His finger itched on the trigger, but he pushed down the manic urge to blast away and forced himself to concentrate. It wasn't the witching hour. Not yet.

He'd been sitting in his car outside Evan's house for four hours, watching the family through the big picture window and timing their activities.

They were entirely predictable. Almost boring. The kid got off the bus at the same time every day. He would check the mail, drag his oversized backpack up the front walkway, open the dark green front door, and disappear inside. He'd go up to his room, turn on the computer, and sit in front of the window for several hours. He probably got online and talked to his friends. Maybe he told his mother he was doing homework. *Little liar.*

He liked picturing the kid as deceptive, impudent, and sneaky. Somehow it made the idea of killing him even more appealing.

Just snuffing out one more lying little bastard. Doing the world a big favor.

The killer put the gun down and shifted the car into drive.

Soon the kid who looked like Billy would be blown away. He smiled and eased into the street. *Soon.*

Chapter Forty-seven

SAM PROTESTED when Andy settled him into his bed.

"I don't need to be in bed, son."

Andy tossed him a stern look and pulled the covers to his father's chest. He tucked around the edges, as if he were a child.

"Dad. You of all people should know enough to follow doctor's orders."

Sam's face twisted into a frown.

"I know. I'm sorry. It's just..." He looked longingly out the window.

Andy bent down to kiss his father's forehead.

"It will still be waiting for you in a few days when you're stronger, Dad. Just be patient. I promise nothing bad has happened out there."

His son smiled, almost patronizing, and turned to go downstairs to help his mother make dinner. Listening to their chatter, Sam flopped against the pillow and denied the pain that ripped up and down his side and shoulder.

"He's so stubborn, Mom."

"Dad will be okay, sweetie. He just can't stand being laid up. That man has to be outside or he pines away for it."

The voices went on and on, until finally Sam tuned them out.

Just a few days.

The marble glowed from his pocket. He reached down to take it out, and rolled it between his fingers in the light.

Billy's calling me.

He tumbled in time, rolling through green mist until the sound of seagulls crying overhead anchored him in the past.

⁂

Billy flew past Sam on the flat wet beach. The musky smell of low tide permeated the air. Seagulls screeched and fluttered around them, vying for choice morsels that lay ripe on the rippled sand.

"Can't catch me!" Billy raced ahead of him, challenging his brother with a smile.

They cavorted on vacation in Brewster, Cape Cod, just a few weeks before Billy had disappeared. The weather had risen to July-like temperatures in mid May. Records had been broken for an entire month.

Periwinkles dotted soggy violet-colored sand. It looked like someone had spilled purple watercolors on the beach. A magenta hue stained the wet sand in a broad irregular area.

Was it a mineral of some kind? Had a whale thrown up on it?

Sam laughed at his own crazy thoughts. His bare feet slid on the pebbly surface of dozens of periwinkles. He ran as fast as he could after his little brother. The kid could really move. The low tide flats ran for miles, scattered with small oases of tall grasses.

Sam called to him.

"Hey! Heads up!"

He drew back his arm and lofted the football high in the air. Billy turned, twisted in midair, and caught the ball.

Unbelievable.

Sam looked around to see if anyone else noticed how good his kid brother was with a pigskin. Unfortunately, there was no one else out except a few fishermen and some kids playing tag. He smiled to himself and caught the ball his brother threw back to him. A tiny hermit crab scuttled past Sam's feet. He leaned down, and squinted at it.

"Look, Billy. A hermit crab!"

Billy sprinted back to his brother, splashing through seawater puddles. He leaned down eagerly.

"Pick it up, Sam."

Sam was a bit hesitant, but didn't want to look like a scaredy cat in front of his brother. He leaned down and gingerly picked up the crab. Little legs wiggled out from the cavity, moving tiny pincers. Sam moved his fingers back, afraid of getting pinched. He held it to his brother's face.

"Cut it out," Billy laughed. "He might get me."

Sam joined in the laughter, then put the critter back in the stream that ran from Paine's creek to the far receding sea. His father waved to them from a rocky promontory stretching from the parking lot to the beach. Both boys straightened and waved. His mother lay on a blanket beside their father. She wore a sweatshirt and khaki slacks and was always cold.

The breeze was cool, but the water was warmer.

"Let's follow the stream back," Billy said.

"Okay. And look for driftwood for Mum."

"Yeah."

Billy slogged his way through the strong flowing stream. The wind blew against them and the tide pushed hard against their ankles. They sunk into the sand, knee deep in water. It shifted down when they stepped through it. Although it was tough to walk in the stream, both boys preferred it to the sand, since it was fun to wade in the warm currents.

"Look! Minnows." Billy said.

A school darted in a tide pool, trying to follow the water disappearing out to sea. One minnow fluttered on the damp sand. Billy leaned down and scooped it into his hand. The silvery fish flipped and flopped in his palm.

"Poor thing," he said. "Here you go. Back with your brothers and sisters."

The fish hesitated, but soon started to swim again in the ankle deep stream.

"You saved his life," Sam said.

"Yeah."

Suddenly, an expression of concern crossed Billy's face. His eyes darkened, and he looked toward the blue ocean sparkling on the horizon.

"What's wrong, buddy?" Sam asked.

Billy's lower lip quivered. He stopped suddenly and sat down in the swirling stream that meandered in winding curves along the bay. Sam dropped down beside him. The warm, brackish water whirled to his waist.

"What is it?"

Billy looked at him with clear hazel eyes.

"Would you save my life if someone was gonna kill me?"

"Of course, silly. In a split second. Why do you ask?"

Billy still looked worried.

"I dunno. It's just that he's been so weird lately. I think he's wicked jealous of me and you."

"What? Who?"

Billy hesitated.

"Bruce. He's been looking at me funny, every time I come along and hang out with you guys. He gives me dirty looks. He told me he wished I—I was dead."

Sam relaxed. It was only Bruce. *Juicie Brucie with the bug-out eyes.*

"Aw, he's harmless. I know he gets a little jealous. But so do Doug and Harvey once in a while. It's because you're my favorite, and I won't pick any of them as a best friend. Each one of them has asked me that lately."

"What? If you'd be their best friend?"

"Yeah. Every one of them. It's too weird. I think they thought it up to test me. I hate it."

Sam looked down at the water. He wished he could forget about his buddies and their incessant need to be his best friend. It was so annoying.

Billy stood quietly beside him.

"I don't blame you. Sometimes those guys can be real jerks."

"Yeah." Sam put Billy in a headlock and rubbed his scalp with his knuckles. "Besides, you're my best pal."

Billy looked up with a broad grin and twisted out of his brother's arm. He shoved Sam into the water. "Likewise."

Chapter Forty-eight

THE KILLER SAT in the now familiar pine grove behind the Moores' house. A plastic soda bottle tilted against a tree stump. The cola had gone flat hours ago. Candy wrappers littered the ground to his left. He'd meant to pick them up, but each day his preoccupation with the Moore family deepened. He'd gone through a whole bag of fireballs and a bag of peanut butter cups.

The outdoor roost was better than watching through car windows. He was well hidden, and there would be no inquiries about his car being parked on the road for hours at a time. It had been easy. He pulled his sedan into a state park near the walking trails, traversed a cornfield and some woods, and reached the back of the Moores' property in fifteen minutes.

The binoculars grew heavy in his hands. He wiggled backwards and sat up again behind the bush he used for cover. Carefully, he drew out his notebook and pen and wrote.

Five forty-five P.M.: Maryellen washes dishes. Evan rides bike—first time in days. Must be feeling better. Andy helps dry dishes, calls someone from kitchen phone.

He put down the pen and picked up the binoculars again. For the millionth time, he wished he'd purchased a little video camera or even a tiny voice recorder. He wanted to hear them, be a closer part of their daily routines.

He watched Andy on the phone. He imagined him talking to Sam. Sam was better now, much stronger. Sam had been tilling his garden when he drove past the house yesterday. It was a good sign.

Evan had been riding his bike around the driveway in big circles. Over and over again. He wore a blue baseball cap, a gray tee shirt, and white shorts. For an instant, Evan stopped dead and looked straight at him. He froze, heart hammering.

Did he see me?

The boy shook his head, as if dismissing intuitive thoughts, and went back to practicing wheelies on his blue bike.

The killer relaxed and lowered his glasses.

It has to be soon.

He had to act before they uncovered his secrets, or spied him in the woods. He'd finally chosen the date.

Sunday night. Two more days to prepare the trap.

Chapter Forty-nine

LATE SATURDAY AFTERNOON Sam slumped on the bench by the fire pit. For the first time in weeks, he wasn't obsessed with the past, or the killer, or the marble. He could only think of Andy.

His boy—so grown up—and yet in Sam's mind, still a child. He'd said goodbye to Andy on the tarmac of the Rochester airport yesterday, and felt a conflicting mix of deep-down pride and absolute dread. He'd hugged his son's wide shoulders and tried not to show it. The strength with which Andy met the news of his impending tour of duty in the Middle East had been inspirational. Maryellen had stood proudly with Timmy and Evan, waving goodbye.

Sam shot a half-smile to no one and sighed. Maryellen would be dropping off the boys any minute now.

He flexed his arms and raised them above his shoulders in a luxurious stretch. The stitch in his side that had limited his activities for the past week had completely disappeared. Sam lowered his arms and examined his hands. They were stained from the spent daylilies he'd been deadheading for the past half-hour. The succulent blossoms of the red-pepper-colored lilies snapped off easily, sometimes clinging to the leaves beneath them. They subsequently dyed his fingers a deep Kool-Aid red.

His gaze wandered to the roadside garden extending along the back of the property. Red Monarda, pink snapdragons, rose and melon colored honeysuckle vines, red Geum, and a blanket of electric hot pink roses shimmered in the sun. Old-fashioned hollyhocks, with their double maroon blossoms, stood tall behind the Monarda. Bright cherry-tangerine blossoms of new phlox had just begun to burst open with rich colors. They would help to carry the gardens through the rest of July and August.

The knotweed patch looked deceptively neat. Sam had finished mowing the entire property an hour earlier. Once again, the knotweed had sprouted ten inches in a week. He was seriously beginning to doubt the theory that one could "mow it to death." It seemed healthier than ever, and even appeared to multiply, flourishing in this new regime of frequent mowing. He shook his head and laughed. He had seriously underestimated the power of the weed. It fought valiantly against him, and had a good chance of winning. The last resort was a chemical assault.

Well, if need be, he would stop in at the garden center in the fall and request advice on how to kill the stuff.

The sound of gravel crunching on the driveway drew his attention. He hopped up and walked briskly toward Maryellen's van, opening the sliding door when it stopped.

"Papa!" Timmy cried from his car seat in the back. "Out! Git down!"

Sam exchanged an amused look with Evan, who sat across the aisle from Timmy.

"Hi, Evan. How are you, son?"

"I'm good, Grandpa. I miss Dad already, though."

Evan's eyes darted to his mother as he whispered, afraid to upset her.

Sam reached over to squeeze Evan's shoulder. "Me, too."

Timmy squealed and struggled against the car seat.

"Git down!"

Maryellen hurried around to the side of the van. She handed Timmy's backpack and pillow to Sam and unbuckled the baby from the seat. He scrambled down and reached for some Teddy Grahams on the floor.

"No, Timmy," Maryellen said. "Those are dirty, honey. Yucky."

Timmy shoved them in his mouth.

"Oh, Timmy. No!"

Sam laughed.

"Typical boy, huh?"

Maryellen rolled her eyes.

"Yeah. I hope they don't drive you nuts this week, Sam."

Sam put down the boys' things, then reached in and unbuckled the car seat from the van. He swung it out onto the lawn and grabbed the backpack and other necessities.

"Oh, don't you worry. These boys are perfect angels when they stay with us. We'll be just fine."

Evan exchanged glances with Sam, chuckled, and took his own backpack out of the van. He led the way into the house. Maryellen carried Timmy, who wrapped his legs around her middle and laid his head against her chest. Once inside, Maryellen lowered the boy to Rachel's waiting arms and threw her arms around Evan.

"I'll be back in two weeks, sweetheart. After Grandpa Nelson's operation, when he can move around on his own. I'll be back before you know it."

Evan nodded. His face was tight.

"It's okay, Mom. We'll be fine. Don't worry about us."

Maryellen nodded, held back the tears, and quickly hugged Sam. She leaned down and pecked Rachel's cheek, then picked up Timmy for one more embrace.

Finally, she handed him back to Rachel and walked slowly toward the door.

"Take good care of my boys." Her voice trembled and she swiped at her eyes.

Sam and Rachel answered in unison.

"We will."

Sam followed her to the screen door. "Don't worry about a thing, dear. They'll be spoiled rotten by the time you return."

She flashed a small smile, waved to her boys, and trotted out to her car.

Rachel sighed.

"Poor thing. Saying goodbye to all her men in the course of one weekend has to be tough."

Sam agreed, then noticed Evan's face.

"We sure are the lucky ones. We're going to have ourselves one heck of a party in this house, aren't we? Who's up for spaghetti and meatballs?"

Evan brightened. It was his favorite. The meatballs simmered in the sauce on the stovetop. Timmy raised his head from Rachel's shoulder. He worked vigorously on his pacifier, then mumbled around it.

"Sketty," he said. "Hungry."

Evan walked over to his little brother and picked him up from the chair.

"How could you be hungry? You just ate a whole package of crackers."

Rachel wheeled to the stove.

"Well, now, we've got two growing boys on our hands. And they're hungry! Sam? Could you please put the boys' things upstairs? I'll start the water for the pasta. It'll be ready in a jiffy."

Chapter Fifty

Timmy reached for another piece of meatball and shoved it in his mouth. Rachel wiped his face with a napkin.

"Messy!" Timmy said proudly.

Rachel laughed. The delightful sound reminded Sam of the wind chimes that jingled on their porch. Memories washed through his brain.

Rachel. On the beach in a one-piece white bathing suit that emphasized her creamy skin, her long hair blowing in the salty breeze, and the tinkling, bell-like laugh that caused a stirring deep in his soul.

Rachel. Standing in front of the stove with a wooden spoon in one hand, two children at her feet, and a faint sheen of perspiration on her brow. She'd suddenly let loose with that magical laugh. It had driven Sam wild with desire.

Rachel. Wrapped in a sheet, standing at the window in the moonlight after an unusually passionate evening, her dark hair tumbling around her shoulders and face in its characteristic untidy fashion. She'd laugh for the pure joy of it, and his reaction to it had almost always started another round of lovemaking.

Before the illness, she'd been light on her feet and full of boundless energy. He remembered the sensuous lover who'd erupted from the chaste, virginal woman he married, and smiled. A deep sense of affection washed over him. Although now the physical lovemaking was practically nonexistent, Sam was an integral part of Rachel. Their spirits were entwined, and he suspected it had been so for many lifetimes.

He watched her with the baby. So gentle. So accomplished, even from the confines of a wheelchair.

Yes. There was no doubt about it. They were lifetime soul mates whose passion had transcended the physical.

Rachel glanced at him, sensing his eyes on her.

"Messy!" Timmy repeated.

She flashed a warm smile at the boy.

"Yes, baby, you're messy. Now finish your garlic bread, sweetie pie, then we'll give you a bath."

Timmy grinned, "Splashin'!"

Evan took a long swig of milk and looked at his grandparents with a bemused smile.

"What?" Sam asked. "What's going on?"

Evan giggled and reached for another piece of bread.

"You'd better wear a raincoat, Grandpa. Timmy splashes all the water out of the tub."

Sam raised an eyebrow.

"Is that so?"

Rachel tittered.

"Want my umbrella, Sam?"

Evan laughed through his nose, snorting loudly. He covered his mouth with his hand, embarrassed that he'd made such an ungodly noise. Sam snorted too, on purpose, of course, then each of them lost control, including Timmy, who joined in the hysterics. When they finally settled down, Sam lifted Timmy from his high chair and carried him up to the bathroom while Evan and Rachel started the dishes.

"Bath!" Timmy squealed, trying to lift one leg over the side of the tub.

"Whoa there, little guy."

He grabbed him by his middle and pulled him back.

"We have to start the water first and get you undressed."

Sam popped the plug into the drain and ran the water, working at it for a while to get it to the right temperature. Evan had already unpacked and placed Timmy's strawberry scented baby shampoo, milk and honey bath soap, and moisturizing lavender-scented skin lotion on the side of the tub.

Sam smiled. Things sure had changed since his kids were little.

He tested the water again and nodded.

"Okay. Now it's getting there."

Timmy tried once more to lift his chubby little leg over the side.

"Bath! Want it!"

Sam gently grappled with him, took off his tee shirt, sweat pants, and diaper, then lifted him into the tub. Timmy splayed his hands under the gushing faucet and sprayed water all over the room.

"Timmy!" Sam said.

The baby squealed with delight, standing in the tub and squirting water toward Sam.

Sam grabbed one of the soft blue towels from the table and held it as a shield.

"Timmy!" he yelled, laughing in spite of himself. "Cut it out!"

Finally, he reached over and shut off the water. The baby looked at him with severe disappointment. His lower lip quivered.

"More?" he asked, looking at his grandfather with his large eyes. "More water?"

Sam smiled, gently pushed him into a sitting position, and soaped his chubby body.

"Not yet, little man. Let's get your hair washed first, okay?"

Timmy whirled around, grabbed a plastic bowl that held his tub toys, and immediately dumped them out.

"Toys. Want 'em."

The pink plastic elephants, blue rhinos, and green dolphins floated happily in the suds. As Sam soaped the baby's hair, Timmy laid the plastic bowl on its side until it filled with water, and heaved it over the side of the tub onto the linoleum where Sam kneeled.

Sam's pants were instantly soaked.

"Oh, Timmy," Sam used the towel to mop the lake that traveled across the room. "What did you do?"

"Dumped it," Timmy said with an expression of concern.

He anticipated being rebuked.

Sam shook his head, smiled broadly, and leaned over to kiss the baby on his wet cheeks.

"No, sweetheart. No dumping. Let's try to keep some of the water *in* the tub, okay?"

"Okay," he said, immediately preparing a repeat performance.

Sam was ready this time.

"No, no, no! Let Papa have this, now. We need to rinse your hair."

Sam struggled with the vigorous and mindful little boy for the next five minutes. Finally, when he had finished bathing him, he pulled the plug.

Timmy watched the water swirl down the drain, grabbed the plug, and tried to put it back in the drain hole. The metal chain stopped it from seating properly. He frowned, moved it around a little, then tried again until he actually pushed the stopper into the hole.

Sam watched in amazement. The child was only twenty-one months old.

After several more attempts to remove the plug and drain the water, Sam finally distracted Timmy.

"How about a movie, Tim? Wanna watch a movie with Evan and Grandma?"

Timmy's eye's widened with interest and he stood up, water sluicing off his body.

"All done. Git out."

Sam wrapped a towel around the slippery boy and carried him to the bedroom to dress him in his pajamas. He chose a pair of tops and bottoms of thin jersey material. Fire trucks and police cars scattered across a white background.

Well, at least some things hadn't changed.

After dressing Timmy and combing his hair, he brought him downstairs to the living room and settled with him in the comfortable stuffed rocker. Rachel and Evan had spread the pieces of a jigsaw puzzle on the card table—a lighthouse and rocky beach scene. A bag of popcorn lay open beside Evan, still steaming from the microwave.

"Booby. Tiger. Now." Timmy insisted.

Sam looked quizzically at Evan.

"He wants his movie, Grandpa. You know. The one with the Tigers."

"Ah! Of course."

He got up, found the movie of interest, and popped it in the player.

"Push pway," Timmy said.

Sam's eyebrows rose.

"What did you say?"

Evan laughed.

"He knows how to push the play button at home."

Rachel and Sam exchanged glances. Sam whistled.

"I don't believe it."

Evan smiled with pride.

"Yeah. He learns real fast. Of course, I taught him everything he knows."

Chapter Fifty-one

THE KILLER PACED across the floor of Healey's Cave. Seething, he kicked the old ball he'd been tossing around in his unique version of caveman racquetball.

The Moores had screwed him. Ruined his plans.

Why the hell did Andy Moore get called to duty now?

In the beginning, it was purely revenge. The first few murders were calculated to eventually implicate *him*. The defiler, the murderer of his dear Olivia.

As time passed, and the murders tumbled on top of each other, the plan for revenge had merged with the unexpected pleasure he discovered from his actions. He began to remember his childhood more clearly—the other kids in the neighborhood. He fantasized about what it would have been like if he'd been Sam's best friend. There'd been so much competition for Sam's affection. He was the most popular boy in his class. Not so much because of anything he did or things he owned, but because of his warm sense of humor and all-American, baseball loving, infectious, little-boy charm. Everyone loved Sam.

He stopped, wiped his streaming brow, and let the delicious dreams slither over him again, soothing him. He pictured the scene as he had a thousand times.

He would wait on the corner for the boy to ride his bike past like he did every evening. He'd sit quietly in his car, ready to entice him inside. The dirt road would be nearly deserted. The boy would be willing, concerned for him.

Sure it's okay. Your grandpa won't mind. We're friends. You know that, right? I just need your help for a few minutes.

He pictured himself popping the trunk and lifting the bicycle inside. He'd tell him to get in.

Go ahead. It's okay. Buckle up, now.

The boy would listen.

Why not? He'd been to his grandfather's house, for Heaven's sakes.

He could use that if he had to.

He ran his hands nervously through his sweaty hair. Although Healey's Cave was normally cool, today the hot, heavy air had followed him inside. He mopped his forehead with the bottom hem of his tee shirt.

Why am I sweating so much? Maybe it's the chemo.

He shook his head, gathered his wits, and sat down on an outcropping of rock to reformulate his strategy.

The plan would have to change since the kids were at Sam's house now. He'd seen Evan riding his bike in the driveway. It would have to happen right on Sam's property.

He couldn't wait any longer. The compulsion to kill was overbearing.

He'd look for an opening. Grab the first opportunity. He'd be ready.

He felt calmer and looked around the cave at the toys and games he'd bought on Ebay. They reminded him of his childhood. He'd lined them up on the ragged stone shelves jutting from the walls. His eyes traveled over the collection, mentally ticking off the list. A slinky, a green metal tractor, a hula hoop, a jump rope, a pair of silver roller skates, a baseball and glove, a wooden wiener dog on wheels, a holster with a pair of pearl-handled guns. Not real, of course. Child-sized.

He sighed happily. The boy would like them. They could play together.

Until it was time.

With a sharp and sudden cackle, he leapt to his feet and ran out of the cave toward his car hidden in the woods.

I'm ready.

Chapter Fifty-two

SAM CLOSED THE STORYBOOK and laid it on the table. Timmy sprawled in the crib on his side, sucking on his Binky and running his fingers rhythmically through the fringe on his pillow. His eyes drooped. Sam leaned over the side rail and rubbed Timmy's back. Moving his hand in gentle circles, he soothed the child in the same manner he'd used to calm Andy and Beth when they were young.

The fan in the window ushered in cool evening air. It was palpably moist, dampening the sheets and blankets with a familiar summery scent. Sam searched his memory and in a flash, he remembered where similar sensations had originated.

Campouts. Damp sleeping bags. Droplets of summery dew on the inside of a green canvas tent.

He thought of Bruce, Doug, and Harvey. Each in his sixties. Each a successful part of the community.

And one of them is a brutal jackal. A killer of boys.

Sam consciously suppressed the atrocious thought. Evan lay on his bed, reading one of Sam's old Hardy Boys' mysteries. The cover was faded and well worn. He flipped a page quietly. His eyes darted over to Sam, then back to the page.

"He needs his bunny," he said. "If he wakes up and Bobo's missing, he'll cry."

Sam smiled, leaned down under the crib to pick up the tattered rabbit, then placed it in the bed beside Timmy. The boy reached out a chubby hand and snuggled the rabbit to his chest.

"Bobo," he mumbled. "Night-night."

"Good night, little man." Sam waited a few minutes, stroking the boy's curls.

He straightened, turned off the lamp on the table by the crib, and walked to Evan's bed.

Evan looked over the top of his book.

"Do you like it?" Sam asked.

Evan nodded.

"Uh huh. A lot. I really like the boys. I wish I was that brave."
Sam sat on the side of the bed and patted Evan's knee.
"What do you mean?"
"Well, they go all over town and follow the bad guys and find treasures. You know, that kind of stuff."
"Ah. I see. Well, maybe someday you could study law enforcement and join the police force."
Evan wrinkled his nose.
"Nah. I wanna be in the CIA. It's cooler."
Sam raised an eyebrow.
"Really?"
Evan's eyes danced with excitement.
"Yeah. And I could travel. Rome. Paris. London. All over the world."
Sam smiled and squeezed his arm.
"Wouldn't that be something? I know you could do it. You're one smart boy."
Evan grinned and closed his book.
"Thanks."
Sam leaned over to give Evan a gentle hug.
"Okay. Don't stay up too late now. Your mother will kill me."
Evan smiled. It was already past his usual bedtime.
"I won't. I'm getting kinda sleepy now anyhow."
"Okay. Night, sport."
Evan put the book on the table and turned off the lamp on the nightstand. He snuggled into his pillow and mumbled.
"'Night, Gramps."
"Sleep tight, Evan. Don't let the bed bugs bite."
Sam padded along the hall to his bedroom. Rachel lay in bed on her side. She'd already begun her soft snoring. Sam picked up her reading glasses and the book that had fallen to the floor. She stirred, mumbled something unintelligible, and went back to sleep.

He leaned over, brushed the hair from her cheek, and kissed her.

Undressing quietly, he put on his pajamas and brushed his teeth. On the way to bed, he stopped and looked at his jeans folded over the chair. The marble was still in the pocket, and a fluorescent green glow shone through the fabric.

He fished it out and held it in his hand. The warmth penetrated his fingers.

Trying not to disturb the sleeping household, Sam hurried down the hall and the stairway to the living room, where he settled into the stuffed chair in the dark. He rolled the marble back and forth in his fingers and wondered about Bruce, and Doug, and Harvey.

Which one is it? And when will he strike?

His thoughts were interrupted by the sound of a roaring freight train spouting green smoke. He plunged once more into his childhood.

Chapter Fifty-three

SAM FLOATED IN THE AIR above Billy. This time, it was different.

Billy raced down the road on his brand new bicycle. The boy's exhilaration spiraled skyward and coursed through Sam's suspended being. He shared stomach-twisting thrills when Billy pedaled hard up and down Sullivan hill. He also felt Billy's cloying disappointment that lingered because Sam was talking on the phone to *a girl*, instead of riding beside him.

The streamers flapped rapidly in the breeze. Billy stopped and looked back, squinting to see if Sam was coming.

No brother appeared on the horizon.

With Billy's shivering sigh, Sam's spirit was drawn into his little brother, and he saw the world through Billy's eyes.

Billy stared hard in the distance, wishing Sam would join him. Nevertheless, he stomped on his bike pedals and kept going.

Down the street, Bruce cruised on his fancy jet-black ten-speed English bike, making slow S curves. Billy waved and shouted to him, anxious to show off his present.

As they drew closer, Billy turned a few figure eights and popped a wheelie in the middle of the street. He skidded to a stop next to Bruce, placing both feet squarely on the pavement.

Bruce noticed, just as he'd hoped. "Keen bike! Did you get it for your birthday?"

Billy nodded. Pride swelled in his chest. Red paint gleamed beneath him in the late afternoon sun.

"Yup. It's brand new."

A wide grin spread across Bruce's face.

"Race ya!"

Billy's heartbeat quickened. Sam sensed Billy's concerns, knowing he wasn't allowed to ride past the intersection of Maple Beach and Morris. But Bruce had already started, and Billy didn't want to be left behind.

"Wait up. Wait!" He pedaled furiously after Bruce.

An invisible barrier held Sam back when he tried to follow his brother, as if he were plastered against a giant fiberglass web. He pushed hard to follow Billy, but was held back by the maddening barricade. He struggled wildly against it, kicking and yelling.

"Billy! No! Don't go with him. Come home!"

The eerie force dragged Sam back to his living room. He awoke, sitting on the chair. The marble still glowed in his closed fist. An ethereal, jade green mist swirled from his hand, and suddenly gushed inward, as if drawn into the tiny glass sphere.

What stopped me? Why was this time so different? Why wasn't I in my own body?

After an hour of frustrating analysis that went nowhere, he shook his head, pushed away a feeling of terrible dread, and went upstairs to bed.

Chapter Fifty-four

DREAMS SOUGHT SAM the minute he closed his eyes and sagged into bed beside Rachel.

He lay face up on the bottom of the pool near the waterfall, suffocating in three feet of water. He knew it was the same spot where he'd pulled up the bleached branches he thought were Billy's bones. Cold creek water flowed over him, smooth and heavy, filling his mouth and nose and choking the breath out of him. Golden shafts of sunlight streamed into the pond and sparkled on the quartz rocks lining the bottom. Suddenly able to breath water, he turned his head to look at them.

So beautiful. So cold.

In a flash, he felt the fear again, his chest pressed down by an unearthly hand. He struggled to stand, but couldn't budge. Sharp stones pressed into his spine when he kicked violently at the force that pinned him underwater.

A bitter argument took place above the water. Faces loomed and wavered overhead, bizarre caricatures of his friends. Although their voices were garbled, he heard Harvey, Bruce, and Doug arguing about him while they stomped on his chest.

"No! He's *my* best friend!"

Doug pushed Harvey. Bruce shoved Doug.

Sam snapped his head from side to side, struggling to free himself from the heavy pressure of water and to slither out from beneath their sodden sneakers.

Amazed he could breathe; he stopped panicking for a moment and looked around. The water turned tepid and clear. He breathed it in and out, easily. A tiny stream of bubbles rose to the surface. Three sunfish sashayed above him, glistening turquoise and silver.

Scuffling feet caused a cloud of dust to rise, obscuring the light. Sam glanced sideways to stare at something moving in the swirling current. It shone through the water, behind the dancing dust motes, but was indistinguishable in the murk.

The water cleared again, and the object loomed toward him.
Billy.

Dead eyes stared at Sam, unseeing. His short sandy hair waved in the water.

Billy reached for him.

Sam yelled in his sleep, waking with a start.

Another scream penetrated the night.

This scream was real. Sam froze.

Evan.

"Sam!" Rachel shook Sam's shoulders.

He bolted out of bed and raced to the boys' room. Timmy sat in his crib, wailing after being awakened by Evan's cries. Evan shivered under the bed sheets in the dim light cast by the nightlight.

"Evan! What's wrong?" Sam asked, trying to catch his breath.

Evan trembled and lowered the covers.

"A bad dream," he moaned.

Timmy whined and bounced on his toes, hanging onto the crib rail.

"Papa!"

Sam found Timmy's Binky and laid him back down in his bed. He pulled up his blanket and pushed the button on the lighted aquarium music box on the side of the crib. The music started and Timmy closed his eyes.

Sam hurried to Evan's side and sat on the side of the bed.

"Was it a bad one?" he whispered.

Evan hugged his knees and rocked back and forth with eyes closed.

"Really bad." He raised his eyes to his grandfather. Fear etched his face. "It just felt so real."

Sam leaned forward and hugged the boy, knowing all too well how real dreams could seem, especially after the excursions on which the marble had taken him. The words tumbled out of Evan's mouth.

"I was drowning. Underwater. And these kids were pushing me down. Stomping on me. Talking about who was my best friend."

Sam froze. His blood ran cold. He looked at his grandson with an expression of absolute disbelief.

"What?"

"They were trying to bury me. And then the water got all dark and gross and I turned my head and saw a little kid. He looked like those pictures you've shown me of Billy, Gramps. And then he reached for me. That's when I woke up."

Sam's hands shook. He stared at his grandson, unable to speak.

We had the same dream. The same goddamn dream.

Autopilot took over. Sam patted Evan's shoulder, calmed him with soothing meaningless words, and drew the covers over him. When Evan's soft snoring finally resumed, Sam stumbled back to his room in a daze.

What the hell? How is this possible? The same dream?

He tumbled back into bed and moved as close to Rachel as he could, taking comfort in the warmth of her body and the regular rise and fall of her chest.

Chapter Fifty-five

SAM TOSSED AND TURNED, in and out of a stupor until dawn with the persistent image of Billy's face resurfacing in his dreams. He finally rose at six o'clock, while Rachel and the boys still slept. He looked in on them, pulled the blanket over Timmy's cold legs. Evan lay on his stomach with his legs sprawled beneath the blankets and his tousled head turned sideways under his pillow.

Sam watched Evan's back. It rose and fell slowly, powered by his young, healthy lungs.

Satisfied, he backed out of the room and went down to the kitchen.

In the light of day, the possibility that he and Evan shared the same nightmare seemed insane. He busied himself filling the cat's water, emptying the dishwasher, and restocking the birdfeeders. He pushed the crazy thought away.

Impossible. It couldn't have happened.

He removed the trash from the kitchen waste can and carried it out back. Lifting it into the rubbish bin, he pressed the cover down tightly, and froze.

Something moved in the woods behind the barn.

He stopped dead and stared. The trees swayed in the breeze, a mourning dove cooed, and a white-tailed rabbit hopped onto the lawn to sample the sweet grass.

Sam laughed at himself.

Just a rabbit. Man, I really need to calm down.

He shook his head and looked up just as Evan leapt off the porch with two gloves and a baseball in hand.

"Grandpa!"

Sam stopped and smiled. The boy had so much energy, was so full of life.

"Grandpa, let's toss a few around."

"Have you had breakfast, sport?"

Evan raced to his side, handed him the glove, trotted backwards toward the woods, and lobbed a high ball toward Sam.

"Nope. Maybe in a little while. I'm not hungry yet."

Sam tossed it back to him, underhand this time. It sailed slowly toward Evan.

"Okay. Let me know when you get hungry. You want pancakes this morning?"

Evan grinned broadly and tossed the ball back to Sam.

"Blueberry?"

Sam nodded, caught it easily, and returned it.

"Sure. We have pecans, too."

After a few minute of back and forth, Evan piped up.

"Grandpa? I'm getting hungry. Talking about those pancakes really did it."

Sam laughed and trotted over to the boy. He ruffled his hair, poked a few fake jabs at his stomach, and turned toward the house. Evan threw the ball straight up. He squinted against the morning sun watching it spin overhead, then stepped sideways and caught it.

"Call me when they're ready, okay?"

Sam laughed. "Count on it. Won't be more than twenty minutes, sport. I'll give a holler when they're on your plate."

Sam walked into the kitchen, stopped, and listened. Timmy was crying. He raced upstairs and into the boys' bedroom. His own bedroom door was still closed. Rachel was probably still asleep. She'd need at least another three hours to be able to get through the day.

"Papa!" wailed Timmy.

He stood in the crib without his pajama pants or diaper. The soiled diaper lay on the floor, and the pants dangled from the changing table.

"Timmy? What the heck?" Sam said as he stooped to pick up the dirty diaper.

"What da heck," repeated Timmy.

Immediately, guilt flooded Sam.

"What happened, buddy?" he asked, hoping to distract him from learning the unlovely new phrase.

"Diaper yucky," he said somberly. "Throw it."

"How the h—, I mean how in the world did you get your pajamas off?"

Timmy smiled proudly.

"Pants off!"

Sam tossed the dirty diaper in the diaper pail, then lifted him up and laid him on the changing table. He cleaned the wiggling boy; found some clothes for him, put on his socks and sneakers, then carried him downstairs. Evan still tossed the ball high in the air in the backyard.

"Ball!" squealed Timmy.

Sam put the boy in the high chair that had been Andy's.

"Phone!" Timmy squealed, reaching toward the toy phone Rachel had donated to his collection.

"Phone!" he repeated, reaching toward the toy box again.

"Okay, okay." Sam grabbed the yellow phone from the box in the corner and put it into the boy's hands.

He tied a bib around Timmy's neck and gave him the Sippy cup full of warmed milk. "Here you go. Here's your milk. Papa's gonna make breakfast now, okay?"

Timmy picked up the phone and held it upside down against his ear.

"Hewwo?"

He smiled radiantly.

"Who is it?" Sam asked, taking the pancake mix from the shelf. He opened the refrigerator door, grabbed the milk and eggs, and set them on the counter. Timmy held the phone away from his ear and grinned.

"Evan."

Sam laughed. It was the new ritual.

"It's Evan? What did he say?"

"Evan hungry. Eat cheese."

"What?" Sam laughed.

This was a new one.

"Evan wants cheese?"

Timmy nodded.

"Cheese!"

Sam smiled.

"Okay, how about I give you a slice while you're waiting, huh?"

He unwrapped a slice of American cheese, folded it into eighths, and broke the pieces apart on Timmy's tray.

"Here you go."

They continued with the telephone game while Sam made the pancake batter and poured it into the hot cast iron skillet. By the time he had cooked a stack of eight, Rachel hobbled down the stairs and slid into her wheelchair. She rolled into the kitchen and yawned.

"Oh, my. Look who's cooking breakfast."

"You're up early. Why didn't you sleep in, hon?"

She grimaced. "Couldn't. I got that pain in my back. It stretched around to my stomach and woke me up."

Sam knew the one. The nurse in the neurology clinic jokingly called it the MS hug. But there wasn't much affection in the gripping pain that ensued.

"I'm sorry, baby. You want some coffee?"

She nodded. Sam poured her a cup and set it on the table. She wheeled to it and took a sip.

"Where's Evan?"

Sam pointed outside and flipped another pancake onto a plate. He poured more batter into the skillet and dropped blueberries on top.

"He's playing ball out back. Wanna call him in? It's just about ready."

She took another sip and smiled.

"Sure."

She rolled a few feet to the screen door and squinted into the sunshine.

"Where is he?"

Sam glanced at her.

"Right out back. Just yell. He'll hear you. He's hungry," he said with a smile.

"Evan! Breakfast is ready!"

She shaded her eyes and waited for an answer.

"Let me try, honey," Sam said.

He laid the platter of pancakes on the table and walked briskly to the door. Pushing the screen door open, he stepped out onto the porch.

"Come on sport, it's ready!"

The mourning dove continued in her plaintive song, but Evan didn't answer.

"That's odd. He was just here."

He hurried down the porch steps and out past the barn. Maybe Evan lost the ball in the woods and couldn't hear him.

"Evan? Where are you, son?"

The sparrows swarmed from the eaves of the barn in daring attacks on Lila. She sat primly on the picnic table, lapping her white fur.

"Where is he, Lila?" he asked, scratching behind her ears. He'd been calm up to now, but in a millisecond, Sam's stomach clenched. Cold panic rippled through him.

"Evan!"

His voice sounded almost shrill in his own ears. He raced around the property, shouting the boy's name.

"Evan!"

The barn was empty. Nobody tossed a ball behind the hedgerow. No smiling face sat on the swing. And no hungry boy answered his call.

Chapter Fifty-six

Sam stood in the warm morning light. A cold tremor passed through him. He looked toward the road, across the back field, then to the woods. The marble burned against his leg.

Billy's trying to help me.

Should he call the police, or follow Billy's lead?

The marble glowed and pulsed through the fabric of his jeans. Without giving Sam a chance to decide, it propelled him across time through a flickering, green glass passageway. His vision filled with green, he breathed green, smelled fresh cut grass. It overwhelmed him. He sped quickly through the flashing realm, and was immediately deposited in the continuum he had left the last time—on the day Billy disappeared.

☙❦

Bruce and Billy raced forward on their bikes. Their pedals spun in frenetic circles and the red-faced boys pushed harder and harder. Bruce was in the lead, but Billy, although a year younger, was taller. He was gaining on Bruce. An excited laugh burst from Billy's lips. They approached the corner where Doug lived. Bruce, afraid he would lose the race, spun into Doug's yard and announced his victory.

"I won!" he shrieked. "I won!"

Billy followed him into the driveway. Once again Sam felt Billy's innermost thoughts. Uneasy, he knew he'd gone out of bounds a while ago. He glanced backwards, wondering if Sam would catch up soon. Would he tell on him? Get him in trouble?

Doug and Harvey tumbled down the Smythe's front steps. Doug seemed so excited to have the older boys in his yard that his eyes bugged out. He was ready to burst.

"Guys! Hey, guys! Wanna go for a ride?"

He swung a scrawny leg over his purple bicycle and laughed with giddy excitement. With one swooping shout, the three boys yelled and began to ride away.

"Come on, Billy!" they called.

Billy stood with his feet astride his new bike, filled with uncertainty. His plastic streamers hung motionless from the handlebars, but when a warm, moist breeze ruffled his hair, they rustled, urging him forward. Sam felt the conflict within his brother and hovered over him in the air, helpless to advise, powerless to change the past.

Sam screamed soundlessly at him.

"No, Billy! Go home!"

Billy followed the gang down the road.

Sam cried out again, this time with every ounce of strength.

"No. Billy! No!"

Billy stopped for a moment, cocked his head to one side as if listening, then shook it as if to dispel a wayward thought. He pedaled hard to catch up to the gang heading for the waterfall.

Sam hovered above them, drawn forward by the ghostly pull of the past. No steel web kept him back this time, but apprehension blackened his heart.

The boys looked hot and tired by the time they'd reached the dirt road leading to Healey's Cave and the falls, but they kept pedaling.

"How far are we going?" Billy shouted when he caught up to Doug.

Dust clouds puffed from the hot dirt road. An oppressive hum filled the air as thousands of insects vibrated in protest. Sam felt sweltering air fill Billy's lungs.

"To the falls. Goin' swimming," Doug shouted back.

Billy was hot and tired. A swim sounded great.

"I don't have my towel," he shouted, coughing from the gritty road dust.

"Don't worry about it, nobody has one. Don't be a baby. We can dry out on the way home."

Billy grimaced, hating to be called a baby by a kid a year younger than him. He pushed harder, passed Doug, and pulled even with

Bruce when they reached the waterfall and the pool below. Bruce flung a smile at him. They leaned their bikes against tree trunks, hopped out of their socks and sneakers, removed their dungarees and shirts, and scurried toward the pool in their underwear.

"Last one in is a rotten egg!" Harvey shouted.

They approached the dead tree spanning the pool. The waterfall glistened upstream, creating a sparkle of moisture in the air around them. Doug went first, balancing carefully along the slippery surface, showing off.

"Wish Sam could see me now," Doug laughed, "Look at me. I'm going to do it myself!"

Bruce motioned for Billy to go next.

"Go ahead! It'll be fun, Billy. Even Doug can do it."

Doug leapt into the water from the log, surprisingly unafraid. Watery circles rippled where he'd gone under. He broke through the surface again and called to Billy.

"Come on in! The water's great!"

Billy balanced on the log. His features were tight, frozen in a mask of fear. Sam always helped him cross the log. He'd never, ever considered leaping from it into the pool twelve feet below.

"Don't slip, now—jump clear of the log," Harvey said, moved cautiously behind him. Bruce brought up the rear.

Sam sensed fear running cold in his brother's belly—along with the primitive urge to be accepted. Since he'd already risked serious punishment by coming this far without his brother, and without permission, he had to make it count. He knew his folks would be worried soon.

Billy hesitated.

"Come on! Scaredy cat! Scaredy cat!" Doug taunted him from below, treading water.

Bruce motioned for him to keep moving.

"Come on, Billy. It's not so hard."

Billy stopped in the center of the log, struggled to keep his balance, and closed his eyes.

"One, two, thr—"

He slipped, arms flailing, and lost his footing. His body sailed through the air, twisting until his head slammed against the log. A split second later, he plunged beneath the water, bleeding and unconscious.

Bruce and Harvey plunged after him. A circular wash of red marked the spot where he went under. All three boys dove and searched.

"Where is he?" Doug screamed. Harvey and Bruce dove beneath the surface again, circling wider and wider.

After several tense minutes, Bruce found him, and all three helped drag Billy's limp form to shore.

"Oh my God!" Bruce's voice reverberated into the woods and back, shrill with fear.

Billy's skin was gray, and he wasn't breathing.

Bruce leaned over his inert body and tried to push on his chest in a juvenile parody of a paramedic.

Harvey kneeled beside him, his face taut with fear. A small trickle of water was expelled from Billy's blue lips, but he remained still.

"He's not breathing!"

Billy lay inert on the sandy shore, hair plastered to his forehead, smeared with blood. Lifeless eyes stared at the sky.

"What do we do?" Bruce sobbed.

Harvey stood up, wringing his hands.

"Oh no, oh no, oh no!"

"We need an ambulance!" Doug screamed, looking around him as if willing one to miraculously appear.

Harvey, overcome by horror, backed up and fell to the ground sobbing. Bruce was the first to recover. He brushed Billy's hair back from his forehead and closed the dead child's eyes.

"We're going to jail," he said.

Doug screamed again.

"What? Why?"

Harvey sat up and turned a tear-stained face to Bruce.

Bruce continued. "We made him jump. Then we couldn't save him. It's as good as killing him. We're going to jail for the rest of our lives." He spoke woodenly, softly.

Sam's soul screamed. He couldn't stop the anguish. He tried to reach for his brother, to comfort him, to breathe life back into him. But the forces that brought him to this realm also held him at bay. Pinned between both worlds, he couldn't move. His insides slid down the same slope he'd traveled when Billy had first disappeared.

This time was different. Now he *knew* what happened.

Billy's dead. I saw it happen.

As he hovered in the netherworld, the boys cried and argued over a course of action.

Unexpectedly, a sense of peace passed through him. A whispery presence hovered above the prone form of his little brother. Sam sensed his freedom. Billy's spirit floated before him, urging him, pushing him. He watched in wonder as the filmy specter connected with him.

Go, he urged, *go home now. Evan needs you.*

When the three boys dragged Billy's body into the pool of water and buried him with rocks, Sam was thrust back into the present. Raging fear gripped him once again.

Oh my God. Evan!

Chapter Fifty-seven

"Sam!" Rachel screamed.

She must have seen him collapse on the lawn. The porch was an insurmountable obstacle for the wheelchair, but she'd discarded it and had made it halfway down the steps.

Sam got up, brushed the wet grass clippings from his shirt and pants, and called to her.

"I'm okay, Rachel. Just stumbled. Call Mac. And tell him Evan's been taken. I'm going after him. I know where he is."

Rachel called him, her voice trembling with panic.

"No! Sam. Wait. You can't. Wait for the police. *Please*."

Driven, Sam knew he couldn't waste a second. Billy urged him forward.

Move!

He started to run with Rachel's cries echoing in his ears. Sprinting across the backyard to the wood's edge, he jogged down the path leading to the falls. Somehow, he knew the killer would be there. He would return to the same location where Billy died to bury his final victim under the water, in the precise area to which Sam had been drawn earlier. When Sam imagined bones beneath the water and instead came up with bleached sticks, he was close. *So* close. Billy had been right there the whole time.

His knees throbbed; his breath came short and raspy. The pain in his chest made him wonder if he was having a heart attack.

Slowing, he caught his breath until the pain subsided, then raced along the path toward the waterfall.

Evan. Oh my God. Evan.

Sam reached the falls in fifteen minutes. Drawing clammy air in ragged breaths, he stopped at the edge of the woods and surveyed the area.

Nothing.

He listened hard.

He has to be here.

In the distance, a faint sound of voices wafted out of Healey's Cave. Sam hurried toward the entrance. He stared at his empty hands and panicked.

He had no weapon—he hadn't even grabbed a garden hoe. Although tempted to call Evan's name, he held his tongue. His only advantage would be surprise.

Instead of using the main entrance, he scrambled up the hillside and located a skylight opening near the back. Poised above the hole in the ground, he paused. A strong wind stirred the leaves of the tree overhead. The two-hundred-year-old oak seemed to sway in the gust. Its massive roots stretched from its base down to the cavern below. Split in a lightning storm years ago, it groaned, buffeted in the breeze. Clouds rolled in, darkening the afternoon sky. A flash of lightning flared in the distance and a light patter of raindrops splashed against his face.

Sam climbed into the hole and down the wet, slippery roots and boulders he'd descended many times as a child. A trickle of water ran along the rocks into the cave below. Thunder and lightning worsened overhead. Using roots as handholds, he navigated his descent carefully.

The climb down was harder to negotiate than when he was a kid. Nevertheless, he hurried, trying not to make a sound.

Sam had just reached a large sandy boulder and placed his toe on it when he heard a laugh, followed by a mumble. Both voices sounded adult. He paused and listened, but as he tried to balance with one foot, he slipped. Down the side of the boulder he went, landing with an awkward thump on the shelf of rock below. He cried out involuntarily.

Oh, God. Did they hear me?

He stifled another moan, waited for the pain in his side to pass, then quickly clambered the final five feet to the floor of the cave to avoid being discovered.

Chapter Fifty-eight

VOICES ECHOED DEEP inside the cavern. Sam followed along the sandy floor toward them.

A light flashed in the distance. At first it looked like lightning, but from the way it bounced off the walls, he knew it had to be a flashlight. He flattened his body against the wall and ducked behind an outcropping of boulders.

Footsteps approached and then receded as if they took a path in the opposite direction.

"Move!" said a raspy voice.

He heard a muffled response, then a moan.

Sam's gut tightened. He recognized the sound. He'd heard it before, when Evan was sick with chickenpox, when he made a particularly bad throw with the ball, when his little brother followed him outside and asked to play. This moan was different, however and it made Sam's blood run cold.

Evan's scared.

Galvanized by the sound, Sam pushed away from the damp stone wall and raced after them. He rounded a corner and ducked through a low archway. They were approaching the section of the cave in which he'd been taunted—the cave with the little boy model dressed in clothes just like Billy's. Sam slowed when he saw figures ahead of him.

Bruce sat on a wooden chair. *Juicy Brucie with the bugout eyes.*

Sam's heart sank.

Not Bruce. Please God, not Bruce.

His best childhood buddy sat with his back to him, facing the back wall of the cavern. Sam moved forward, looking for Evan.

There he was, slumped against the wall in front of Bruce. Rope secured his hands behind his back and his mouth was covered with duct tape. He looked so small, so helpless. As he was about to challenge Bruce and storm into the cave, a voice spoke from the far side of the cavern, out of sight.

"So, my dear Senator, you're without protection tonight? Where's your gorilla? What was his name? Ruby? No. Ruben? Oh, right, Rufus. How much do you pay him, anyway? Or is it our tax dollars that foot the bill?"

The voice sounded oddly familiar, yet twisted. Sam couldn't place the eerie singsong tone. Bruce appeared to be simply sitting on the chair, but when Sam's eyes adjusted to the dim light he was startled to see his childhood buddy was also bound. Surrounding Evan on the floor were dozens of toys, including a slinky, a green metal tractor, a hula-hoop, and a holster with a pair of pearl-handled guns.

Bruce turned his face to the right and answered the voice.

"Let the boy go. He's an innocent child, for God's sake. If you have a beef with me, so be it. We'll face it, discuss it. It doesn't have to be like this."

Evan raised his head and spotted Sam. Sam raised one finger to his lips and shook his head. The boy nodded imperceptibly and shifted his eyes.

"We'll 'discuss it'? We'll 'face it'? Where do you think you are, on the campaign trail?"

Who the hell is he? Sam's mind boggled with the possibilities.

Bruce's shoulders slumped and the thunderstorm above grew more violent, shaking the walls of the cave.

"No. I'm sorry. Whatever I've done to you, I want to rectify it. Let the boy go. He's done you no harm, Stew."

Stew?

Sam frowned.

Who the hell is Stew?

"I need the boy. His murder will be the perfect culmination of your villainous career. Since you and your buddies watched Billy drown, there's been one poor boy eliminated every five years. No one knows Billy died accidentally. Thanks for sharing your deepest secrets with me, by the way. It was most entertaining during those long, drunken college blasts."

Bruce's jaw dropped.

"What?"

"Don't remember spilling your guts to me, Senator? Oh, it happened several times. You told me all about it. After a six-pack, you were a regular Chatty Cathy. You and your pals buried Billy right outside in that pool of water by the falls. Didn't you?"

Black sludge filled Sam's heart, but he pushed it away.

Don't think about it now. Concentrate on Evan. Get him out of here.

"After I arrange convenient accidents for Doug and Harvey, it will be clear that you were at fault. Each murder occurred in the vicinity of…YOU. Surprise, surprise." The man chuckled. "The evidence will be linked to you, my dear Senator. In the end, you will be convicted of this murder, then ultimately charged for each of the others. The proof will be damning. And I'll be back in the headlines again. 'Hotshot FBI agent identifies serial killer. Psycho Senator kills self after murdering final victim.'"

Sam strained to hear the words over a loud crack of lightning and the thunder. The man had lowered his volume when he reached the end of the diatribe. Sam slowly inched forward, hoping the argument with Bruce would divert attention from Evan. Following the left wall of the cavern, he slinked in the shadows, straining to see Stew's face on the far side of the cave.

Bruce tried again.

"Stew. Why are you so angry? Was it something that happened at Everdale?"

Everdale—the private boarding school Bruce attended each fall. He hated it there and couldn't wait to spend the summer at home with his friends, especially Sam and Billy.

"You really don't know, do you? You pompous idiot!" The man's voice rose in pitch. "I suffered my whole life because of you, and you don't even know what I'm talking about?"

The voice grew louder, ending in a screeching, raspy wail. Again, Sam recognized something about the tone, but the memory continued to elude him, like a child playing hide-and-seek behind sheets drying on the clothesline.

"Stew. Please. Just tell me. I'll fix it. I promise. Whatever you need. It's been a long time since we were in boarding school, man. A hell of a long time. We were just kids, for crying out loud."

"Let me refresh your memory."

Sam moved forward again. He blended into the shadowy recesses of the cave well, and realized at this point he was hidden from Stew's view. He strained to see the man behind the voice, but was unsuccessful. As he crept along in the shadows, he listened to him vent about his past.

"She was the love of my life, you slime ball. *Senator.* And you threw her away."

Stew spat the words "senator." Sam thought the man might break down. His voice had turned wobbly and unsteady.

"Who? Who are you talking about, Stew?"

Stew sighed.

"Did you really pay so little attention to those around you, Senator?"

Sam inched forward. He was halfway across the room. Stew continued.

"Olivia. I'm talking about Olivia Richardson."

Sam looked up in surprise. He remembered the story. It had been all over the news. The young woman killed herself by jumping off the roof of the Everdale Boy's Academy. Bruce told him a little bit about the girl, that he dated her before it all happened. It had been quite the mystery. They never learned why she jumped or how she had gained entrance to the institution that night.

Bruce stopped protesting and stared into the darkness where Stew waited.

"You knew about that?" he asked softly.

Stew answered, venom pouring from his mouth.

"Knew about it? Hell, we all knew you were screwing her. After I introduced you two at the football game, she wouldn't *look* at me! All she could do was talk about you, pump me for information about you, and ask me if you liked her. And I *found* her! I'm the one who went every day for three months to order ice cream at the shop where she worked. It took me three months to work up courage to ask her out. She finally agreed to go to the game with me, and that's where I made the mistake of introducing her to you. You pretentious bastard! She wasn't good enough for you or your family, was she? Not high class enough to bring home to mom and dad? Is that why you rejected her?"

Bruce squirmed. He seemed more worried the ancient secret would be revealed than the fact that he was tied up in a cave by a maniac.

"Listen. I didn't actually reject her. I just said we had to cool it. She was getting on my nerves, too clingy. After we were, uh, intimate, she started talking about getting married. I was only seventeen, Stew. You have to understand that. I wasn't ready for a commitment."

He paused for a second and quieted his voice until it sounded senatorial.

"You're not going public with this, are you? I'm about to be nominated for the Presidential election, for God's sake. Come on, Stew, it's been over forty years."

Stew stepped forward into the light and backhanded Bruce. The Senator's head snapped sideways.

Sam froze against the wall and stared.

Mac Stewart stood before him, enraged. He slammed his fist into Bruce's jaw, nearly knocking him over.

"I loved her! I *loved* her! You used her and threw her away. She couldn't take it! She was so ashamed she threw herself off the roof. It was because of you, you moron! She was gonna have your baby! She told me. She told me about the baby, and that you didn't want her. I tried to calm her down, but she got away from me and raced up the stairs to the attic. I stumbled. I was…" His voice broke. He stopped momentarily and finally regained control. "I was too late."

No one spoke. Evan, who had been watching with wide eyes, looked down at the ground.

The thunderstorm grew stronger overhead. A puff of cold air blew across the room, stirring dust on the ground.

Finally, Bruce broke the spell.

"She was pregnant?"

Mac barked a false laugh. "Ha. You didn't know? Sure you didn't."

Bruce answered hurriedly. "No. Honest to God. And I didn't know you had feelings for her. You have to believe me, Stew. I thought you were just friends."

"Friends? Yeah. Right."

Mac leaned against the wall near Evan, took a gun from his belt, then pointed it directly at Sam.

"You might as well come out now, Sam. You've been lurking in those shadows far too long."

Chapter Fifty-nine

"Hands in the air, Sam."

Stunned, Sam moved slowly into the light with his hands up.

"Sit. Next to the boy." Mac motioned to Evan with his gun.

Sam followed directions, burning with shame. How could he have been so stupid? Mac had known he was there all along.

Thunder rolled and rumbled above. Each clap boomed louder as the storm approached.

"Now I have to change the plan. Geez, Sam, why did you do this? You're screwin' up everything."

Sam's mind raced.

Rachel! Did she call the police?

His heart sank. He'd asked her to call *Mac* when he ran into the woods. No wonder he'd known Sam was lurking in the shadows. He'd probably been waiting for him.

Mac kept the gun trained loosely in Sam's direction and paced like a caged animal. His voice became more familiar and assumed an analytical, thoughtful tone.

"Well, let's see. You followed Bruce out to the caves, in vain, but courageously attempted to save Evan. Bruce took care of both of you, then turned the weapon on himself. End of story." He flashed a sick grin at Sam. "Okay! No more dilly-dallying here. Let's get you lined up properly. Let's see, you, kid, over here."

A loud clap of thunder cracked overhead, galvanizing Sam. He lowered his head and lunged, ramming Mac in the gut; then wrapped his arms around Mac's waist and knocked him to the ground. Mac reacted swiftly, pried Sam's arms apart, and flung him to the floor.

Sam's head hit the dirt floor with a thud.

"Grandpa!" Evan screamed, struggling against his bonds.

Mac held the gun to Sam's temple. "Shut up, Billy."

"I'm not Billy!" Evan yelled. "And you really screwed up, you stupid moron!"

Sam's head shot up. He stared at his grandson in surprise.

Mac shoved Sam with his foot when he tried to get up.

"Stay put." He turned to Evan and frowned. "What the hell do you mean, you little bastard?"

Evan spoke evenly and with confidence.

"You messed up. You'll be found out. They'll figure it out in a snap."

"Spill it," he growled, prodding Evan's chest with the gun.

Evan looked directly into Mac's eyes. "We found you online. Me and my friends. Tracked your IP address to your FBI office in Washington. Those fake Commando1070 bids all came from one computer, routed remotely through your office in DC. We found you, and so will the cops. My friends will tell if I don't turn up soon. I was supposed to be at Sean's an hour ago."

Sam looked at Evan with surprise. He sat up slowly and rubbed his shoulder.

"Evan?" he asked. "Is that true? You made the connection online?"

He nodded.

"Yeah. Last night, Grandpa. I didn't tell you because I was up after you and Grandma fell asleep. Sean helped me. I'm sorry."

Sam's heart melted. The boy was facing death, and still felt the need to apologize.

"It's okay, buddy. You may have saved our lives."

The sound of splattering grew louder. A rivulet of rainwater trickled down one of the tree roots that snaked through a hole in the ceiling. It pooled on the sandy floor of the cave.

Mac spat at Sam, truly angry now.

"No way, Mr. Rogers. It's not gonna end pretty this time. I don't give a crap if they can trace it to me. It could have been anyone in my office. Someone who sneaked in, like Bruce here. He's in Washington often enough. Besides, the medals were a brilliant touch. Bruce was going to try to pin it on Harvey, the vet. Until I 'discovered' his elaborate plan to trick us all."

Bruce's face darkened. He flung himself and the chair to which he was attached at Mac. Mac's knees buckled; he went down hard. Bruce lay on his side, still tethered to the chair. Sam lurched toward him, but Mac jumped to his feet, the gun in his hand pointed at Sam's chest.

"Hold it, Sam. You wanna get plugged first?"

Mac wobbled and leaned against the cave wall, touching a gash on his temple.

The puddle of water at his feet enlarged.

He shoved off the wall and reached Bruce, righting him in his chair with one superhuman effort. With a glower, Mac slugged Bruce on the chin, knocking his head back.

"You son of a bitch!" Mac shouted.

He reached around and squeezed the rope looped around Bruce's neck.

Bruce's face reddened, then turned a sickly gray-blue.

"Stop it, Mac! You'll kill him. Do you think they'll believe he strangled himself?" Sam shouted.

Mac released his grip on Bruce's neck.

"Good point. Guess a shot to the head is neater, anyway. But first, the kid."

He dragged Evan to a standing position. Sam lunged at him, but Mac sidestepped just in time.

"What? You want to die together? So be it."

Sam shoved Evan behind him. Mac laughed, backed up, steadied himself against one of the large roots of the tree that wound down to the cavern, and aimed.

A bolt of lightning struck the oak tree. Twenty thousand amps shot through the tree, boiling sap and splitting bark. A sharp boom sizzled in the cave, followed by a crackling blue flash. The massive explosion ripped along the tree trunk, through the stream of water beside it, and into the pool in which Mac stood.

Current passed through Mac's body, entering at the shoulder, moving through his heart and muscles, and exiting through his feet. Mac dropped to the ground, twitched twice, and lay still. A burning stench filled the air.

The tree roots exploded like a wooden grenade. Oak shrapnel pierced the air. Sam felt a sliver stab his upper arm. He threw himself over Evan, wrapping his arms around him until it stopped. Bruce's face was bloodied, pricked by several wooden splinters. Sam freed Evan's hands from the ropes and released Bruce from the chair.

"Come on, let's get out of here!" Bruce said, swiping at the blood on his face and taking the lead.

Sam hid Evan's eyes when they passed Mac's charred body and headed down the tunnel. Another massive crash came from above. The tree root pulled from the ground and out of the rocky nest in which it grew. Rumbling filled the air. Stones began to rain from the ceiling.

"The old oak is down," Sam shouted. "Watch out!"

Bruce, Evan, and Sam ducked and ran through narrow tunnels, out to the next stone chamber. The air filled with dust, and rocks tumbled around them. They made it to the entrance, but stared at it in horror. Already caved in, the exit hole was blocked with rocks and debris. Bruce moved forward to investigate, while Sam and Evan flattened themselves against the wall to avoid the stones raining from the crumbling ceiling. Sam wrapped his arms protectively over his grandson.

"Gramps. I'm scared."

Sam hugged him close.

"I know, sport. Just hang in there. We'll figure something—"

Before he could finish his sentence, the earth opened beneath their feet.

Chapter Sixty

Instinctively, Sam locked his arms around Evan. They slid through a hole in the earth and landed in an underground stream. Water propelled them through a dark tunnel, rushing around them and knocking them into rocks along the way.

Sam's head smashed against a boulder. He saw stars and nearly blacked out, but fear for his grandson strengthened his resolve and he managed to hold onto the boy. A surge in the current slammed them into the tunnel wall, spinning them in the water and forcing them, tumbling, beneath the surface. Sam fought in the shallow stream, moaning from the intense pain where his hip and shoulder crashed into the wall. He nearly lost hold of Evan when they went under, but managed to raise their heads above water. The torrent pulled them along.

"Gramps!" Evan cried. His voice gurgled with inhaled fluid.

The water churned around them, driving them along the rocky terrain. Evan locked his arms around Sam's neck when they were flung around the next corner.

"Hang on," Sam shouted.

The flow of the water increased and multiple streams joined with the one in which they struggled. The water level deepened, allowing Sam and Evan to float more easily, although they could not fight the strong current that moved them forward.

"Hang on, buddy. Just hang on."

Evan's face glimmered before him, covered in scratches and bruises. His left eye was swollen.

"I won't let go, Grandpa," he sobbed.

They bobbed in the dark water. It swept them through the tunnel. The ceiling grew higher. Floating like human flotsam through eddies and streams, they were thrust forward.

The interior of the cavern brightened. A roar in the distance tightened Sam's insides.

Oh my God. The falls. We're going over the falls.

It happened in seconds. In spite of Sam's efforts to fight the current, he and Evan were catapulted over the waterfall. Sam lost his grip on the boy; they flew over the edge and into the pool below. Cold green water bubbled around Sam, filling his mouth and nose. He swam through the turbulence, making his way to the surface. Finally, his head burst through into the air. He tread water and frantically searched for Evan.

He spotted the boy face down, wedged near the shore. Sam's heart leapt into his throat. He stroked hard in Evan's direction. He reached him, pulled his face out of the water, and dragged him onto the shore. Cold fear ripped through his stomach.

He's not breathing!

Sam turned him on his side and pressed his stomach. Water trickled out of Evan's mouth.

Oh my God, not like Billy. Please not like Billy.

Sam stopped, forced himself to think, and rolled Evan onto his back. He slid Evan's jaw forward, hooked his thumb into his mouth to hold his tongue, pinched his nose, and breathed into his mouth. The boy's lips were cold. His chest didn't rise.

Sam began to panic. Tears streamed down his face. *No! No! No! No! No!*

As if an angel entered his body, a calm presence filled him. His head cleared and he realized Evan's airway must be blocked.

He turned him on his side again, pushed between his shoulder blades and tilted him as much as possible.

More water flowed out of Evan's mouth.

Sam tried again, rolling him back over as his own sobs threatened to break through. He leaned forward, pinched his nose, tilted his head back, and breathed into his mouth. Again. And again.

Finally, when Sam had almost given up hope, a burst of water spewed out of Evan's mouth. He spluttered. His eyes opened, and he coughed fiercely, drawing in long, ragged breaths.

Sam collapsed on the ground beside him, completely spent. An overwhelming sense of exhaustion rippled through his body.

"Gramps!" Evan spluttered.

Sam looked at his grandson, felt his eyes roll back in his head, and was engulfed in a black void.

Chapter Sixty-one

"Grandpa, please. Please wake up."

Sam felt Evan's hand stroking his face. He wanted to wake, but pain seared his head, back, hip, and shoulders and a heavy blanket smothered his senses. Rain dripped steadily from the leaves above. The thunderstorm had passed.

"Grandpa, I need you," Evan sobbed.

Slowly, Sam crept closer to consciousness and finally broke through. His eyes opened as if sealed with thick molasses and his jaw swelled in pain. He looked at his grandson who leaned over his chest, crying hard. Evan's shoulders shook; the sobs wracked his body.

Sam reached up and touched his grandson's back. "Evan. It's okay."

The boy raised a tear-stained face to his grandfather, eyes wide with surprise and relief.

"Gramps!"

Sam's insides hitched when he saw Evan's swollen eye and scratched face. He slowly sat up and reached for the boy, holding him close in spite of the pain that ripped through every muscle and joint in his body.

"We made it, son. We made it. It's gonna be okay."

Sam's brain gradually cleared. Sitting on the wet grass, he remembered. Again, he pushed aside the fresh knowledge of Billy's death.

Bruce.

"Where's Bruce?" he asked. "Have you seen him?"

"No," Evan said with downcast eyes. "I think the whole thing caved in."

"Come on. We have to find him," Sam said.

He stood. A bolt of pain seared through his temple. He idly wondered if he had a concussion. He automatically patted his jeans pocket to check for his wallet and the marble, then froze.

Oh no.
It's gone. The marble's gone.
He gazed at the pool of water beside him. A sinking sensation filled his soul.
The marble's gone. Billy's gone.
No more visits, no more family vignettes to relive.

Evan put an arm around Sam's middle to steady him when he lurched sideways. He looked down at his grandson. Realization flooded him.

Evan's here. Alive. Full of love and humor and spunk. Just like Billy.

He squeezed his grandson's shoulder, flashed a smile, and started to walk. Moving unsteadily toward the main entrance of the cave, Sam fought nausea and dizziness.

"How long was I out?" he asked, leaning on his grandson's shoulder for support.

"I don't know. Maybe twenty minutes."

A grim realization hit him. If Bruce was trapped in an airtight chamber, every second counted.

They reached the tunnel entrance. A massive rockslide had sealed the opening with boulders only a bulldozer could move. Sam shook his head.

"We'll have to get help. There's no way we can move those."

He froze. A faint cry came from within the cave.

"Up there!" Evan shouted, scrambling up the side of the hill.

Sam followed, calling on every ounce of his strength. He made it to the top of the hill and stared.

The ancient oak had toppled, pulling its roots partially out of the rocky caverns. It had crushed younger trees in its wake and gouged the earth, forever altering the landscape. Sam tried to get his bearings, to locate the skylights that had been their tunnels in his youth.

They both heard the cry again.

"Help! Please help me."

Bruce sounded desperate and weak.

They called his name and carefully picked their way across the top of the hill, stepping lightly, fearful they might fall into the abyss from which they had just escaped.

"Bruce," Sam cried. "Where are you?"

"Senator McDonald!" Evan yelled.

A dirty hand reached into the air twenty feet in the distance.

"Here! I'm here."

Darting toward him, they approached the hole gingerly and inspected below. Bruce had climbed nearly to the top, but stopped a few feet beneath the opening. Several rocks packed the side the of exit hole, leaving a gap too small for a human to pass.

"My hand's broken, Sam. I can't move the rocks. They're wedged too tight."

Sam looked down into the eyes of the senator, but saw only his childhood friend, the boy who craved a normal family. Fear, hope, and trust passed over Bruce's face simultaneously. Sam pushed away feelings of betrayal, ignoring thoughts of Bruce's involvement in the secret of Billy's fate.

"Hold on, Bruce. We'll get you out of there."

He ignored the pains shooting through his arms and shoulders when he leaned over and tugged at the first rock. Eighteen inches across and heavy, it didn't budge. Evan looked at his grandfather as if struck by an idea, and ran toward the woods. He came back with a rusty wrought iron rail.

"Where did you find that?"

Evan tossed his head in the direction of Manfred Healey's house.

"An old fence by the hedgerow. It was falling apart."

Sam nodded, proud of his grandson's ingenuity, and used the bar to pry the rock. When he stabbed beneath it several times, dirt and gravel fell onto Bruce's upturned face.

"Move away, Bruce, just in case."

Bruce moved back against the wall.

"Okay. I'm clear."

Sam pried the rock once more, finally shifting it enough to gain a purchase. He leaned over, slid his hands around one end, and lifted with all his might. It budged, but then fell back into position.

He turned to Evan.

"I need your help, son. When I lift, you slide the lever in further, okay?"

Evan nodded.

Sam tried again, and this time when he had raised the stone a few inches on end, Evan plunged the pry bar deeper beneath it, securing it. Sam shoved at the stone, pushing with all his might, and half rolled/half carried it out of the hole. It landed with a heavy thud on the soil above.

They continued removing rocks for fifteen minutes, until they opened a hole wide enough for Bruce to squeeze through.

"Okay. I think you can make it now, Bruce. Come on."

Bruce squirmed to the opening, popped his head through the hole, and raised his good hand to Sam.

"Careful of his other hand," Sam said.

Sam and Evan both pulled him up and out.

They dragged him to a safe spot on the grass, panting like runners after a cross-country race. When a soft rumbling hummed beneath them, all three scrambled to the edge of the woods. The earth vibrated once more, the old oak shuddered, and the hole Bruce was in seconds earlier collapsed, spewing a cloud of dust into the air.

Falling onto the soft grass, they gaped at the scene.

"Wow," Evan said. "You just made it, Senator."

Bruce, covered in dust and dried blood, smiled at Evan. He took Sam's hand with his good left hand and thanked them both.

"If you hadn't heard me…"

His eyes filled and his head dropped to his chest.

Sam flopped on his back and looked at the clearing sky. The storm clouds skittered away, revealing blue sky streaked with lavender. Emotions yo-yoed in his heart, banging against its walls with manic persistence. He'd finally learned what had happened to Billy, but rage flowed in tandem with relief. Bruce must have sensed his thoughts.

"Sam?" Bruce turned to him and touched his hand. "I'm *so* sorry about Billy. We should have told you. But we were scared. And then you went, well, crazy, and they put you in that place. We all thought it would push you over the edge again if we told. We didn't want to be responsible for another breakdown, even if it meant keeping the accident a secret." His voice broke, shaking with emotion. "I've harbored two horrendous secrets. Billy and Olivia. They've ripped me apart inside." He buried his face in his hands. "I can't live like this anymore."

Sam looked away, unsettled. The knowledge was too fresh for him to tender his forgiveness. He needed time. His friends saw his little brother die; yet remained silent for fifty years. It was hard to fathom, especially when his own life was haunted by the eternal question of Billy's fate. He imagined Olivia's parents felt the same persistent questions about their daughter. Did they know she'd been with child?

Bruce finally raised his head, wiped his eyes, and looked at Evan.

"Hey. I found this in the cave while I was stuck there. I think it was Billy's, if I remember right. He won it off me in a fierce game of marbles when we were about your age."

Evan looked with interest at the cat's eye that shone from Bruce's hand. Sun glinted on the smooth glass. A mourning dove cooed in the distance and the wet leaves on the trees overhead rustled in a sudden breeze.

"Cool," Evan said, picking it up and holding it to the light. "You can see through it if you turn it just right. Thanks, Senator."

A lump formed in Sam's throat. The marble was home.

He slid an arm around Evan's shoulders.

"Come on, men. Let's get out of here."

Chapter Sixty-two

A RED DRAGONFLY lit on the small coffin, wings winking metallic in the sun. It paused as if paying respects to the occupant, then flitted toward the weeds behind the trees.

Sam stood at his brother's grave, squinting in the bright light. He sighed, stirring hot heavy air with his breath. Anguish settled in his stomach, rolling with familiarity.

Reverend Hardina droned words intended to comfort, opening and closing his worn Bible to predictable passages. Feeling dizzy, Sam shifted from one leg to the other. Sunlight dappled the green cloth that draped a mound of freshly dug dirt. It mocked him, dancing cheerfully over brass fittings on the child-sized casket.

Billy's in there.

The sudden thought crushed him. He reeled, shocked by the blast of emotion. Searing, it ripped him down the middle.

It's not really Billy. Just his bones.

He staggered, catching himself on Rachel's scooter. Evan noticed and slid closer.

"You okay, Gramps?" he whispered.

Rachel glanced up; worry pooled in her eyes. Sam found his balance and quieted her concern with a half-smile.

"I'm fine," he whispered. "Just tired."

Evan slid under Sam's arm, steadying him. He patted the boy's back to reassure him and noted the bruise on his eye now flamed yellow and lavender. It had almost healed. He tried to focus on the minister's words. He needed to find his center, but it eluded him as bizarre thoughts tumbled through his mind. Trying to fit the puzzle pieces together, Sam longed to make sense of it, but they jarred against each other, jumbled and misshapen.

He still couldn't quite accept the truth. Bruce, Doug, and Harvey had witnessed Billy's death. Watching in horror as a red cloud blossomed in the water, they'd panicked. Their amateur attempts at resuscitation had been futile. Hysterical and fearful of being blamed, they'd buried the body beneath rocks in the pool.

The same three men shuffled in agony on the opposite side of the coffin. Each had delivered mournful apologies to Sam when the story broke.

When Bruce explained why they were afraid to come clean, Sam had bristled. They'd considered their silence an act of protection. To Sam, it had felt like an act of betrayal.

He remembered his stint at the psychiatric hospital. Numb from pain, he'd felt nothing but isolation from the world in which he suffered, surrounded by the mentally unstable. He didn't speak for weeks, almost a month. When he returned to the "real" world, his three so-called friends remained silent.

Protection?

Bruce claimed they were afraid to "set Sam off" again—afraid he'd lose his marbles—this time, for good.

Evan squeezed his hand and looked up, youthful eyes glimmering with concern. Hazel with flecks of orange and gold, they reminded him of Billy's eyes. His hair, sandy and wavy, resembled Billy's in color and texture. Evan's look of affection warmed his heart. *He really understands.*

The minister closed his Bible, signifying the end of the service and bittersweet closure.

Dropping his grandfather's hand suddenly, Evan reached down and patted his pocket. A warm green glow shone through the fabric. He glanced up at Sam and fished out the cat's eye.

Sam wiggled his fingers for it and the boy quickly dropped it into his earth-loving hands. He caught it and rolled it between his fingers, absorbing the warmth; it illuminated his flesh with a green glow.

He willed Billy to whisk him away, aching to speak to him. He wanted to feel Billy's small hand in his, to jump down from the top bunk and comfort him after a nightmare. He wanted to walk the hot summer pavement barefoot, race through the cornfields, ride bikes together—just one more time.

Evan pulled Sam down to his level and whispered in his ear.

"You should keep it, Grandpa. Billy would want you to have it."

Sam's eyes brimmed. He brushed away the moisture and pocketed the marble. It cooled and quieted, satisfied to be home.

"This concludes the memorial service for William Moore. The Moore family extends their appreciation and wishes you well."

It was a polite way of telling the others not to expect a reception at the Moores' house. Sam didn't want to make a big deal out of the ceremony. No food, no fancy gathering. He really wanted only Rachel and Evan at his side today. Of course, Timmy was home with Maryellen. Eighteen months was far too young to stand at a gravesite. He would have liked to have his son and daughter at the ceremony. But Andrew, somewhere in Iraq, continued to fight for the liberty of an oppressed people. Beth had been called back to work in Manhattan for an emergency. Her boss, a slave driver, had refused to let her stay away more than one week. Apparently, she was indispensable. They'd said tearful goodbyes at the airport two days ago.

Sam looked beyond to the graves of his parents. Three Moores lay in a row, their headstones glistening pale in the morning sun. The red daylilies he planted between the graves last spring glowed bright crimson, their luscious color punctuating the dense summer air. He looked at the simple marker he'd chosen for Billy. The smooth rectangular granite was appropriately sized for a young boy.

He glanced across the flower-strewn coffin. Bruce, Doug, and Harvey had insisted on coming. Though they were collectively responsible for the conspiracy to hide the truth, they pushed aside their guilt in favor of this well-intentioned support. Sam chanced a look at Bruce, who seemed miserable. After all, it had been his idea to hide the body. One hand still hung in a sling.

Bruce shambled to Sam's side. Rachel took Evan's arm.

"Come on, honey. Let Grandpa talk with his friends."

Despair and anger welled in Sam's chest. He held it in over the past week, feigning gracious forgiveness. But it wasn't real, and the pressure of lying had wrapped him in resentment. Sam swallowed hard when Bruce put a hand on his shoulder.

"Buddy?"

He raised his eyes to Bruce's, careful not to let the real feelings seep through.

"Yeah?"

Bruce looked at Sam with such misery and compassion that Sam lost it. In seconds, he was engulfed in a warm embrace as they both shook with emotion, consoling each other. Bruce needed redemption. Sam needed deliverance. When they parted, Harvey stood close by, looking like a guilty sheepdog under his shock of white hair.

"Sam. I… I…"

He couldn't get the words out. Sam reached for him and was crushed in a bear hug.

"I'm so sorry."

It was all Harvey could manage.

Doug stood behind the group, shooing his young wife toward the parking lot. He planted his feet wide, as if to hold himself steady. Sam looked over Harvey's shoulder and met Doug's eyes. He mouthed, "Gotta go. Take care," as he fluttered one hand in the air. What Sam read in his eyes was, "I screwed up. Can you ever forgive me?"

Sam blinked his eyes slowly and nodded to him. Doug choked, spun on his heels, and took off across the cemetery.

A breeze whistled in the maple trees above the coffin, rustling green leaves that shimmied overhead in the August sun. A mourning dove cooed in the distance. Her mate answered, sweet and low. Sam reached into his jacket pocket and closed his fingers around the yo-yo. He laid it on the headstone.

Here you go, buddy. This is for you.

The marble pulsed in his pocket.

Chapter Sixty-three

THE HOUSE HUMMED with a quiet deeper and more intense than Sam remembered. Maryellen and the boys had left hours ago. Evan had stuck close to Sam for the duration of the visit, needing proximity to reassure him. He'd started seeing a therapist, but Sam knew it would take more to help him fully recover. He needed the love of his family, laughter over the dinner table, the safe return of his father from the war, and playing numerous games of catch with his grandfather. Sam looked forward to each moment with Evan and Timmy. He knew, in spite of his past obsession with Billy, it was time to focus on the living.

Rachel sat across from him, deftly weaving strands of cane over and under until the pattern evolved. A chilly breeze pushed through the opened window in the living room, fluttering the curtains and sending a shiver along Sam's back. Rachel felt it, too.

"Honey? Would you…?"

He didn't need to hear the rest of the sentence. They knew each other so intimately they barely needed words to communicate. He put his book down and rose from his armchair. The window whooshed shut when he applied pressure to the frame. No peepers now, no crickets. All Sam heard was the squeak of Rachel's wet cane as it slid through the neighboring strands.

The paper lay open, announcing things Sam didn't want to think about tonight. Yet his eyes kept drifting back to the bold headlines.

Serial Killer Exposed—Plot to Destroy Senator Thwarted.

On his way back to the armchair, Sam flipped the newspaper over. He eased into the chair, still pampering his sore hip and shoulder.

Rachel watched him surreptitiously. She continued with her work, glasses poised on the tip of her nose, sitting up in the wheelchair with pillows stuffed behind her back.

"Sam?"

He stared off into space, tapping absentmindedly on the chair.

"Mmm?"

She reached into the water dish for another coiled strand of cane, plucked the clothespin from it, and shook water droplets back into the container.

"Are you okay?"

He shifted, turning toward her with eyes downcast.

"Not really."

Rachel shot him a sad smile.

"I wish you'd talk about it."

Sam grimaced, running his fingers through a strand of gray hair that had fallen over his eyes.

"About what? Billy? Mac? Bruce? The other guys?"

She spoke softly.

"Anything. Everything. I don't care, just talk to me. You don't have to be gracious or forgiving. I understand."

Her deep brown gaze zoomed into his—searching, pulling it out of him. He slumped in the chair, pursed his lips, and blew at the stubborn lock of hair.

"I need a haircut," he muttered.

"Sam. Please."

He tossed an apologetic look.

"Sorry. Where should I start?"

"Start with Mac. Tell me why he did this. What happened to him to twist him so? And why did he choose you and Billy to fixate on?"

Sam leaned forward and rested his arms on his thighs. He studied his hands and began to speak.

"Well, you know Mac lived down the street from us."

Rachel nodded. "Across from the Healey's, right?"

"Kitty corner. He watched the Healey's a lot, I guess. In the beginning he pretended not to know where I lived. That's when he went to see Bruce to 'ask for directions.'"

"He couldn't have forgotten where he used to live. Was it just an excuse to see Bruce?"

"Right. And he's been hunkering down in his mother's old house every since the case was reopened. Apparently the people who'd been renting it had some sort of car accident. We'll never know if he caused it to free up the property, or if it was a bizarre coincidence."

"Did you say he was your age?"

Rachel picked up a fresh strand of cane and wrapped it in circles around her hand. She pinned it with a clothespin and laid it in the water.

"No. He was a few years younger. Used to watch us when we rode bikes past his house. I don't think he ever had a bike, come to think of it."

Rachel sighed.

"Makes you wonder what made him turn so wicked. Did his family seem happy?"

"I'm ashamed to admit I rarely thought about it. I guess if I think back, there was talk about his dad drinking. He worked for the town. Drove the snowplows. I have a vague image of him standing on his porch in his white tee shirt and shorts, yelling at Mac. I used to peddle fast on that part of the street, anyway, because of the Healeys."

Rachel picked up a wooden peg and secured a piece of cane in a hole.

"So Manfred Healey was only implicated in the first murder?"

"Right. Mac spilled his guts to Bruce and Evan before I arrived. Apparently he witnessed the accidental killing and burial of Tommy Donahue by Healey and his pals. Mac used to go back to the gravesite frequently. Got obsessed with it, I guess. Liked the idea of it."

Rachel shivered. "You mean Mac was out in our backyard?" She glanced through the nearest window toward the woods.

"Years ago. When we were kids."

"Sometimes abused children need to feel a sense of power when they have little or no control over their own lives," Rachel said. "At least that's what I've heard on Oprah."

Sam chuckled.

"You would have made a good psychologist, honey. You've got excellent insight, you know."

She smiled.

"Back to the topic, though. Will Healey be charged?"

Sam frowned.

"I'm not sure. Bruce said he's been taken in for questioning. And they're searching the woods for his mother's body."

Rachel rearranged the pillows behind her back.

"And the rest of the murders? They were all Mac's doing?"

"Yeah. He's been trying to set up Bruce since their college days."

She grimaced. "Such an elaborate plot of revenge. Did Mac actually follow Bruce to Maine and DC?"

"I guess so. The fact that they both attended Everdale was pure coincidence. But the death of that poor young girl was the catalyst."

She pushed back the chair she was working on and rolled over to Sam's side.

"What exactly happened?"

Sam settled back in his chair, crossing one leg over the other.

"I guess it was a case of unrequited love. Mac fell for Olivia. They dated. Then Mac introduced her to Bruce and it was all over. Bruce was a real charmer back then."

"Still is," Rachel laughed.

Sam raised one eyebrow.

"Really?"

She quickly restated her words.

"Well, so I hear. He's not my type, of course."

Sam grinned. "Good recovery."

"Was Olivia really pregnant with Bruce's child?"

Sam nodded. "Apparently. But she never told him. When she hinted about marriage, he pulled back and broke it off."

"And that's when she jumped?"

Rachel's eyes filled with empathy.

Sam nodded. "Yeah. Mac had become her confidante, instead of her boyfriend. She blurted it out to him, then climbed up the tower. He followed, but wasn't fast enough. I guess the poor girl died instantly."

Rachel brushed a tear from her eye.

"There was so much shame in those days. Enough to push her to suicide. It's horrid."

Sam reached over to pat her arm.

"I know. I feel bad for her parents. And apparently it was the breaking point for Mac. He spent the rest of his life pursuing Bruce, planning and executing murders all over the East Coast to implicate him."

"But why not try to implicate him with just one murder?"

Sam paused. "I'm not sure. Instinct tells me he liked it too much. Loved the preparation, reveled in the actual killings, savored the idea of getting back at Bruce. And as Bruce's career moved ahead, he must have relished the idea of taking down someone who was so high and mighty."

"It almost worked, Sam."

He studied his hands and nodded.

"I know."

"Why did he target you and Evan?"

Sam sat up straighter, breathing deeply.

"Bruce told Mac about Billy's death. He spilled the secret after getting drunk at a frat party. Mac knew he could use it to destroy Bruce, but waited until the time was just right."

"You mean until he was about to be nominated for the presidency?"

Sam nodded. "Yeah."

She sighed and looked at Sam with deep compassion.

"Will you ever be able to forgive them?"

He knew exactly what she meant, shifted uncomfortably in his seat, and blurted out the words.

"I don't know. I just can't believe they kept it from me. All those years. Years of worry. Years of hell."

She wheeled closer and put one hand up to his cheek, brushing it gently with the backs of her fingers.

"I know, Sammy. I know. It hurts, doesn't it?"

He took her hand and brought it to his lips.

"I'll get over it. Eventually. I still care for the guys, in spite of everything."

"I know you do. You have a great big heart."

The room grew quiet again, punctuated only by the ticking of the grandfather clock and their soft breathing. Finally, Rachel wheeled over to the stairs, pulled herself up from the chair, and balanced on the stair railing.

"I'm ready to go up. You coming?"

Sam smiled and jumped to help her.

"You bet, lady. My pleasure."

He took her arm to steady her.

"Come on," he whispered. "Let's go to bed."

The End

About the author

After writing in the early morning hours, Aaron Lazar works as an applications engineer in Rochester, New York. Additional passions include vegetable, fruit, and flower gardening; preparing large family feasts; photographing his family, gardens, and the breathtakingly beautiful Genesee Valley; cross-country skiing across the rolling hills; playing a distinctly amateur level of piano, and spending "time" with the French Impressionists whenever possible.

Mr. Lazar resides in Upstate New York with his wife, daughter, son-in-law, three grandchildren, step-grandson, mother-in-law, two dogs, and three cats. Although he adored raising his three delightful daughters, Aaron finds grandfathering his three grandchildren to be one of the finest experiences of his life.

Learn about Gus LeGarde mysteries and more. Read excerpts from the novels at:

http://www.legardemysteries.com/

http://www.mooremysteries.com

Mazurka

When Siegfried receives a puzzling invitation to visit an ailing relative in Germany on the eve of Gus and Camille´s wedding, their honeymoon plans change. Siegfried — Gus´s socially challenged brother-in-law — can´t travel alone, so they gather the gentle giant under their wings and fly to Paris.

After luscious hours in the city of lights, a twist of fate propels them into a deadly web of neo-Nazis. A bloody brawl on the Champs Élysées thrusts Siegfried and Gus into the news, where a flawed report casts Siegfried as the Nazi leader´s murderer, sealing his death warrant.

While Siegfried recovers in a Parisian hospital, Nazi terrorists stalk Gus and Camille. Hunted and left for dead in the underground Parisian Catacombs among millions of Frenchmen´s bones, they barely escape. Siegfried is moved to safety at his aunt´s in Denkendorf, where he learns a shocking family secret about Chopin´s steamy past. The calm is soon shattered, when the threesome is plunged into a cat-and-mouse game where the stakes are lethal and the future of Europe hangs in the balance.

"Lazar delivers a masterful display of heartfelt emotions, need, and compassion. That he wraps this present in a thrilling, mysterious package for us just makes it all the more enjoyable."
Thomas Fortenberry, Literary Critic

"You'll be looking for other books by this imaginative author and enjoy every one of them."
Anne K. Edwards, author of *Shadows over Paradise*

"The author has outdone himself with this book! Each page propels the story forward with a series of clever surprises. There is a sense of history and destiny within these pages, as the characters seek to reconcile the past with their futures. Gus and Camille start their lives together, but need to understand the mental abuse she suffered with her former husband. Frieda Hirsch has a story to tell that is filled with the melody of love. And the Neo-Nazis live with a historic hatred for a group of people. There is an amazing blend of the past, present and the future, as these situations tie together.

Sorrow-filled scenes, delicate details and exciting escapes will satisfy all readers. Well-turned phrases and excellent writing causes the plot to come alive with a sense of reality and purpose.

Mazurka marches forward with a solid story that beats with passion!"

Joyce Handzo, *In The Library Reviews*

Tremolo

Summer, 1964: Beatlemania hits the States, and the world mourns the loss of JFK. For eleven-year-old Gus LeGarde, the powerful events that rocked the nation serve as a backdrop for the most challenging summer of his life.

After Gus and his best friends capsize their boat at his grandparents' lakeside camp, they witness a drunk chasing a girl through the foggy Maine woods. She's scared. She's hurt. And she disappears.

The camp is thrown into turmoil as the frantic search for Sharon begins. Reports of stolen relics arise, including a church bell cast by Paul Revere. When Gus and his friends stumble on a scepter that may be part of the spoils, they become targets for the evil lurking around the lake. Will they find Sharon before the villain does? And how can Gus—armed only with a big heart, a motorboat, and a nosy beagle—survive the menacing attacks on his life?

"...It is easy to see that Aaron Paul Lazar loves to write, as his style is lilting and beautiful. He weaves childhood memories of the lakes of Maine into a stylized whodunit that is original and breathtaking. His characters are children living in a fishing resort with a very special visitor whose presence lends an air of melancholy to an otherwise carefree environment. Lazar gives the reader an idea of what real pirates can be like as the villains, making the tale even more tempting. There is no code of honor among these thieves. A great read."
Midwest Book Review

"Beautifully written, with the perfect touch of nostalgia and suspense, the pages of this book tremble with a strong emotional appeal. Set in Maine during the summer of 1964, there is a vivid sense of traveling back in time, as memorable moments of this era provide the framework for the story. The author has captured both the coziness as well as the craziness of the sixties, thereby making the plot realistic and riveting...."
Joyce Handzo, *In the Library Reviews*

Forthcoming

Firesong: an unholy grave

Firesong: an unholy grave, pits Gus and Camille against drug lords with a backdrop of a tornado, forest fire, collapsing salt mine, and the discovery of a fantastic local link to the Underground Railroad. The entire town is threatened as Gus and Camille unravel the truth behind reprehensible dealings in their country church and the scandal of a missing town supervisor.

Don't miss any of these other
exciting mainstream novels

➢ Death on Delivery
(1-931201-60-9, $16.50 US)

➢ Death to the Centurion
(1-931201-26-9, $16.95 US)

➢ Embraced by the Shadows
(1-933353-90-2, $18.95 US)

➢ Mazurka
(1-60619-160-8, $16.95 US)

➢ Murder in the Pit
(1-60619-110-1, $16.95 US)

➢ Murder Past, Murder Present
(1-60619-206-X, $19.95 US)

➢ The Golden Crusader
(1-933353-91-0, $16.95 US)

➢ Tremolo
(1-933353-08-2, $16.95 US)

Twilight Times Books
Kingsport, Tennessee

Order Form

If not available from your local bookstore or favorite online bookstore, send this coupon and a check or money order for the retail price plus $3.50 s&h to Twilight Times Books, Dept. GB810 POB 3340 Kingsport TN 37664. Delivery may take up to two weeks.

Name: _____

Address: _____

_____

Email: _____

I have enclosed a check or money order in the amount of

$_____

for _____ .

If you enjoyed this book, please post a review
at your favorite online bookstore.

Twilight Times Books
P O Box 3340
Kingsport, TN 37664
Phone/Fax: 423-323-0183
www.twilighttimesbooks.com/